QUIMBY

QUIMBY

Arthur Adams

A Joan Kahn Book

St. Martin's Press   New York

This novel is a work of fiction. With the exception of actual historical personages and political organizations, which have been used fictitiously, the characters, organizations, and events are entirely the product of the author's imagination.

QUIMBY. Copyright © 1988 by Arthur Adams.
All rights reserved.
Printed in the United States of America.
No part of this book may be used or reproduced
in any manner whatsoever without written permission
except in the case of brief quotations
embodied in critical articles or reviews.
For information, address
St. Martin's Press, 175 Fifth Avenue, New York, N.Y. 10010.

Copy Editor: Leslie Sharpe

Library of Congress Cataloging-in-Publication Data

Adams, Arthur E.
  Quimby / by Arthur Adams.
      p.   cm.
  ISBN 0-312-01504-6 : $17.95
  I. Title.
PS3551.D26Q5   1988
813'.54—dc19

First Edition
10 9 8 7 6 5 4 3 2 1

To Jan

QUIMBY

1

Harare, October 22, 1986—Zimbabwe Deputy Minister of State Security Godswill Malunga said today that three National Executive Committee members of the African National Congress (ANC) have been shot and killed in Harare since late September. "These murders appear to be the work of assassins sent into the country by a foreign power," Comrade Malunga said. "The ANC is the most prominent group seeking violent overthrow of the government of South Africa, and we know of course that the apartheid regime has sworn to crush it."

Malunga said that if military groups secretly invade Zimbabwe's borders, or organize inside our boundaries, our security forces will destroy them wherever they are discovered.

The Herald

PETER Chitepo paced across the hard concrete floor and peered through a dirty window at sun-baked pink clay and dusty rows of whitewashed shanties. Chitungwiza— ugly and poor, home of more than a hundred thousand blacks, many of them with jobs in Harare, the capital of Zimbabwe, thirteen miles away. The workers were coming home now—on bicycles, or packed into rickety old cars, in trucks serving as pirate taxis, in overcrowded buses. They came walking up the street in scattered clusters—filling the air outside with the sounds of people glad to have most of the day's work done.

Chitepo smiled sympathetically at the sight of a mother and three children who rushed out to greet a man who rode up on a bicycle, grabbing him so enthusiastically around his legs and waist that he had to struggle to keep his feet.

When he turned back toward his guest, Chitepo's thin-fleshed black face became stern again. He wanted passionately to win the point they had been discussing, but his visitor was far too important to be yelled at; therefore, Chitepo spoke courteously, trying to conceal his impatience. "But you do agree, sir, that the ANC may be destroyed here and now? You agree that the work of years is being wiped out by these assassins?"

"Of course, but that does not justify our taking risks that could destroy our party."

Chitepo's visitor was Herbert Nkala, member of the African National Congress' National Executive Council, a small, controlled, quiet man with a round, lined face that spoke of heavy responsibilities carried for many years. He had served his terms in South African prisons, and between prison terms he had organized and led ANC activists inside the country, fighting for the right of blacks to participate in the government, fighting for justice. Now he was one of the leaders, one of the heroes whose calls to action were heard and followed by millions.

Nkala's voice reverberated with basso resonances like distant rumbling thunder; it was a voice meant for commanding troops or swaying crowds, reined in now to stay within these shanty walls. "We must be sensitive to our situation," he said. "We are refugees in Zimbabwe, tolerated only so long as we do not bring trouble. You are advocating that we start a war within our own party, but the men you want to attack are backed by the people who supply Zimbabwe's weapons and military training, the Russians and their German friends. If we start an open fight, the Prime Minister could be forced to drive the ANC out of Zimbabwe simply because he *must* have these weapons. And what if you are wrong in thinking that the Communists in our party are causing these murders?"

Nkala picked up a heavy white china cup, stared into it a moment, then swallowed the rest of the lukewarm tea it contained. "Consider the probable consequences of the fight you want to start," he said. "It is not only the Soviet Union I am concerned about. Look to the south. If it were to become known that the ANC is having trouble with its Communist members, the leaders of South Africa's government could use this 'new Communist threat' as an excuse to invade Zimbabwe and drive the ANC out. They are using similar pretexts with considerable success in Angola and Mozambique, and in Namibia. We could bring disaster to the ANC as well as to Zimbabwe."

Chitepo, tall and skinny, thin lips pursed and eyes angry, shook his narrow head in frustration. Here in Zimbabwe, he was the ANC's counterintelligence chief, responsible for the safety and security of the ANC's local staff and of the leaders who visited Zimbabwe from time to time. It was his duty to protect the lives of these people, but Nkala had spent the better part of the last hour flatly prohibiting him from taking any action against men he believed were engineering the murders of the ANC leaders.

For Peter Chitepo, exiled from South Africa, not yet thirty, but veteran of five years of civil war in Zimbabwe, the life of the ANC was all-important. For him the party was *sacred*. The great African National Congress, the mother, the umbrella party that accepted members from all other reform groups in South Africa—labor unions, church councils, youth organizations, and hundreds of other parties and fighters, including even the South African Communist Party—this African National Congress was leading *all* the people in the fight against apartheid. For him, only the ANC—democratic, tolerant of many opinions, but totally committed to bringing change to South Africa by whatever means were required—only the ANC could succesfully lead the great revolution that was already under way.

He did not agree with the suggestion made by Zimbabwe's Deputy Minister of State Security, that South Africa was sending in its assassins. Instead, he believed that the SACP, the South African Communist Party, which had its own members on the ANC National Executive Council, was making its long-expected effort to gain control of the ANC—by murdering the ANC's non-Communist leaders.

For more than an hour, he had begged Nkala's permission to go after the SACP, arguing that the ANC must fight off these internal killers. But Nkala had struck down every argument Chitepo had offered for direct ANC involvement, rejecting every option that might damage the party. Now, Chitepo decided, it was time to present the proposal he had been keeping back, the proposal that *had* to win Nkala's approval. It was time to show the leader what could be done *without involving the party in any way.*

Chitepo pulled a rough wooden chair close to Nkala, turned it around and sat down, folding his long arms over its back. He leaned over his forearms, his narrow head thrust forward, daring to look boldly into the leader's eyes.

"I have a proposal for action that will not involve the party."
"Yes?"
"There is a man here in Harare who can help us. An American."

"A white man?" Nkala's gentle question only partly hid his surprise. His dark eyes studied Chitepo's face intently.

"No. This man is black. His name is Taylor Quimby. From a city named Detroit. We fought together under Robert Mugabe for Zimbabwe's freedom. He has had much military and intelligence experience—in Vietnam, later in what is called the Special Forces, and in another organization the Americans call the Delta Force—an elite counterinsurgency group like the British Special Air Service. He came here in 1978 and fought under Mugabe, not as a mercenary, but as one of us, because he knows that if black people want freedom they must fight for it. He led one of our liberation army's most feared and successful groups against the Rhodesians' Selous Scouts. He was so successful and so ferocious in those days that we called him 'The Destroyer'—*Muparadzi.*"

Chitepo paused, his thoughts turned back to those days of hardship and death. He rubbed calloused fingers along his taut, flat cheeks, and went on quietly: "After Mugabe was elected Prime Minister, Muparadzi stayed on in the security forces and helped with the pacification of the country. When Joseph Nkomo rebelled against Mugabe, Muparadzi was in the thick of it, helping our people's liberation army because he was determined that the new state would be successful."

Nkala fiddled with his tea cup, put it down carefully, and looked up, shaking his head doubtfully. "What can one man do?"

"This one is intelligent and experienced. He has a wild sort of daring that solves problems others find impossible. We would ask him to find out who these assassins are, who is behind them. If it is necessary, he will not hesitate to eliminate them. Let me repeat that, sir: *If it is necessary, he will not hesitate to eliminate them.* He knows that we can win only by meeting force with force."

Chitepo hesitated, watching for some sign of approval on

Nkala's face. He added, hopefully, "I could help him—in complete secrecy—with information, with weapons if he should need them, with transportation. He would have to be told what we know and what we guess. I would maintain contact with him but keep the party out of it."

It was Nkala's turn to stand and pace the floor, to stare through the dirty window into the fast-gathering darkness. He stood before the window several minutes, a small, broad-shouldered man in a dark suit and white shirt, curly gray-black hair clinging tightly to his round skull. He turned and wandered about the dreary room, stopping to look at a shelf of African animal figures carved from wood and stone. He smoothed the six-inch-long back ridge of a red-granite rhinoceros, then picked it up in his right hand and studied it, touching its head and hooves and horn with the fingers of his left hand. Looking at Chitepo over his shoulder, he asked, "Your work?"

"Yes, sir." Chitepo's face softened with love and pride.

"If it were not for our political struggle . . . Even so you are a distinguished sculptor."

"Thank you. I work at it when I can. The money these pieces bring helps me stay alive."

Nkala smiled sympathetically. He went to the door and opened it for a moment and listened to the shouts of children playing on the worn blacktop of the uncurbed street. He turned away and came back to the packing-box that served Peter Chitepo as a table. He lifted the teapot and held it tipped to his cup, pouring nothing because the pot was empty, considering Chitepo's proposal.

Chitepo saw that the wrinkles around Nkala's eyes had become very deep, as if he were trying to see through darkness into the future. The heavy lips were pursed in an almost childlike pout, and the broad shoulders bowed forward. Chitepo sensed the weight of responsibility this man carried, and for a moment he pitied him, but he maintained his silence.

Nkala said, repeating himself, "It could mean disaster for the party and for our effort to help the people of South Africa if it became known that the party is attacking its Communist members. Can we trust the discretion of an outsider?"

"He is not an outsider. His values are ours."

"And you trust him?"

"I owe him my life several times over. If he decides to help us, he will proceed wisely but stop at nothing."

Nkala nodded his round head emphatically, making his decision. "May God forgive me," he said. "We will ask this man to help us. I see no other way." He raised his voice, and Chitepo heard the soft Bantu aspirants whispering like ancient Africa behind the English words. "But only you and I and he shall know. My colleagues in the National Executive Council are not to be involved. If I have decided incorrectly I will take the blame and go down alone. May I meet your Muparadzi?"

Chitepo smiled exuberantly and brought his hands together the way the Shona people of Zimbabwe do, making a slow clapping sound. "I was hoping you would want to," he said. "Three years ago, he retired from Mugabe's security forces and went into business in Harare. We should go to his house late tonight when people are asleep."

WHEN Taylor Quimby decided to retire from Mugabe's Special Security Service three years after Mugabe had been elected Prime Minister, it had seemed to him that six years in Rhodesia/Zimbabwe were enough. But Mugabe's Minister of Commerce and Trade had summoned him and said, "We hate to lose you.

The nation needs educated and vigorous black people who will work for our prosperity. We want you to stay. Go into the import business, into pharmaceuticals. We desperately need penicillin, terramycin, tetrocyclin, and other drugs—for our wounded, for the diseases that have increased during the fighting, for the people who spread venereal diseases as if they were giving away honey. Because you are an American, you can make good contacts in the United States and Germany and England. We will loan you enough money to get started; we will clear your requests and expedite your licenses and see that your goods come through the borders without difficulty. But we will not bail you out if you fail to make profits, and if you do not repay our loan, the business will revert to us."

Quimby had been thirty-three then, tired of war, feeling his age. He had stayed, and worked hard, and now he had money in British and Swiss banks, excellent credit ratings in New York and Chicago, a tight little house in the Mount Pleasant suburb of Harare, and an almost unbearable burden of restlessness.

He knew very well that he should be content to live in a city where blacks and whites ruled together, where a man's worth was recognized regardless of his color, where he had friends. But the spurs of impatience with himself and with the work he was doing roweled constantly at his conscience.

When that restlessness first began to plague him he had thought he was suffering from homesickness, and had despised himself. Was he truly pining for the filthy streets and racial sickness of Detroit? Was he such a miserable, soft-headed idiot that he wanted to get back where he could be insulted and hated every minute of the day, where he would have to live in certain parts of the city, walk fast past the police with his head down, and be thankful if Whitey let him have a steady job? Was he so damned stupid he could be homesick for that?

When he examined his restlessness more seriously he quickly understood that homesickness was not the problem. He was chafing at the bit to get started on new and useful work.

He possessed training and experience that had to be used in the struggle for black equality, and he was letting the sharp edge of his ability grow dull with peace and money making.

His skills were of no use in the United States; he had learned that years ago. There, too many blacks spent their time on welfare, whining that Whitey owed them more. In the worst parts of the cities at home, they huddled in the slums, trading drugs and women and booze, rapping on the street corners, living on what they could scrounge or steal, or taking the scummy, part-time jobs white people handed down to them like raggedy old clothing.

And in the cleaner parts of the cities where the whites just barely tolerated them, other blacks lived at the edges of the middle class, desperate to keep what they had won, wanting no trouble, no trouble with anyone, terrified that they might lose the little they had.

There were the others who had got themselves through the universities and into the professions; they were struggling hard to hold their places, scrambling for their share of the spoils so hard they couldn't look back without shuddering. And there were a few thousand young people, trying to climb upward by getting education, moving through the universities, keeping their heads down, working hard.

All kinds of blacks lived in America, he knew that. But the one thing very few of them were prepared to do was fight for their rights.

And fighting was his profession.

In Vietnam he had sloshed around in rice paddies and mud as an infantryman for two years and got himself shot through the chest. He'd come back to Wayne State University, where he had already put in two years, and he'd earned himself a degree in political science and a wife who wanted life to be nothing but booze and pot parties. When she realized that he was what she called "a mootherfookin' drone," which took her six whole months, she walked out without a word one day, and he'd never heard from her again.

That was the year when all the Vietnam veterans came home; the best job he could find with his degree in his pocket was carting parts up to the line at Ford's River Rouge Plant. He wanted dignity and respect; he wanted to do something useful, something significant with his life, to make a contribution, and he wanted his share of the rights and freedoms the Constitution promised. But what he got was insults, people who called him "Nigger," as if that was his name, white people who hated and feared him and everyone else with a black skin because they couldn't see past the black, and a couple of friends who wanted him to help them run heroin in through the St. Lawrence Seaway.

Remembering the comradeship of Vietnam, he had fled back into military service, talking his way into the Special Forces. But Vietnam was over. Training the Green Berets, who were considered incredibly tough, was easy and repetitious for him; peace had come; macho talk and stifling routine monopolized the time of men whose duty it was to keep themselves fit for action they might not see for decades.

That wasn't what he was hunting for.

A new unit was being formed at Fort Bragg in late 1977, the Delta Force. Scuttlebutt said that it had developed the toughest training known to man—learned from the British SAS and the West German Grenzschutzgruppe 9. It was training for counterinsurgency, for fighting terrorists, boarding planes to free civilians, breaking into buildings to free hostages. He talked himself into the Delta Force, lived through three cycles of the training, and began to train others.

For months he fired every small-arms weapon known to man three or four hours a day, made endless treks alone or with a small team in the dead of winter and on the hottest days of the summer through West Virginia hills and forests and Georgian swamps, practiced assaults in every kind of closed space—subways, alleys, planes, buildings—learned French and studied international politics. . . .

And after he had been around the cycle once too often he realized that his whole life boiled down to waiting for the moment when the President or some general might order the unit to assault a hijacked plane or an occupied building, or dash into a foreign country to rescue U.S. citizens from some crazy bunch of terrorists. Meanwhile, more macho, more training dreamed up by sadists trying to prove that they and their men were the toughest bastards in the world, more desperate efforts to keep from going batty with boredom, and the endless round of getting more and more prepared for whatever was going to happen but never did and probably never would.

He brooded for months about the futility of training that was never used. Men looking for mercenaries who would sign on to help save one or another African country for its rulers offered him high pay in gold. He rejected their offers, but began to study those African wars. His attention focused more and more on the struggle of the black people of Rhodesia for the right to govern themselves, and one day when he was on furlough, he walked into an office in New York and volunteered to serve in ZANLA, the Zimbabwean African National Liberation Army.

At first the people he talked with thought he wanted them to hire him as a mercenary, but he insisted that he would work at the pay level of everyone else in the guerrilla forces, which was exactly nothing with a little food thrown in, and they accepted him.

He worked out his resignation from the Delta Force, taking a lot of criticism in the process, got himself into Africa with the last of his savings, landed in a guerrilla camp southeast of Salisbury near the Mozambique border, and within days knew he'd found his niche. He and his comrades fought arrogant units of well-armed whites who thought God had personally selected them to rule and exploit the blacks of Southern Rhodesia forever. And at least on some days his experience and knowledge and the way he managed his units helped win battles and save black men's lives.

Now he worried that he was getting old in this import business; thirty-five, almost thirty-six. He had helped Zimbabwe. He and other black men had fought and won their freedom; they were building their own society; they were responsible for their own government, and they had not thrown the whites out. On the contrary, Mugabe had meant it when he said there would be an end of racism. Most of the whites were still here, and prospering.

But Quimby was profoundly uneasy about getting old and rich while millions of blacks were still oppressed by whites—in South Africa and back home. If his life was to have any real meaning, he was convinced, it was absolutely essential that he use his skills to fight for the only thing he believed in, the only thing worth giving his life for—the right of black people to govern themselves and live with dignity.

In the evenings, when he was not with a woman or other friends or down in Mozambique trying to hand-carry a shipment away from the wharves of Maputo and across the border into Zimbabwe without being robbed of more than half its value, he worked at a hobby that helped keep him sane. He pored over maps of Botswana and Namibia and Zimbabwe's border with

South Africa, pondering how the war in South Africa would have to be fought when it came.

He followed with intense interest the grim game the African National Congress was playing, putting its guerrillas across borders into South Africa, building military strength and political experience among the people there. Twenty-four million blacks were under the Afrikaners' guns, resisting in any way they could. Sooner or later they were going to explode. The struggle would be bitter and long, and he intended to do his bit.

But the time wasn't ripe. Not enough of South Africa's blacks were ready to fight; they supported the ANC but trembled at the power of the Afrikaners. South Africa's army and air force and police and security organizations were too immense and terrifying; the Afrikaners were clever and ruthless, and they knew how to make themselves appear to be invincible. They manipulated their instruments of politics and terror skillfully, splitting political groups, terrorizing the townships, slamming thousands of opponents into jails where no one could find them, killing hundreds.

Nonetheless, the great rebellion was coming. He could feel its heat the way a person feels the heat of lava dripping from a volcano. There would be war; he wanted to be ready and hoped to God he would be young enough to help and wise enough to know where in the cities and in the countryside the kinds of actions he could lead would be most effective.

This was one of those nights when he was poring over his maps. He looked up quickly when someone tapped at the window in his bedroom. He walked into the bedroom without turning on the light, hearing the tapping again, and he stood against the wall trying to see into the dark. Two men. He could not make out their features. He went flat on the floor and raised a hand to open the window slightly, and he heard a man outside whisper, "Muparadzi, we need to talk with you. Turn out your lights and unlock your back door."

A few years back certain men had called him Muparadzi, and he and they had sworn to be friends forever. Quimby went through the house turning out lights, unlocked the door to his little kitchen, and stood away against the wall as the two men entered.

THE shade was drawn at the bedroom window and a blanket was stretched over the shade. The bedroom itself was wild color—carved African figures stood close together on two tables, bright woolen squares and carved heads hung against pale yellow walls, and a queen-sized bed was covered with a red, black, and white Zulu-styled spread.

While Peter Chitepo sat on the bed explaining the reason for their visit, Quimby walked about the room and studied Herbert Nkala's face.

He had heard much about Nkala. Everyone in Africa knew his story. One of the senior heroes of the African National Congress. Eight years on Robben Island locked up near the famed Nelson Mandela, chief of the ANC. Removed to a hospital at Pollsmoor on the mainland, he had escaped by taking the place of a dead man in a coffin, and he had immediately gone back to work, organizing attacks on police stations. Arrested again, and freed. Arrested again, and freed: too stubborn to back away until a sentence of death was put on his head and the party ordered him to leave South Africa and come to ANC headquarters in Zambia, at Lusaka. Even then, he had returned to organize new fighting groups and manage the sabotaging of the power station at Johannesburg. For years he had been one of the five or six leaders who held the movement together and drove it forward. In his mid-fifties now—one of the great men, one of the brave men.

Quimby was impressed by the air of modesty in the quiet, controlled face, the careful way Nkala studied him, and the way he listened to Chitepo's words, nodding his approval. It seemed to him that this man had outgrown the idea of fear; he was dedicated to a cause that could never be abandoned, and he would remain in the struggle until it was won or he was dead. He was what a man was supposed to be. . . .

"You know how the ANC is organized," Chitepo told him. "A great umbrella over members from many parties, unions, church groups, and so on—all the people who stand for democracy and majority rule in South Africa. And although each individual who joins our party may have differing opinions because of his other affiliations, the Congress is great because it has found room for all those who want change and who stand for equality and majority rule."

Chitepo paused and pointed a long finger at Quimby. Speaking carefully, he said, "Here are some facts: First, three of our ANC leaders who are also members of our National Executive Council have been murdered in the last three weeks. Second, three weeks from now, on the fifteenth of November, there is to be an international conference of the ANC in Lusaka."

He placed the glass of whiskey Quimby had given him on the floor untasted, and he looked up, glaring furiously. "Now here's the point: None of the Communist leaders who are in the ANC's National Executive Council were present at the meetings where the attacks were made; the three who died were all non-Communists. And what does that mean? Three weeks ago the National Executive was made up of thirty members. Nineteen were ANC, the other eleven were also members of the South African Communist Party. At this moment, given the deaths, there are eleven Communists and sixteen non-Communists on the National Executive Council."

Quimby interrupted from the other side of the room. "And you believe the SACP intends to kill more of your non-Communist ANC leaders because it's going for total control?"

"It is a possibility," Nkala murmured, watching his eyes.

Chitepo nodded his narrow head emphatically, as if he wished to blot out Nkala's moderation. He got up from the bed and pounded a fist into the open palm of his other hand. "I'm sure of it. The Communists are denouncing non-Communist members, beating them up; they call our people 'paid agents of the CIA'; their thugs threaten to kill rank-and-file members who are anti-Communist or non-Communist. I'm convinced that the SACP leaders intend to create more vacancies in the National Executive and fill them with Communists before the international conference, and at the conference they intend to gain total control of the National Executive Council and the ANC."

Quimby swung his hands and arms outward, relaxing the tension in his muscles. He was about five-foot-ten, compact and slender-looking with good shoulders and chest and a flat stomach. He still faithfully drilled himself with the rigorous calisthenics the Delta Force had taught him and jogged too many miles each morning before heading for the office, keeping himself ready.

The regimen showed in his shoulders and neck. Swinging his arms that way in his dark blue sweatsuit, he looked like a light-heavyweight boxer loosening up for a fight. The skin of his face had a sheen like dark mahogany in the yellow light of a lamp, and his high cheekbones threw the almost hollow cheeks into darkness. He moved about the room frowning thoughtfully, black brows down over his eyes, heavy lips parted.

Nkala leaned forward with one hand lifted, politely asking for moderation. "You must understand, sir, we are not naive; we know what the long-range Communist objectives are, but for the moment we want them contained inside our coalition where every viewpoint can be represented. However, we *cannot* permit them to seize the ANC and use it as a battering ram for their proletarian revolution."

Quimby nodded that he understood, although he was not as certain as Nkala seemed to be that the Communists could be contained. He stood at a table that held the carved figure of a naked Shona hunter facing a lion with only a slender spear. He touched the point of the little spear, looked up at Chitepo and saw by Chitepo's flickering smile that for him too the lion was the SACP.

Although he had already guessed what they wanted from him and knew what his reply would be, Quimby asked, "Gentlemen, how can I help you?"

Peter Chitepo went prowling along the other side of the bed. He turned back to Quimby and spoke too loudly, sounding as if he were almost afraid to make his request. "We want you to find out who is doing the killing. We want you to stop them."

Quimby glanced quickly at Nkala, seeing that he was in agreement.

"You understand," Chitepo went on, "the ANC cannot be directly involved because if our involvement became public the consequences could be ruinous. There are too many possibilities: What if Russia and her little whore, the GDR, are back of this conspiracy? They provide us with weapons and training. Will they hold these back if they learn that the ANC is fighting the SACP? At the same time, if it should suddenly appear that the SACP has taken over the whole ANC, South Africa might use the threat of Communism as an excuse to invade Zimbabwe to end Mugabe's regime and get rid of us at the same time. They're trying to do this kind of thing right now in the other Front Line States. Someone outside the ANC must identify the assassins and stop them before it's too late." He rubbed his hands nervously along his thighs, and added: "I can provide weapons, information you will need, money to pay fighting men."

Quimby put his hands flat against his stomach and let out a great breath that was almost a sigh of relief. This was the meaningful work he had been wanting; his decision was already made.

He spoke to Chitepo: "Give me a cut-out for communication with you, someone not known to be ANC, someone who can move messages between us quickly. And—" His tone changed and became more respectful as he turned to Nkala. "I must ask that neither of you tell anyone at all that I am involved. I will try to get to your assassins before they know we're looking for them."

Chitepo and Nkala exchanged glances, Chitepo's tight-skinned face wrinkling into a delighted smile, and Quimby asked, "So when is the next meeting of ANC leaders?"

"Tomorrow night," Chitepo replied, ducking his head apologetically. "Four of our leaders. Here in the city."

"You don't give me much time."

Quimby stood perfectly still, thinking hard, working on the outline of a plan. In a moment, he said, "We'll have to tell the members not to be there. You do it, Peter, personally. Speak directly to the leaders themselves; make sure they don't discuss the change with anyone in the SACP, not even their secretaries. Don't tell them what we suspect. Just say the meeting has been canceled." He put pillows against the head of the bed, sat on the mattress and leaned back. "Tell me about the meeting place, how the others were killed, and how I am to contact my cut-out."

QUIMBY crouched in the darkness, watching the approaches to the house. He carried a heavy knife with a six-inch double blade, and he strained his senses to see or hear the men who might be coming to kill the ANC leaders who were supposed to be meeting inside.

Earlier in the day he had looked up two of his old fighters, men he knew felt as he did about the ANC. He had squatted on the ground outside George Mungu's shanty in Highfield and discussed with him and Shodiksa Shara the plan he had in mind and the help he needed. Mungu, bandy-legged, stolid and powerful, with a heavy jaw and watchful eyes, ran an unregistered secondhand goods store from the junk piled high at his shanty, inside and out. During the war and the pacification actions he had been absolutely fearless in battle, but in day-to-day matters he was ruled by his Shona belief in tribal and ancestral spirits, good and bad, and in the witches he discovered almost everywhere.

Shara, slender and tall and hollow-cheeked, his black skull close-shaven, worked at the Shell Company in Workington, and had been reminded by both Quimby and Mungu of the old days when they had called him *Mutota,* The Wet One, because of the way his sphincter had once let go during a nighttime firefight.

"It is the same cause," Quimby had explained. "The same enemy, but there are more of them this time. Outsiders want to tell Africans how they will be governed, and they are murdering the ANC leaders in order to have their way." He had explained carefully how he thought they might discourage the assassins.

Both men heard him out silently, and when Quimby had finished, Mungu shrugged his powerful shoulders and said, "It would give my life meaning to serve with Muparadzi again. He is a powerful spirit who will not leave the land until Africans have won back their freedom."

Mutota nodded his head in agreement, laughing with excitement. "Like the old days, eh? We have a big purpose in life again. That is more than I have found in these starving days of peace."

Quimby had never fully understood all the reasons for the kind of friendship that grew up in a fighting unit, but he knew well how powerful it was. When the chips were down, it wasn't God or the nation or equality that moved men to fight; it was the comradeship, the fine pleasure of working together when every man knew that his buddies could be trusted to the death and every man knew that he was trusted. In Mungu and Shara he had friends who would fight. . . .

Near the front door of the one-story bungalow, hidden by flowering bougainvillea, Mungu, armed with a knife and a short iron bar, knew exactly what he had to do. On the low roof above the door, Shara lay ready to make an attack from the air if that became necessary.

Quimby had been concealed in a stand of bushes at the curb for three-quarters of an hour when he heard a car motor cut off on a nearby street. He clicked his tongue twice against the roof of his mouth, alerting the others. And he peered intently through the darkness in the directions from which they had already calculated an attack would have to come—along the line of violet-flowered jacaranda trees near the curb, along the low fence-line sheltered by bushes that surrounded the neighboring house, or from the back of the house through the fir trees that bordered the garden.

Earlier in the day, they had done what they could to give the living room of this house owned by an ANC member the appearance of a place where men were holding a meeting. Mungu had ransacked the piles of junk around his shanty and had turned up four naked clothing store dummies they had dressed from the waist up in dark clothing, fitting the bald plastic heads with what looked like tight black heads of hair. They had placed the dummies in chairs around a table, elbows on the table, dark-stained faces bent downward as though each man was studying the papers in front of him.

Only one weak globe lighted the scene, but even so, Quimby knew, the deception could be effective for only a second or two. A glance would tell anyone who entered the room that the figures at the tables were not men.

He saw a shadow move from one tree to the next along the street seventy yards away. Another followed, and another, and as he watched, still another.

Four of them. His heart began to thump hard, and he breathed deeply, pumping oxygen into his blood, watching the men approach.

They were damned good; they moved swiftly with the forceful purpose of highly trained soldiers in top physical condition, advancing one man at a time in an orderly but silent drill that must have been rehearsed somewhere many times. Sure of themselves . . .

When they reached the trees near the front of the house they delayed for a moment; then two of them dashed forward to blend into the fence-line at the west side of the house. Another ran forward to the east corner, and as that one ran Quimby saw the shape of a gun held high, an extravagantly thick barrel pointing upward, and he knew that these men were carrying silenced guns.

He felt a coldness clamp down on his mind, and perspiration suddenly dampened his skin. It was certain now; there could be no negotiating with this group, no attempt to take its members alive. They were loaded for bear and it was kill or be killed. He felt a sadness, a regret that it had to be this way, and he eased his shoulders forward, bowing his back, loosening his muscles for what would have to be intensely swift action, concentrating all his attention on the front of the house.

The fourth man left the cover of the tree that had been hiding him and ran straight to the front door. The men at the west corner of the house joined him, and in another moment the other flitted in that direction across the close-cropped lawn.

The door splintered loudly as they hit it; then they were all inside, and Quimby was racing forward, wanting to get as close to that open doorway as possible, and as he ran he heard the loud-whispered "phut, phut" of the silenced guns. Then he was at the door, and he knew from the sound of a muttered curse and the following silence that the killers had realized they were in a trap. Now they knew they were the prey, not the hunters. Now they had to surrender, or run, or turn and fight.

They poured through the door in a rush, moving in disciplined, muscled hurry, and Quimby grabbed the first one by the arm, using the man's forward impetus to swing him away from the door, pulling him into his knife so that the blade sliced across the throat hard enough to cut it through and silence the voice box. He caught at the man's gun, knocking it away, and as he dropped that one, he saw that Mungu had taken the second one out with his iron club and was straightening up, turning back toward the doorway.

Mutota's dark figure plunged down from the roof on top of the third man, and Quimby counted that one finished. He grabbed at the fourth man, hearing the "phut" from the gun in this one's hand, seeing the spurt of the flame from the barrel and feeling its heat on his cheek. He wrestled the gun hand upward, stamped on a foot, lifted his knee into the man's crotch, and stepped back to put his knife into the man's gut, hearing the gun repeat its soft popping sound, aware that he had a powerful and determined fighter on his hands who meant to shoot his way out of this. Then the vigorous strength that resisted him seemed to suffer a sudden shock, and he realized that the struggle was over, that Mungu had crushed the man's skull with his club, and he let the man fall.

The three of them stood breathing hard, hearts beating too fast, listening to silence, their eyes beginning to search the darkness for the backup these four might have brought along.

When there was no movement along the street, Quimby whispered, "Mungu, bring the van to the alley. Shara and I will carry the bodies back. Get the doors open as soon as you stop."

Mungu melted away in the darkness, and Quimby knelt to turn a body in preparation for lifting it. He remembered the guns and felt along the ground until he found one of them—a machine pistol with a heavy silencer; he could not tell any more than that. He put it under his arm, and whispered to Mutota, "I have one gun. Be sure we have three more. We wipe out every trace."

He heard Shara grunt as he lifted a body over his shoulder. He bent and gathered the corpse at his feet into his arms, and they moved along the side of the house to the service road. Mungu had not yet arrived, and they laid the bodies at the edge of the alley and went back for the others.

When they returned, Mungu had loaded the first two. They lifted the others in, and returned to retrieve the dummies inside the house. Of the four dummies, the heads of two had been smashed by bullets, the chest of the third had been flattened. The fourth had simply fallen off the chair, and Quimby wondered if someone had kicked it to the floor in fury.

They carried the dummies to the van, closed the doors quietly, and moved to the front. They climbed into the front seat, and Mungu moved the van away without turning on the lights.

They were heading for the Bluestone Farm twelve miles out on the Chinhoyi Road, and until they were out of the city all three sat tense and silent, staring straight ahead, each of them thinking his own thoughts. Then Quimby said, "When you get there drive right into the barn on the left, about a hundred yards from the house. The place has been abandoned."

Mungu drove carefully, eyes on the road. "Taylor?"

"Yes."

"When we put those bodies in, did you see it?"

"Did I see what?"

"Those are white men with black stuff on their faces and hands."

Quimby felt a sudden jerk of panic and disbelief. Had they killed Zimbabwean police? Some of those British police advisers who were still out here? That couldn't be. Why would they be sneaking into that particular house in the middle of the night?

With his mind searching anxiously for other explanations, he climbed over the seat to get into the back. He knelt and turned a body to face him, ripped open the dark shirt and saw white flesh; he scraped a fingernail across the face of a second corpse and saw the pale cast of skin where he had scraped. He swore aloud; then, struggling to suppress the queasiness of his belly, he began a methodical search of the bodies, looking for something that would tell him where these men came from.

Whoever they were, they had been carefully drilled and thoroughly inspected before they had left whatever center had dispatched them. Nothing in their pockets, nothing around their necks or wrists; the labels had been cut from their clothing. He studied the clothing in the half-light of the dashboard—civilian trousers of four different kinds, different makes of soft-soled shoes, dark shirts, two of them woven jerseys with long sleeves, two of them heavy cotton. He touched their hair, looking for telltale, military brush-cuts, but the haircuts differed, from dark and shaggy to almost bald. Civilians then?

He lifted one of the machine pistols and examined it, recognizing the make now. A Skorpion, made in Czechoslovakia. An old gun with a complicated silencer created for clandestine work, the whole thing fairly short, much shorter than the widely used British Sterling. He wondered where these men had got their hands on Skorpions, and thought at once of the East German advisers who were in Zimbabwe helping Mugabe shape up his security battalions.

He gave the silenced gun to Shara, asking him to examine the cartridges, and Shara, leaning close to the dashlight, shelled bullets out of the gun's magazine, and said, "The bullets are manufactured in South Africa."

Quimby knelt behind the front seat and examined a cartridge himself, seeing the South African designation on its rim, and the skin at his forehead tightened. He felt the impact of this discovery in his belly and scrotum, in the sudden tautness of the muscles of his back and shoulders, and in the way his fists clenched. His mind had already leaped to the conclusion that he had killed South African commandos sent here to murder the ANC leaders, that he had given the Afrikaners an excuse for coming into Zimbabwe with all the force they had, and he felt the beginnings of panic.

He had been trying to step on a spider and had fallen into a tangle of vipers. The possible consequences of what he had done tried to surge through his brain all at once in a frantic mass, and he knew that he had to think this out rationally, objectively. South African commandos? How could they be involved in a struggle between the Communists and the ANC? How in hell could they be mixed up in this game?

He realized that he was perspiring heavily, more frightened than he had been for a long time, and he knew that for the moment he must forget the fact that he might have a load of dead South Africans in the van. First he had to get rid of the bodies and do a good job of it, covering every trace of this night's action. Then and only then could he take time to think about the consequences of what he had done.

In a rickety barn on a farm abandoned four years ago by a white

Rhodesian farmer, the three of them dug into sandy soil, making a grave deep enough for the commandos as well as for the shattered dummies. They threw the guns in after the bodies, covering everything and stamping the soil down until it was almost even with the old surface. Mungu drove the van back and forth over the grave, packing down the earth; then they patiently stamped and smoothed the soil and finally roughed up the surface again.

Mungu retrieved his bicycle from the roof of the van, and came and put a hand on Taylor's shoulder, a somber expression on his broad, homely face. "This will not be the end of it," he stated. "An evil *ngozi* caused this to happen. Your spirit must fight the ngozi until what is proper for Africans has been restored."

Never quite sure what Mungu was telling him about the spirits, Quimby said, "It is just the beginning, my friend."

"Your spirit has great power, Muparadzi." Mungo's white teeth shone in the darkness in a quick smile, and he pedaled away.

Shara waited while Quimby brushed the steel floor of the van with sand and swept the sand out and inspected the walls to be certain that no telltale signs of the corpses remained.

Quimby inspected the ground once more, quickly, under the van's lights. Then Shara waved a hand and drove the borrowed van away.

Quimby walked two miles in the darkness along a pathway at the edge of planted fields, aware now that for October the night was very cool, shivering under his damp shirt. His car, a white Toyota Camry, was parked at the end of a wheat field under several graceful brachystegia trees. He pulled into the road and drove toward the city.

AT home, not needing lights because it was almost sunrise, Quimby brewed coffee and showered and began dressing for the office, letting his mind come back to the whiteness of those corpses. Perhaps they weren't South Africans at all. Perhaps this was just one more effort by a few soured white Rhodesians to breed trouble for Mugabe that might help them return to power. Or they could be mercenaries—from anywhere—here to do a cash killing for the SACP.

He wondered about *Umkhonto We Sizwe*—the Spear of the Nation—the ANC's military organization. It was common knowledge that its training, tactics, and leadership were dominated by Communists. Its best soldiers went for their advanced training to Angola and Cuba, to East Germany or the Soviet Union, and the man who had led them for years was now Chairman of the SACP. Were some of its members doing these killings? Or for that matter, were the German Democratic Republic's security advisers trying to provoke trouble that would weaken Mugabe and help to bring his rival, Joshua Nkomo, into power? Nkomo had always been the Soviet's choice. That fight wasn't over. . . .

He was more than half convinced that he was trying to lie to himself by considering these possibilities. If he had come eyeball to eyeball with the South African defense force, the fact had to be faced.

The thought of being up against South Africa's power turned his mind back to the first time he had come into open conflict with what had seemed then to be an all-powerful and hostile authority.

That had been almost twenty years ago. . . .

DETROIT. July 1967. Black people were rioting in the streets, breaking into stores, looting, carrying booze and television sets and shoes and even big overstuffed chairs down the middle of the street. Houses and stores in the area were burning; the air stank with the thick black smoke of burning tires and old wood.

Police clustered at street crossings around their patrol cars, letting crowds of noisy looters walk past them, trying only half-heartedly from time to time to stop someone, watching the whole thing with sick smiles as if they were part of a crazy circus.

Quimby was sixteen, cutting high school for the day. He had wandered for hours through the streets, scared but curious, trying to understand what was happening and why.

He knew the feeling of blind frustration well enough, the anger and resentment these others felt. He felt the way they did, but their actions seemed irrational to him. These were their own houses burning; some of the stores being looted were run by black brothers. Looters his age were giving away some of the stuff they had stolen, or throwing it into the gutters, and others were deliberately mocking and challenging the police to do something about it, almost as if they were trying to get themselves killed.

He understood what was happening well enough; his brothers were expressing their hatred of Whitey's system; they were saying that they hated the filth of the tenements they lived in and the lives they lived, that they wanted something better *right now*. They were saying that if it couldn't be better, they didn't want anything at all; they'd rather burn down the whole goddamned city; they'd rather be dead.

He had a sickeningly strong premonition that all this would come to nothing. Envy and hatred and anger weren't going to achieve anything useful unless a lot of black people were willing to settle down and work like hell for what they wanted. He had the idea that real progress would take years and years of uncompromising struggle. What was happening here was just a spontaneous explosion, a symptom of crazy, pent-up anger.

He came out of an alley to Twelfth Street, and a fat, white policeman not much older than he was yelled at him: "Hey you! Boy! Stop right there!"

Quimby stopped and turned, seeing the patrol car beyond, the cop's gray-haired partner lolling on the far side of it, a shotgun held upside down on his shoulder.

The young cop came closer and Quimby saw sweat pouring down his fat throat into the fuzzy red hair on the cop's chest; he caught the reek of sweat and tobacco and sour beer and saw what looked like a mixture of fear and curiosity in the man's eyes.

The cop poked his billy at Quimby and commanded: "All right, back up into the alley. Put your hands up against the wall. Lean forward. What you been stealing?"

Taylor did as he was told, and answered the question. "Nothin'. I ain't been stealing nothin'. I'm just lookin'."

"Don't give me that, you fucking nigger!" The billy slammed into the kidney area on Taylor's right side, starting an immense pain that sent a paralyzing shock through his whole body. And while he groaned and cringed under the pain, he felt the billy track its way up the center of his back and come down sharply on his left shoulder.

Taylor craned his neck around, crying and shouting: "It's true! I swear I ain't done nothin'!"

"Bullshit! You're like all the rest."

In the cop's frowning, meaty face, Taylor saw the white man's hatred and frustration and the desire to take his hurts out on somebody else. More—he sensed the urge to kill and realized that the cop must hate this life in the slums almost as much as the blacks did. *He wanted to punish someone. He wanted to hurt someone because he was suffering.* He swung his club across Taylor's rump, slammed it across the backs of Taylor's thighs. Then he snickered and the billy came poking up between Taylor's legs, searching for his genitals.

Taylor twisted around and tore the club out of the white man's hand. He reversed it, and holding it with both hands, he drove it hard into the fat belly; then he lifted it and slapped it down solidly on the blue-billed hat.

The look of astonishment and fear that had suddenly appeared on the sweaty red face turned to dazed helplessness. With his eyes wide open the cop fell on his back and rolled into the fetal position, his arms up over his head, moaning.

The partner would be coming, wanting to know what was happening in the alley. Quimby remembered the shotgun. He pulled open the young cop's holster flap, yanked out the pistol, and turned and ran.

And all the way down the alley as he ran, he told himself that he was not running because he was afraid. He was mad, yes, crazy-mad at being treated like a dog, and determined not to be abused any further. Humiliated, yes, but not afraid. Not one goddamned bit afraid of those fat white bastards.

Behind him, too far away to be dangerous, the shotgun boomed. He threw the pistol away, turned the corner, ducked into an open-doored, gray-sided, clapboard house, and ran right through it. He came out on a fenced backyard, crossed it under the eyes of an old woman and three black children playing there, and went through the back gate. He trotted over to Virginia Avenue and ran on to West Euclid. He hid for two hours in a friend's cellar, sobbing out his fury, telling himself that he should have stayed and fired the pistol at that old son of a bitch with the shotgun. . . .

THAT had been a long time ago. Since then, he'd seen a lot of violence more terrible than those riots, and lived through it. He was going to live through this thing too.

He would find out who these people were and stop them. He had promised Nkala.

2

JUST after eleven o'clock the next morning, Quimby left his office on Manica Road and walked up the First Street shopping mall with its huge pots of trees set out in the street. Earlier in the month, down in Mozambique on the Maputo wharves, he had stifled in the humid heat, but up here on Harare's high plateau the dry air invigorated him. This fine, clean city was his home. He loved it.

He walked in bright sunshine, wearied by the night's work, but determined to keep his normal routine going through the day. Importing pharmaceuticals was as good a cover as he was going to get.

He was dressed in a dark blue springweight suit and cordovan loafers—a narrow blue tie over a white shirt. He was a Harare businessman in good standing, well enough known in the city to be greeted by several men as he turned east on Stanley and walked past Cecil Square.

The square itself was in all its glory, trees and bushes covered with blossoming flowers—pale violet, white and yellow and red. Even the Mexican feather-duster tree by the fountain waved its long tendrils at him as he passed.

He entered the elegant Voorman Hotel, walked through the busy lobby where employees who had seen him many times before nodded or smiled their recognition.

He stepped into an elevator, got off at the fourth floor, looked right and left, saw the maid's cart halfway down the hall at his left, and walked that way. Just after he reached the cart piled high with towels and soap and bottles of cleaning fluid, he passed an open door, glanced inside, and saw a chambermaid moving purposefully at her cleaning. He stepped through the doorway, noting the defensive swiftness in the way the woman turned to face him.

"Tandy?"

She was in her late twenties, attractive, with the short, flat nose, dark eyebrows, rounded cheeks, and smooth forehead of a dark-skinned Cleopatra. A white *duka*, or scarf, covered her hair, emphasizing her black lashes and large eyes. He had a quick impression of a good figure under her yellow smock, not terribly slender, but high-breasted, full-thighed, and strong, two or three inches shorter than he was.

"Actually, I'm Thandiwe," she said pertly. "That translates into English as 'Beloved,' but since I'm beloved by no one, they call me Tandy." Her smile was cautious, her eyes watchful.

"I'm Chifamba," he said, as Peter had told him to do, completing their recognition ritual.

A quick welcoming smile lighted her face, and she moved to the door and closed it. "I didn't expect to see you so soon. Peter said—We don't have much time to talk. My supervisor will be—"

He interrupted. "We don't have any time at all. Tell Peter I must see him at noon. There's some kind of conference going on out at the Sheraton. Tell him to come in the hotel entrance and drift toward the conference hall. I'll pick him up along the way."

"Peter said I was to keep you two apart."

"Tell him this is urgent."

"Yes suh! Right you are, suh!" Her voice mimicked the British-like overloud submissiveness of a Rhodesian trooper, mocking him.

He held out his hands asking her to forgive his abruptness. "This *is* urgent, Tandy. We're not playing a goddamned game. *Tell him!*"

He was out of the room and moving. He climbed two floors of stairs and took the elevator to the lobby. Outside, he made his way through a crowd of Indian women in bright sarongs who were coming off a bus that had taken them to see the wild animals at the McIlwaine Reserve. He rode in a taxi to the Sheraton, hoping that its latest conference had collected enough people to cover his meeting with Peter.

PETER came past the big front entrance and went on through the huge lobby; he stopped to look into a bar, then ambled on toward the corridor that led to the conference hall. That gave Quimby time to look around at the people gathering in the lobby from various meeting rooms and watch the entrance for another half-minute. Peter was too skillful to drag a tail behind him. After all, he was the ANC's counterintelligence chief in Zimbabwe, but there was no harm in making certain.

Quimby sauntered after his tall friend, pausing as Peter had done to look into the bar but actually checking the long mirror there to see if anyone was following. Most of the traffic was in the opposite direction; the two of them breasted a crowd of conference participants surging out of the meeting rooms under the gallery of the great conference hall.

These rooms would be empty now, Quimby guessed. He overtook Peter at a door, and pushed it open to glance inside. A man and a woman sat in the huge room about halfway down the ranks of chairs, heads together, discussing a paper they held between them. Quimby did not know either of them; he looked up at Chitepo's thin face questioningly, but Peter shook his narrow head and led him up a stairway to the gallery of hundreds of steeply rising empty seats.

They leaned against a wall just off the stairway, a position that gave them a view of the whole hall, and Peter said disapprovingly, "I gave you a cut-out so that we would not have to take the risk of being seen together. You see her once, jump down her throat, and demand to see me."

Quimby said, "Your assassins came in last night, four of them."

Peter's left cheek twitched. He lifted a hand to place two fingers on the twitching and squinted intently at Quimby, waiting for him to go on.

"They were white," Quimby said. "The only pertinent evidence I have—very thin—says they're from South Africa."

Peter grimaced and put both hands flat against his stomach. "God!" he said with a sound like a groan. "Where are they now?"

"You don't want to know."

"Will they be found?" Dark eyes regarded Quimby fearfully.

34

"No."

Peter sighed, and rubbed hard at the tic in his cheek. He kept his voice down, but Quimby heard the panic. "Why would South Africans be hitting just the ANC leaders? Maybe SACP keeps its meetings secret better than we do. Jesus, Taylor! We've got to pull out of this. I'll tell Nkala—"

Quimby put a hand on Peter's bony shoulder and squeezed hard. "We can't pull out. Not now, not ever. Get hold of yourself."

Chitepo threw him a frightened grin, thin lips pulled back against his teeth. "How do you know they were South Africans?"

"They were white. They carried Czech guns loaded with South African cartridges."

"That doesn't prove anything," Chitepo objected. "The only thing that makes sense is that the SACP is behind this."

"So I'll keep an open mind. The important point right now is that you've got an informer in your organization."

Chitepo groaned again. "We're riddled with informers, black Judases who spy on us for anyone who will pay. But I've checked—the ones we know about don't have access to information about the leaders' meetings."

"So there's someone you don't know about. Can you review everyone who has access to that information or to people who do? We want anyone who's acting jumpy, who's mad at the system, or spending too much money, or got himself a new woman. And if you turn up anyone who deserves attention can you put him under surveillance?"

Peter said regretfully, "I don't have enough staff." He looked into Quimby's impatient eyes, looked quickly away, then added, "I'll start as soon as I get back to the office."

"Think SACP, but don't forget South Africa."

"Ah, Sweet Jesus, yes," Peter said. He waited a moment, and when Quimby did not go on, he asked: "Why did you jump on Thandiwe?"

"She thinks we're playing games. Is she smart? Reliable? Steady?"

"Smart *and* reliable. Trained in a teachers' college—in math, and of all things, music. Motivated. She's given up teaching temporarily to do odd jobs around the city where I need her. She lost both her brothers in a police action at Alexandra outside Johannesburg last year. The police abused her."

"Abused?"

"Kept her locked up for months. Beat her with whips. Played with her. She won't say whether they raped her, but they usually do. She's carrying a big hate."

Quimby remembered her friendly smile, the warm grace of her movements, and regretted his sharpness with her. "I'll apologize." He came back to his first concern. "Can you give me a rundown on the ANC's administrative organization, on the people who have access to information about these meetings?"

"I'll give some paper to Tandy for you."

"And while you're looking, if you think you've found your informer, tell me before you do anything about it."

"Maybe you want to do it all?" Peter asked.

Quimby heard the resentment, and put out his hands in a pleading gesture. "Peter, please. What I meant was—you're counterintelligence; I'm operations. If you uncover the guy we want, let me follow up the lead and keep the ANC out of it. I'm anxious. The way those commandos handled themselves last night convinced me there'll be more of them. Find the informer for me, and I'll have a talk with him; then maybe we can go for the people behind this."

Peter's stare seemed to hold resentment or fear, and something else unaccountably hostile. He shrugged his shoulders almost imperceptibly, and Quimby sensed that he was being condemned for killing those commandos, for suggesting they might be South Africans.

Peter looked out across the conference hall, the tic pulling again at the tight skin below his eye. He waited a moment, and when Quimby shook his head, indicating that he had no more questions, Peter nodded good-bye and hurried away down the stairway.

Quimby saw a set of stairs at the far corner of the gallery. He walked between rows of seats to that stairway, waited several minutes, giving Peter ample time to clear the area; then he left the hotel, wondering if Peter was getting too old for this kind of work, if he was going to be too frightened to be useful.

WEARING faded jeans, a light blue polo shirt with short sleeves, and an old pair of jogging shoes, Quimby sat at a raw wooden table and smiled. His biceps and triceps and forearms bulged impressively, and the beer-server was quick and polite. The Chief's Den—at the northern edge of the industrial area called Southerton—was not the wildest nightclub in town, but neither was it a *shebeen*. What he had called a "blind pig" in Detroit was a "shebeen" in Harare; both were operated illegally by people selling home brew and rotgut in their parlors. Here in Harare the rotgut was called *kachasu,* and *The Herald* was constantly full of stories about people blinded or killed by a poison batch. Like Detroit.

The Chief's Den sold its beer and scotch legally to a good crowd.

He was here to see the floor show.

He sat drinking sour African beer out of a plastic mug and listening to the thumping of a four-piece band in the back room that made up in volume for what it lacked in finesse. Definitely not Louis Armstrong. Through the dark entrance to that room he could see several crowded tables, the corner of the band platform, black waitresses clad in brief yellow skirts and green blouses moving back and forth with their drink trays, reflections of orange lights playing on a tiny dance floor.

It was almost eleven o'clock. He drifted into the club and let himself be guided to a tiny table at the far side of the room. Another beer, this time a bottled Polish Pilsner, at five times the price he had paid for the African beer. Cover charge.

The dark room, crowded with tables and people, was suddenly filled with sounds of squeaking chairs and excited laughter as tables were turned and chairs moved so that everyone could see the floor show that was about to begin. After a few minutes people settled down and expectantly watched the small patch of light focused on a curtained entrance at the left of the bandstand.

A drum began to play a soft rhythmic pattern of sound, spreading its music through the room. Slowly, almost tentatively, an electric guitar picked up a cross-pattern that wove through the drum's rhythm, improvising a melody. Then a second drum, louder and more insistent than the first, began to pound out a steady beat that throbbed hard under the sounds of the other instruments.

Members of the audience began to move with the music, tapping the floor with their feet and the tables with their fingers, moving heads and shoulders and torsos, eager and excited. When the high, woody cry of a clarinet moved in and added a second complex improvisation that went singing in and out of the other rhythms, men and women in the room shouted with pleasure and grinned happily into each other's faces.

The drums increased the tempo, as if to test the ability of the audience to endure a swifter pace; the second drumbeat became more and more insistent until it was almost unbearable, rattling glasses, making everyone feel its percussive beat on their eardrums, in their bellies, on the edges of their teeth. Then, abruptly, the sounds fell to a whisper, the underlying beat pounding softly like someone's heart, and Tandy moved through the entranceway to the center of the dance floor.

She was dressed in the thinnest of Indian silks, wearing gold and silver anklets, her hips and legs naked but for a dark G-string beneath the swirl of translucent silver cloth that covered her almost to the ankles. A silver breast cloth only partially contained the full swell of her breasts. Her brown arms and shoulders were bare; her cheeks were boldly rouged; gold eyeshadow tinted her eyelids, and her lips were scarlet.

She began a dance that Quimby thought must be a blend of African and Hindu, fertility and the temple, but her own exuberant movements and the complex rhythms of the Shona tribal music that whispered through the drums, added a wild, strongly sexual excitement that seemed to compel her to strain against the more formal restraints of the music. She danced with muscled abandon, swaying, stamping, moving more quickly as the drumbeat increased its tempo, becoming almost frenzied when the second drum forced her on.

The pace of her undulations increased, her provocative smile seemed to light on every man in the room, her body promised pleasures beyond all ordinary pleasures. The pounding of the drums became almost unbearably loud, making Quimby's ears and diaphragm vibrate with the same frenzy that shook her hips and shoulders. He felt himself being caught up in the excitement, responding with a powerful hunger to have that hot body in his arms. He admired the fine, strong thighs, the perfectly rounded buttocks, the heaving belly and chest, the seductress look in Tandy's eyes as she came close to the edge of the dance floor and seemed to stare straight at him. Lusting for her, he stared back.

The music reached its crescendo. The breast cover went flying and Quimby caught his breath and strained to see and remember every detail of the shape and movement of those breasts as Tandy whirled. She made a final, climactic leap and ended on her knees, bowing forward, then leaning far back, her arms over her head. For an instant her breasts showed clear. Then the spot was extinguished, the drums stopped, and the sudden silence in the room seemed like a new and hurtful kind of sound. Men began to stamp on the floor then, yelling their approval, and they went on with that for many minutes, but Tandy had disappeared and she did not return.

Quimby went back to the bar, impressed by this new aspect of the impudent chambermaid he had seen in the morning. She was a beautiful and talented woman. Carrying a big hate, Peter had said. Devoted to the struggle against the apartheid rulers.

He wondered what life held in store for her, and could not erase the picture of her strong thighs and full breasts from his mind. This was no tall American black girl starving herself to look as if she had no hips, no breasts, no bottom, no curves in her legs; this was an African woman—proud and strong, with Cleopatra's face, thick full lips, expressive eyes wide-set above her short, broad nose, and the strength to dance like that and appear to love it. The sexual hunger she had roused in him still held him and he tried to shake it off, telling himself regretfully that she was a working partner, a colleague who had been brutalized by the South African police. She deserved respect and honor, not these hot fantasies he was having of seizing her and thrusting himself into her to the beat of those drums.

Outside The Chief's Den, he stepped out of the light at the

doorway and studied every shadow and doorway along the street; then he slipped along the building to a side entrance and told an ancient doorman that he wanted to see Tandy.

"Not unless she wants to see you," the old man told him.

Quimby gave him two Zimbabwean dollars and asked him to tell her that Chifamba wanted to see her.

The old man came back and pointed to a closed door of a compartment built inside a larger room stacked with crates and boxes. Quimby walked to the door, knocked, and opened it when Tandy called.

She wore a long red dressing gown, and her face was running with perspiration. She smiled warmly at him, as if he were an old friend, pulled him inside quickly, and closed the door behind him.

"Fantastic!" he said. "Beautiful! Where did you learn to dance like that?"

She laughed aloud at his enthusiasm. "Here and there. You do what comes naturally."

He didn't believe her. Her movements were too beautifully disciplined to be something she'd just picked up. "And where did you get that music?"

"Did you like it? It's Shona tribal music. Mixed with native Christian music and hard rock. That's my own arrangement."

He stood shaking his head. "I'm much impressed, not only by your talent but by your energy. If I tried to go through half the movements you make, I'd break my back or have a heart attack."

She ducked her head gracefully, thanking him for his compliments. She sat before a mirror and rubbed a white cream on her face, wiping away her makeup with soft paper napkins, and said, "Peter gave me whole pages of information for you. They're at my apartment. D'you know the employees' quarters beyond the parking lot back of the Voorman Hotel? Mine is the fourth one in the second row from the hotel. Number fourteen. Come at twelve-thirty and don't knock. Walk in and speak quietly so you don't wake my neighbors. I have to return the papers in the morning."

He felt the strong pull of the body whose lines he had memorized during the dance. He wanted to think up some excuse for staying. Instead, he nodded and smiled, and went back into the darkness, still hearing the pounding of the drums that had accompanied her dance. He had heard drums before; he had never seen a woman dance them alive and make them part of her life.

THE three rows of one-story concrete buildings behind the hotel were a cut better than most of the miserable shanties in the townships. They reminded him of the old-fashioned motels out on Woodward Avenue in Detroit and of a brothel the Chinese had built in Saigon. Paved ways between the rows were swept immaculately clean, and the lights at each end wiped out every shadow.

Quimby entered into darkness at number 14, closed the door at his back, and stood waiting. Tandy turned on a lamp and faced him, her back against the opposite wall. A narrow bed stood on one side of the room; closer to the doorway a woman's bicycle leaned against a wall; flanking Tandy, a straight chair, a long table with a lamp, books, papers, and sheets of music. Slave quarters. A nun's cell.

She was dressed for bed in a short green nightgown that displayed her legs and concealed her breasts but let him see them move under the material, and she held out a sheaf of papers to him.

She said, "I've got to be up at six. You've seen what kind of day I put in. I'm going to sleep. You can sit here at the table and read those, but leave them when you go. Put them under the newspapers."

He had hoped . . . He had wanted to get better acquainted. He had wanted to apologize for being so abrupt at the hotel. He riffled quickly through the sheets she had given him and said, "Tomorrow, first thing, tell Peter that I also want to see any information he can give me about the SACP members on the ANC National Executive Council. The people here are all ANC."

She yawned in his face, a healthy black leopardess too tired to stay awake. "All right. Will you come here for them tomorrow night?"

"Peter said that you work in the Mubare Market by the bus terminal in the afternoons."

"Tuesdays, Thursdays, and Saturdays till seven-thirty."

"I'll come buy something from you about one o'clock. . . . Give me the papers then, and I'll return them here tomorrow night. Same time?"

"Fine."

He hurried on. "Tandy, I'm sorry I jumped down your throat this morning. We've got to be very careful to keep what you're doing hidden so that you can be an effective cut-out, and that means no one should see you with me or be able to connect you with me. I broke the rules this morning because I thought Peter needed to know something in a hurry, but I didn't want to stay and debate things until people came by."

She gave him a forgiving smile. "You Tarzan, me Jane," she said, grinning impudently. "We will kill the lions together." She put a hand on his cheek affectionately, and said, "Good night, Ole Chifamba. You're going to keep your distance?"

He understood and grinned ruefully. "Not that I want to. You're quite a woman."

"And I'm damned tired. See you tomorrow."

She lay on her side in the narrow bed against the far wall and drew a sheet and a blanket up over her hips.

He pulled his mind away from her and spent an hour going through the papers Peter had sent. Vitae of low-level informers Chitepo had been watching for some time, with notes from Chitepo. None of them seemed to have any connection with the people who dealt with high-level meetings.

He studied the ANC organizational chart. Three sections here in Harare, subsections of the headquarters in Lusaka: the Secretariat, led by a woman, with four assistants, a much larger operations section for political action and propaganda, and an organization section that dealt with subordinate groups in the country. He guessed that the Secretariat would deal with scheduling meetings, setting up agendas, and getting out correspondence.

He wrote a note along the top of the chart: *Tandy, Ask Peter to watch the Secretariat people. I think the informer has got to be in there. Chifamba.*

He put that page on top of the others and went back to the informers Peter's notes said could be working for the SACP or South Africa. Any one of them could be the person he was looking for. Peter would be focusing on them now, checking their friends, finding out where they lived and who lived close by, where they had their lunches and spent their evenings, what they did in the darkest hours of the night and whom they did it with.

He tried to think more about the dossiers but felt his mind swirling off to sleep. He shook his head to wake himself and glanced over at Tandy's bed, where a foot poked out from under the sheet. She was sound asleep, purring comfortably. He rose and turned the lamp off and got out, disappointed by the lack of answers he had found in Chitepo's materials and by his feeling that with Tandy he had failed a challenge he had wanted to accept.

* * *

THREE nights later a scratching at his window woke him and he let Tandy in and turned on a lamp by his bed.

Two-twenty-one in the morning.

Tandy wore a wet, gray raincoat, a dark pantsuit, and wet red slippers; her hair was covered by an unattractive, transparent plastic bonnet, and she looked frightened. Standing just inside the door, she spoke quickly: "Peter said you are to go at once. Four ANC people have been killed in a house out in Zengeza. He wants you to look the place over, see if it's part of what you're working on."

Quimby moved behind a closet door to pull off his pajama bottoms and step into a pair of shorts, and when he came back in view Tandy stared at him without comment.

"These were ANC leaders?" Quimby asked. "At a meeting? Why wasn't I told?"

"Peter said they were middle-level people having a social evening. He doesn't know if this is a part of what he called 'the other thing.' He wants your opinion."

"What about the police?"

"A friend called Peter. Peter said he'll have someone discover the bodies after you leave."

Quimby pulled on a dark jogging suit and soft-soled shoes and found a short waterproof windbreaker in his closet. He went to the chest of drawers and rummaged behind his folded shirts and put an eight-inch blackjack in his hip pocket. One thing he *had* learned during his short life—never to get caught in a fight with his hands empty unless there was absolutely nothing loose in the world that could be used as a weapon. He stood thinking ahead for a moment; then went to another drawer, searched in it until he found a pair of thin leather gloves, and put them on.

Tandy followed him into his tiny kitchen and watched him take a flashlight from its place on a shelf. He tested it and got a strong beam of light. He said, "I'll drive you home—"

There was a glint of determination in her eyes. "No. Peter said you'd want a lookout."

IN the African township of Zengeza, on Dunster Street just beyond Hunga Road, Tandy led him between shanties and rubbish and little vegetable gardens to the back of a one-story corrugated iron shanty with a white asbestos roof. She took him by the arm, pointed a finger at the shanty, and whispered in his ear. "The back door is supposed to be open. I'll throw some gravel against it if anyone comes."

He pressed her hand, acknowledging her help, and stepped out across hard, wet ground, concerned about the tracks he was leaving. He would have to get rid of these shoes tomorrow.

The door moved at his touch. He went in quickly and stood with his back against the wall, trying to see the shape of the room and the position of its furniture. Shades or drapes covered the windows. He waited, letting his eyes get used to the darkness, and in a few seconds he saw what looked like a square, white-topped table ten feet away. He took two steps in that direction and fell over a body.

He pulled himself up quickly, on all fours, startled and sickened by the sudden contact with soft, wet flesh. He squatted where he was, got his flashlight out, put his hand over its lens, and turned the light from between his fingers on the corpse.

A middle-aged black man, his mouth wide open, as if he had been screaming when he died. Someone had gutted him, put a knife in his belly and ripped it upward, spilling his intestines over the linoleum floor. Quimby retched and drew in a big breath and held it to control himself. He realized that his gloves were wet

46

with the man's blood and repressed the instinctive desire to wipe them off on his jogging pants; instead he wiped them across the man's shirt, retching again, tasting the sour contents of his stomach.

Squatting back on his heels, still with his fingers over the flashlight lens, he played a tiny beam of light across the floor and picked out two other bodies, one that of a woman who lay on her side, knees drawn up, head down on her chest. He moved cautiously in that direction and put the light on her face. Her throat had been cut, and the cut gleamed wetly under his light. These people had been alive an hour or two ago. Pity for them settled on his mind—pity, and anger at the killers.

The second man, his body large and flabby, his face misshapen by bullets that had cut across it from the jaw to the forehead, lay flat on his back, bloody, staring eyes wide open, arms flung out as if he had been trying to catch himself as he fell backward from the chair that lay on its side across his feet.

Quimby aimed his light at the floor, swinging it back and forth. Over at his right something glistened; he duck-walked to the glistening and picked up an empty cartridge case, continued to look around, and found another. He put the light on their rims: 32 caliber, made in South Africa. The weapon must have been one of those silenced Skorpions; no one would have heard the shots.

He waddled back to the man who had been shot, deciding that there had been two killers—the knife man, the gun man.

He wiped his fingers on the corpse's leg and felt for a wallet in the hip pocket. He did not look for the man's name since he assumed that Peter knew who these people were, but he noted that there was money in the wallet, and he put the wallet back in its pocket. He stood and approached the table, where several beer bottles lay on their sides; he put his beam on the tabletop and saw cards and some bills and small change. Not robbery then. Or at least not robbery for money. Tandy had said "middle-level" ANC members. Playing cards, having a beerdrink.

He played the covered flashlight beam around the room. Tandy had said there were four dead. He stepped slowly across the room searching for the other body, avoiding the corpses and the blood around them as well as he could.

He did not find the fourth person in the neat bedroom, nor in the closet in that room, nor in the little space for coats set into the wall near the front door. He unlocked the front door, opened it a crack, and peered into the sandy front yard and the tarred street. Nothing. He searched through the house again, guessing that someone might have tried to escape from one of the windows, but the three windows in the house were closed tight and the ground outside them was clear and smooth.

He left the house and went to the spot where he had left Tandy. He whispered to her, "I found only three bodies. You said four."

"Four. Peter said four."

Quimby faced the house again, looking carefully along its sides. He turned to look at the lean-to behind the house and realized that there was a separate building behind the lean-to, an outside privy. He walked to the privy, pulled at the door, and felt pressure on it from inside. He opened the door slowly against the pressure, and a woman's heavy body slid forward to the ground. He stepped back to look at her, got out his flashlight again, and squatted on his heels. She wore an orange dress, up around her knees now, her underdrawers down around her ankles. The back of her head was a bloody mess.

He turned off the flashlight and placed it on the ground. Then he turned the woman's head so that he could see her face, picked up the flashlight, covered the lens, and put a glow of light on her.

A burst of bullets had struck her full in the face, destroying it, pounding it into a messy blob. The man who had done these shooting jobs had stood so close he couldn't miss.

Driving back in the rain, he told Tandy what he needed to know from Peter. Had anyone in the neighborhood heard gunshots? Had any of these four people been important enough to be killed by the SACP or the SAs for some specific reason? Were they known to have personal enemies? Were the women the wives of those men, or somebody else's? Could Peter discover any reason at all why these four had been executed by professional assassins?

"Tell him," Quimby said, "it wasn't robbery, it wasn't rape, the house was not torn up, the murderers weren't looking for something to take away. Tell him that these killers were from the same place as the others; I have their spent cartridges. Tell him, if these people were not important enough in the ANC for South Africa or the SACP to have some specific reason for assassinating them, then I assume that this job was done in retaliation for the four we killed. I think this is a case of innocent victims being slaughtered to make a point. The killers are saying they have the right to do any goddamn thing they want to do in Zimbabwe, anything they want to do to ANC people, and we're supposed to sit still and take it."

"Ah God!" Tandy groaned. "It has to be the South Africans."

He ignored her comment. "And tell him I don't think this will affect the other thing. Whoever is behind this has only two weeks before the international conference. They still want their majority. They'll be back."

Tandy moved closer to him along the seat and put a hand on his forearm. "I'm not supposed to know what this is all about?"

"The less you know the safer you may be."

"But I can guess. You and Peter think someone is trying to kill

49

our ANC leaders before the conference, and you're trying to stop them."

"You'd be better off not even guessing."

She turned to face him, leaning closer, her voice suddenly shrill with anger. "Don't talk to me as if I were a stupid, useless bird, Taylor Quimby. I'm as tough as you are, maybe tougher. I've lived through shit you'll never have to take. Stop trying to protect me and let me help you."

"Professionals killed those people, Tandy," he countered, defensively. "The next thing you know they'll be after you."

"Well, dammit all, do I have to go around with blinders? Tell me what the hell is going on!"

He drove in silence, and she came closer and leaned her head against his shoulder. After a few miles, she asked, "Do these killers scare the bejesus out of you?"

"You'd better believe it."

Another long silence; then he said, contritely, "Hell, you already know practically everything I do about what's going on. If you know the rest it may help you protect yourself."

She squeezed his arm. "We can be partners then?"

"You've got to be awfully goddamn careful."

She brushed his warning aside. "Listen, can I go home with you now? Sleep with you? Seeing those dead people wasn't good for you. You're all strung out."

He thought about that, and after a moment he put a hand under her raincoat on a warm thigh. "Ordinarily that would be exactly what I would want," he said. "But if I try to make love to you tonight, I'll be thinking about a man back there—probably a good, peaceful man—with his guts spilled out on the floor. I fell on top of him. There was a woman with her throat cut. You saw the other one. Give me a raincheck."

They drove on in silence for a moment; then he smacked the steering wheel with his palm and laughed with sudden delight. He put an arm around her shoulders and pulled her close, and he said, "Hey, when you say 'partner,' you really *mean* partner, don't you! Ah, Tandy, goddamn—you are something else!"

3

IN the early afternoon Quimby squatted on his heels with his back against the wall of a building and read a newspaper. Wearing sandals and old jeans, a knitted brown shirt and a shapeless canvas hat, he merged in well with the other groups of men lounging outside the market.

The Herald played up the murders in Zengeza as one more shocking example of the bloodshed still being caused by what it called "terrorist-bandits" who refused Mugabe's call to come in and help build the peace. Even their own leader, Joshua Nkomo, it pointed out, had repeatedly begged these men to drop their arms and join him in helping Mugabe build the new black nation. But some were too wild and stubborn, the paper concluded; therefore, the government should move at once to arrest all dissidents and put them in jail.

Since the government owned controlling stock in the paper, Quimby guessed that a new campaign against the dissidents was about to begin.

Never willing to pass up a chance to make a good piece of propaganda, the paper also printed an editorial that suggested that the bandits still on the loose were well-armed because South Africa was equipping them and paying them good money to keep their destabilizing opposition alive.

The Herald's facile coverage of the murders made Quimby uneasy, for he assumed that the police would recognize them as another killing of ANC members. They would be looking for reasons why these four had been singled out, and they too would have found spent cartridges stamped with the SA identification. He wondered how clearly they had identified the tracks he had left in that blood and was glad that he had cut up his jogging shoes and gloves this morning, burned them in his fireplace, and scattered the ashes in a downtown rubbish bin.

He turned pages, looking for other mention of the killings, saw that another white landowner had been "shot by bandits" on a farm thirty miles southwest of the city, and learned that Mugabe was accusing the South Africans of concentrating armed forces near Beitbridge for an invasion of Zimbabwe, "on the pretext that Zimbabwe is harboring ANC guerrillas." They were always doing that, and he was always saying that.

A court had given a man seven years for buggering a mule. An article explained that the man, working on road construction, had wandered off the road to relieve himself, seen the mule, and tied its front legs together. Quimby sat for a moment wondering why the front legs. He'd had no experience with mules, but if he were going to try that experiment he thought he would want to tie the back legs. . . .

He watched Tandy walk by on her way to her job in the market. Dressed Zimbabwean fashion—sandals and bare legs, a white smock open at her throat, a sky-blue duka over her hair. Even that kind of camouflage failed to hide her fine figure and the graceful walk that made him see her in his imagination coming out on the dance floor in her Indian costume. He remembered the look of her when she danced, and regretted having turned down her offer last night. He meant to present his rain check pretty damn soon.

Last night, he'd been sickened and angry. It didn't matter that he had seen dead men by the hundreds. Civilian dead always hit him with a feeling of despair, setting him thinking about innocent lives shot to hell all in an instant. It was always terrible seeing the victims lying sprawled in their own blood, like great, awkward pieces of meat, and there was never a good reason for it. There never could be.

He got to his feet and dawdled through the busy marketplace, where women stood under a long open shed at brick counters topped with concrete, hawking everything from vegetables and flowers to plastic raincoats packed in little squares—green-canvas traveling bags, cheap hand-woven baskets, bright plastic children's toys. Other men, dressed as he was in beaten-up sandals and jeans and nondescript knitted shirts, wandered between the stalls, pricing goods, joking with the women. Black and colored women from the city, most of them looking businesslike and fretful, moved from stall to stall, bargaining fiercely.

Tandy spoke to the woman working with her. She left her stall and walked slowly through the throng of people toward the open-air bus terminal, and Quimby followed.

Out on this blacktopped area of several acres, hundreds of

people milled around buses, carrying boxes and bags and suitcases of every description, going home to townships and *kraals* for the weekend. Portable radios blared, vendors sang about the quality of their wares, children ran about and yelled, family groups rushed laughing and screaming to push their way into one or another of the white-and-pale-blue buses parked around on the blacktop. Men stood on top of the buses shouting for their women to pass the baggage up, and women desperately pulled their children inside through open windows. Pandemonium.

Quimby saw Tandy turn into a shadowed way between a line of buses, and when he came to that place, he turned, did not see her ahead of him, but went on between the buses.

When he came into the open, she had disappeared. He hesitated, trying to decide whether to step over women and children gathered around their boxes and paper bags, eating their lunch, or to turn to the right where a narrow pathway between other groups would lead him toward some shanties. He saw a hand wave from under a canvas-roofed lean-to by the shanties, and went that way.

Tandy sat in the shadows on a piece of cardboard laid on the ground, legs tucked under her, her back against a low wooden wall. Just beyond her were the wooden benches of the beer garden where men talked and laughed loudly over mugs and cartons of beer. Quimby sat down close to her and Tandy began to talk at once: "First," she said, "Peter Chitepo agrees with me. I am to be more than your cut-out. I know the city and the townships, and I am of the ANC. This is my struggle as well as yours."

Quimby grinned. "But we decided that last night, partner. You have this great wish to put your head into a noose with me. We decided to hang together."

He leaned forward, looking into her eyes, reaching to touch her hand, not wanting to be pompous but wanting her to know the seriousness of her decision, and he said, "You must remember that if we take the wrong step we may damage the ANC more than is permissible. Because of a thing I did the other night, you could be shot by the government or by these men who are killing your leaders. Be careful always, as if you were living in a world of crocodiles. Watch your back so that you know if people are following you. Will you remember these things?"

Her eyes searched his face as if she were surprised by his concern for her. "Whatever has to be done, I will do," she said firmly. "Now . . . Peter says about last night: 'No shots were heard, so the guns must have been silenced; the police believe this was a political killing since nothing appears to have been taken from the house; they found tracks in blood made by three men inside the house, but the rain washed away all traces outside. They know the murdered people were members of the ANC, but nothing more.' Peter agrees with your theory that the killers did this in revenge, and he asks, 'What now?'"

"Tell him that I need weapons for at least fifteen men. Uzis, AK 47s, a couple of RPDs, hand guns and grenades, an RPG if he can find one, and enough ammunition for the weapons to keep me fighting for at least twenty minutes. These things should be located here in the city where I can lay hands on them. If he has money I can use to feed and pay some fighters, fine; otherwise, I will use my own money. Tell him I will put together four or five teams of men who used to fight with me. When the next commando attack comes, we will be ready."

He paused and looked at her. She repeated: "Uzis, AK 47s, hand grenades, ammunition. What is an RPD?"

"A Russian light machine gun."

"An RPG?"

"Antitank rocket. Looks something like a bazooka."

"All right."

"And tell him I want to meet him and learn what he and his counterintelligence group know about how people infiltrate our borders."

"I don't understand about the infiltration."

"I want routes used, border crossing points, hideouts. Where they stash their weapons, how they get out, who helps them."

"Okay. A meeting. When?"

"As soon as he's ready. At my house."

When he said nothing more, Tandy rose with the fluid motion he had seen in the finale of her dance. She put a hand on his shoulder and bent over him. "Partner," she said, "watch your back, too."

THREE nights after her first visit to his house, Tandy came again, at one o'clock in the morning. She woke him from a sound sleep by tapping at his window until he opened it, and he let her in, wearing only his pajama trousers and yawning himself awake.

"It must be love," he told her, grinning. "You couldn't keep yourself away. You had to come to me."

"Absolutely. I'm fascinated by your beautiful body and the scars on your chest. What did you do, go head-on into a couple of Zulu spears?"

"Viet Cong bullet holes, in the front out the back," he said, twisting his body so that she could see his back. "What have you got?"

"A woman walked into John Kado's house about half an hour ago. Peter said this may be the break you've been looking for."

Quimby was suddenly wide-awake. John Kado was Secretary-

General of the South African Communist Party, and the most important Communist member of the ANC's National Executive Council.

"Is she still there?"

"Yes."

"Do we know who she is?"

"No."

He reached for his shirt. "I want to get out there."

"It's at thirty-three twenty-four Tudor Avenue. One of Peter's men is watching the doorway from a Nissan truck down the street, in the thirty-two hundred block. You're supposed to check with him when you get there."

"Do I have to dress in front of you?"

She looked at him with an exaggerated leer. "Oh, would you? You've got so many pretty muscles. I don't see why I shouldn't see the rest." She grinned saucily at his frown and turned to the doorway. "Okay! Okay! I'm going."

He called after her, "Tandy, thank you."

He parked his car a block north of Tudor Avenue, and walked south to the dark-colored Nissan truck parked near the corner. A face he could not see clearly in the darkness moved forward to the open window when he stopped at the side of the truck, and the man inside waited for him to speak.

"Is that woman still inside?"

"Right."

"Which house?"

"Second from the corner." A hand came out of the window and a finger pointed. "It's a duplex you enter from this side. You see the doors? She went in the second one. There's another door at the back."

"If she comes out the back door?"

"There's no alley. She has to come around this way."

"You may as well get some sleep," Quimby suggested. "Why don't you take my car and go home? I'll stay here in your truck."

They worked out how they would get the vehicles returned the next morning, by parking them both in a parking lot near Quimby's offices. They exchanged keys, and Quimby watched the other man walk away.

He settled into the truck seat, slouching down, not wanting his head to be sticking up if the police drove by, and he reviewed what he knew and what he felt about John Kado.

Kado was a crowd-pleaser—tall, handsome, what the Africans called "colored." Indian blood had given him a high-bridged nose, straight gray hair, brown skin, and all his pictures showed him with what seemed to Quimby a carefully posed look of intensity in his dark eyes. Peter's dossier on him had said that he was ruthless and ambitious, skillful at telling people what they wanted to hear, and a schemer whose pawns moved the way he wanted them to or found themselves driven out of play.

If the Communists were involved in a plot to take over the ANC, Quimby thought, it was certainly possible that Kado could be at the center of it. But this woman's visit might mean nothing more than that old John was doing his best to keep his love life out of the newspapers. That would be especially important for him, because everyone knew that his wife was in a South African prison.

Kado was probably in bed with a good-looking woman—nothing more serious than that.

He could just as easily be planning the next set of assassinations or trying to find out what had happened to those four commandos who were supposed to have done a job for him last week. But despite what Peter believed, there wasn't any really good evidence that Kado was involved in a plot to kill ANC leaders.

Quimby shifted restlessly in the truck seat. The woman had been in that duplex over two hours. . . . She was probably in there for the night. Servicing Number Two. Winning herself a seat in the Marxist heaven at the right hand of the prophet Lenin, shaking her proletarian pelvis for world revolution.

He turned his thoughts to Tandy. She was a bold one. Gave the impression she held nothing back, but she had major reserves of strength and intelligence behind those big eyes. Blunt and curious. Asking him right out about his chest scars; men saw them, looked at his face, and kept their mouths shut. She just looked at him with that bold stare, asked her question, and filed the information.

A cut-out wasn't supposed to have a personality and a mind; a cut-out was supposed to be a cipher, anonymous, a message center, but Tandy was cutting a place for herself in his life. Calling him "Ole Chifamba," trusting him to let her sleep that night he went to her quarters; then, the night before last, wanting to bed with him because he was strung out. And beautiful—from her painted toes to her bright eyes and the luxurious black hair on her head. She was friendly and curious, warm and honest, very much her own woman, doing her own thinking. That girl he'd married long ago had been all lies and sleazy pretenses and self-indulgence. Tandy was brains and courage. He liked the way she laughed, the way she told him right out what she was thinking. . . .

Something moved at the doorway. He did not see the door open, but picked up a flicker of movement in front of it, and as he watched, a woman in a light-colored dress came to the front of the house where he could see her figure more clearly against a dark background of bushes. She walked to the street and turned left, going away from him.

He studied the area around the doorway, wanting to be sure no one was following her. He got out of the truck on the side away from the house, pushed the door far enough so that the latch held it shut without making a loud snap, and followed her from the other side of the street.

She walked swiftly, not looking back, four blocks along Tudor, south another four blocks. Abruptly, she turned into a walkway leading to the entrance of an old three-storied apartment building.

Quimby sprinted forward, wanting to catch a glimpse of her before she was gone. Too many people would be living in that apartment house for him to guess which one he'd been following; he needed to see her face.

He pushed his way into a hedge of bougainvillea just after she went through the first door. From twenty yards away he saw her pause to bend toward a mail slot, but her face was turned away. She lifted the cover of the mail box and appeared to be taking out some letters, still with her back to him.

He sensed that her figure was a little exaggerated through the hips, but could not see her face. Dressed in peach-colored silk or nylon, with an open collar like a man's shirt and a sashlike belt. Black skin, black hair, tiny braids clinging close like a tight skullcap.

He needed to see her face. He pushed further toward the doorway, out in the open now but taking advantage of the darkness away from the soft-edged spot of light shining above the entrance.

As she entered the inner doorway, she turned her head, looking back for a fraction of a second. He did not think she saw him, or if she did, the sight appeared to make no impression on her for she went on through the door into the hallway.

He turned away and trotted back across the street, taking up a position behind a tree where he could see the front and one side of the building, hoping that he would see lights turn on somewhere, but that didn't happen, and he stood considering his next move.

He could not afford to lose the woman, but it made no sense to drag out forever the effort to identify her.

He went back across the street into the small anteroom outside the locked entrance, and he copied into his notebook the names and apartment numbers of nine apartments where they showed above the mail slots. Three other slots held no name card, and he noted their numbers.

He went outside and jogged back to the truck, hoping that she lived in that building and would be getting into bed now. He moved the truck to a place on Baines Avenue, close enough to be able to see and recognize anyone coming out of the apartment house, wishing that he had some way of knowing that she had not simply gone into this end of the building and walked out the other. Then he sat recalling the look of her, memorizing what he had seen in a single instant.

Clear features—a high-bridged nose, her face broad at the eye level. Prominent cheekbones, round cheeks, protruding lips sharply defined by bright red lipstick, a firm, strong-looking chin. She had held that chin high. Either she had a good opinion of herself or a stiff neck from too much lovemaking. In her thirties. His age. Also, as she had stood pressing that button, it had seemed again that she had a little more than her share of hips and bottom. Big in the rear then.

AT seven-thirty in the morning, she came out of the building, dressed in a dark maroon skirt and white blouse, wearing white-thonged sandals, her hair covered with a gray duka. Long strings of red and azure beads hung around her neck and the same colors flashed at her right wrist from rows of bracelets.

The face was the one he had seen at the entryway. The hips and buttocks confirmed his identification. A magnificent, oversized rear, a magnificent way of swinging it along as she walked.

Quimby got out of the truck and followed.

Walking purposefully, she went east for half a mile, turned south on Prince Edward, and marched along steadily, swinging her hips and a tan briefcase as if she intended to move that way all day.

She crossed Samora Machel Avenue and walked further south on Pioneer Street to Abercorn, turned at Abercorn, and about halfway down the second block took a set of stairs that led to the second floor over an Indian shoe shop.

Quimby came slowly past the front of that building, looking for a sign that would tell him what offices were upstairs but finding nothing.

She had been carrying a leather briefcase. Briefcases held papers, lunches. Probably she had gone inside to work, but he had no idea whether she was sending out messages to South Africa or having her palm read. He could wait for her to come out, or he could try to find out what was upstairs in that building. He didn't have time to wait; he wasn't going to show his face up there; he needed help.

He thought about the alternatives. He could go to his office a few blocks away and call Peter, but they had agreed that such communications were not advisable. The government probably monitored Peter's telephone. Tandy had no telephone. In this whole country there were no more than three hundred thousand phones for something like nine million people.

He wrote a note on a sheet of his notebook:

Abercorn at Charter Road by 0900. Later, home or office. 710496 and 715576. Chifamba.

All over the city there were always young boys called *mujibas* who delivered messages and packages and performed other kinds of odd jobs for people. The local Federal Express. He stood on the corner of Abercorn and Victoria Street for ten minutes before one turned up, and he sent the boy with his message to Tandy's quarters.

TANDY came and went, taking his list of the names of the people in that apartment house and his questions about the woman's identity.

Quimby went home in a taxi for a shower and breakfast and a change from the dark trousers and sweater he had worn last night into his business clothes. He was going to have to arrange for a vacation from the business, he decided. He was getting to work so bleary-eyed these days that his assistant and his secretary were telling him he ought to marry the girl and settle down.

He walked a brisk twelve blocks to the place where he had left the borrowed truck, drove it down to Speke Avenue, and put it into the parking lot, seeing his own car parked twenty yards away. As he walked away from the truck, a starved-looking old man dressed in a one-piece set of blue overalls and wearing a knitted red ski cap down over his ears came across the lot and asked him for a match.

Quimby stopped to search his pockets. He didn't smoke, but he had a habit of picking up match folders in restaurants and stuffing them into his pockets. While he searched, the old man said, "Get in your car and drive out Enterprise Road."

Quimby gave him a match folder from the Monomatopa Hotel. He walked to his car and got in, seeing that Peter Chitepo was hunkered down on the floor of the backseat, long legs folded awkwardly, resting his torso on bare elbows, his bony, square bottom projecting upward.

Quimby drove out Manica Road to Enterprise Road and turned north. He kept quiet until he was well past the Sports Club, and turned off Enterprise Road to drive through the residential streets of Newlands. Finally, he said, "You can sit up now, Peter."

Chitepo came up on all fours and rolled into the seat, dusting his knees. Sitting low, still trying to keep out of sight as much as possible, he said, "We've hit the jackpot, but I don't know what kind of money we win. The woman you followed home last night is Florence Mubaka. She works in our Secretariat. She has a history of absolute loyalty and service to the ANC, and until now we believed her to be an ardent anti-Communist even though she's had two years of management training in the Soviet Union. In other words, we have trusted her completely. The office over the shoe store is one of ours."

"So she's having an affair with Kado?"

"She has a reputation for enjoying her pleasures. She's said to be proud of her looks. Thinks she's a queen. Looks like one."

"You think she's shacking up with Kado and that's all there is to it?"

"I don't know. But I have to say that you can't automatically assume she's an underground Communist just because she spent two years in the Soviet Union. Hundreds of us have been trained in Russia and Poland, the GDR and Czechoslovakia, even China and North Korea. I had a year in Poland, but that didn't make a Communist out of me. Sure, they force-fed me with Marxism-Leninism every day, and I found some of the ideas pretty useful. You have to remember that if refugees like me want education we have to go where we can get it."

"How do you feel about Mubaka now?"

Chitepo grinned a little sheepishly. "Suspicious. We'll watch her closely now and see if we can't get something concrete on what she's doing."

"You do that. I'm going to get acquainted with her."

"You'll put her on her guard."

"Why? I am smitten by her ravishing beauty. Maybe she likes beautiful American fellas."

"The Communists could have a file on you."

Quimby considered that and knew he would take the chance. They might know he'd fought for Mugabe, but that would be a plus for him. They could have no reason for suspecting he was working for the ANC.

He asked: "What about Kado? Is he a womanizer?"

"I don't think you sit around in the middle of the night talking about soccer with a woman like Florence Mubaka, even if you *are* almost sixty."

Quimby nodded. "So it's sex, or politics. You'll have to get under the bed. . . ."

"Yes . . . ah . . . Taylor. Something else . . . People are going through the sheebeens and squatters' camp asking oblique questions that mean they're trying to find out what happened to those men you killed."

"Who are they?"

"Local thugs. They don't know themselves who's paying them. 'White men,' they told one of my people."

"Don't fret it, Peter. They won't learn a thing."

HIS preparations had been almost as elaborate as those he had made in the old days when he was setting up an ambush against the Rhodesian Selous Scouts. Possibly for the same reason, his plan worked almost perfectly.

He came into the crowded Coffee Shop of the Meikles Hotel and walked past several tables.

A woman's voice hailed him from one of the tables.

"Taylor! Hey, Taylor! How are you?"

He stopped, and let his eyes discover Roberta, heavyset and broadly grinning, and he put on a surprised smile. "Roberta!" he said. "Haven't seen you for ages. What's happening?"

She was young and comfortably plump, cheerful and noisy, with a great broad nose and heavy lips. After Peter had sent her around the previous evening, Quimby had coached her until she grew downright impatient with him, but he had wanted her perfect and had kept drilling her even while she pleaded that she knew everything about him she would ever need.

Now for the payoff.

Roberta reached out for his hand and pulled him closer. "I've got a new job," she announced. "Working down close to you for the tobacco auctioneers. And I've moved. You've got to come see my new place." She glanced at her companion with a quick show of hesitation, and rushed on: "Are you alone? Why don't you sit with us?"

Quimby kept the smile on his face and looked at her companion, waiting to be certain the invitation was unanimous. Florence Mubaka glanced up at him, catching up with Roberta's enthusiasm, and nodded her welcome.

Roberta flowed on: "Plenty of room over here by me. Come on, Taylor, sit down. Florence, this is an old friend—Taylor Quimby. You've heard me talk about him. He's American, and he fought with ZANLA for five years, and now he's in business here. He's the only American in the country you can trust because he's one of us. Taylor, this is Florence Mubaka. When we're not trying to make a living, she and I work together in the ANC."

Roberta rattled on in her high voice while Quimby and Florence Mubaka spoke to one another, agreed that the weather was wonderful, that the jacaranda blossoms were more attractive than they'd ever seen them, and managed to get a waitress to bring him a menu.

Quimby was all smiles and politeness. He answered Florence's questions about the state of his business, the last time he'd been to Maputo, where, in the history they had concocted together, he had met Roberta, and he talked easily about the markets in Zimbabwe he supplied with pharmaceuticals.

And while he talked, he gazed at Florence openly, letting her see that he was admiring her, that he found her attractive and pleasant. And she *was* both. Her hair was put up in many tiny braids that clung tightly to her small head and ended in little gold clips; her dark eyes were alert and watchful, her face and lips going through swift changes of expression as she listened and talked. In a pale, lime-colored linen dress, she looked cool and lovely, and her manner seemed to say that she appreciated his admiration.

She seemed to be a well-balanced mixture of easy self-confidence and careful watchfulness. She commented tartly as they talked, showing a touch of contempt—for Mugabe's agricultural policies, for the stupid people *The Herald* reported were in the hospital after drinking poison kachasu, for the United States and its failure to go all out against South Africa's government. Her self-contained gaze and the way her mouth curled up at the ends when she smiled, made it evident that she considered herself superior to the world around her and meant to keep things that way, and yet her eyes included him among the "superiors."

Although she was infinitely delicate about it, she managed to question him closely about his work in ZANLA, compelling him to name places and battles and when they were fought and whom he had served under, and he understood that she was competently making certain that he was what he pretended to be. More than that: it became clear that she had a surprisingly good knowledge of those events. Behind her flattering smile, he sensed a powerful intelligence and an almost grim determination to get at the truth about him, and he wondered if this was the familiar wariness of a woman instinctively carrying on the male-female duel, or the suspiciousness of a woman who had a great deal to hide.

His intention was to win her confidence. Because she questioned him so directly, he talked freely, telling her about his military training in the United States, the war in Vietnam, and the months of operating in the forests on the slopes of the Inyanga Mountains against the Selous Scouts. He recounted stories he thought might interest her about Mugabe's struggle to bring Joshua Nkomo's guerrilla opposition forces into the new Zimbabwe. He told her how Mugabe's Minister of Commerce and Trade had asked him to stay and go into business, how the business had developed, and how he had come to Zimbabwe originally because the cause of black justice was the only cause he wanted to fight for.

She was quick and alert. They laughed about things at the same moment; they found that sentences did not have to be completed because the other understood what was about to be said; and they joined forces to tease Roberta about her huge appetite, which she took in good humor, boasting about her fitness.

He tried to pick up the check, but the women would not permit that. Then Roberta announced all in a rush that she had a long report to type and she hurried off, and as Florence and he sat over their coffee, Florence pressed him almost defensively to talk about himself.

In answer to her specific question, he tried to explain why he had turned to military service: "About halfway through the Detroit riots, the President finally agreed to send troops into the city. The police and the national guards were trigger-happy; they fired whole volleys at shadows, and their overreacting kept the hysteria spreading. In some ways we couldn't take them seriously because we could see they were outnumbered and scared half to death, but at the same time the anger kept building because there were reports they were killing blacks in certain houses and beating us up at the police stations. . . . Then these troops came in—the Eighty-second Airborne Division, veterans from Vietnam. They were tough and they looked tough; they didn't go shooting off their guns in all directions; they weren't about to panic, but it was obvious that if someone else started trouble they would damn well put a stop to it. Things calmed down in a hurry. I guess I wanted to belong to something like that."

Quimby paused and looked at Florence very soberly. "May I ask you a serious question?"

A mask of self-control settled over her face. "Yes?"

He put on a little show of embarrassment and hesitation. "I've been thinking about this for a long time. Well . . . you're in the ANC . . . you may be able to help me. I've told you about my pharmaceutical business, but the truth is, I hate it. I'm a professional soldier and I want to get back into military work. Do you think there would be any chance of my getting into Umkhonto We Sizwe?" He saw the quick tightening of the skin at the corners of her eyes, the firming of her lips, and he went on: "I've had a lot of training, a lot of experience. I think I could be useful."

All the play acting of polite interest was gone from Florence's face. She sat staring at him sternly, a hint of excitement and calculation in her eyes. "You're serious?"

"Absolutely."

"You know that Umkhonto We Sizwe is controlled by our Communists?" she asked, warningly. "I think all the officers and instructors are Communists."

Quimby said, approvingly, "They're well-trained, well-disciplined. They're making life painful for the South Africans."

She continued to study him as if she were trying to look inside his brain. "You would probably have to join the SACP before they would take you into Umkhonto We Sizwe."

"I'll do that if they'll have me. I'm throwing my life away, playing businessman."

She had not moved her hands since he had asked his question; now she rearranged the silverware with her fingers but her eyes still clung to his. "You're a strange man, Mr. Quimby," she said. "But God knows the ANC needs trained fighting men. Let me ask around and see if I can find out how you should make your application."

"Many thanks. It would be a great help."

Quimby leaned back in his chair and changed the subject, sensing that she was seriously interested in him now. He asked: "Do you get to know the big shots in your work, the men like Oliver Tambo and John Kado and Joe Slovo?"

Her modest laughter was quick. "Oh, no! The leaders are much too busy to talk to people at my level. Besides, Kado and Slovo are members of the SACP. I'm ANC all the way."

He changed direction again, hiding his thoughts behind his smile.

"This job you have sounds like a lot of responsibility. Where did you get your training?"

"In the Soviet Union, would you believe it? I was there from March 1981 until July 1982, almost a year and a half, at the School for Public Administration in Leningrad."

"That must have been a fascinating experience."

She frowned as if he had insulted her, and her voice growled with what sounded like fury. "I hated it. I was cold, and sick of their sour rye bread and rotten frankfurters and the rancid sunflower oil they pour on everything, and I was so lonely—I wanted to cry all the time."

She seemed ready to cry again, but her strong chin came up and she shook her head so hard that the little braids flew about. She picked up her purse and pushed her chair back from the table, giving him a tight smile. "I'm sorry. I really must go. I'm very late. . . . I enjoyed talking with you. . . ."

He stood with her, smiling and bowing, and watched her walk away, admiring again the familiar roll of her big hips.

4

IN the later afternoon, two days after his luncheon with Florence Mubaka, Quimby went through the reception line at the Soviet Union's new trade center on Dreary Avenue. He met the ambassador and his wife—two sturdy-looking, middle-aged bureaucrats, and walked on into the crowd around a table weighted down with smoked sturgeon, steely-gray caviar, ham and chicken, cold sliced beef, plates of rich-looking chocolates, vodka, Armenian cognac, and champagne.

Serovski, the round-faced, blond attaché for trade who had invited him the day before, brought him a goblet of Georgian white wine and wasted no time in turning their conversation back to the subject that had brought them together.

"But we want your business," he said, smoothing his blond hair. "And you know that the standards of our pharmaceutical industry are the highest."

"And you know I'd like to work with you," Quimby said, smiling into the Russian's blue eyes. "But the problem is still there. You want American dollars. I want lower prices because of the conditions you set."

The attaché, zealous and pushy, probably under pressure to put new deals together, smiled regretfully. He knew what Quimby's objections were: trading with the USSR pitted a tiny private company against a powerful state bureaucracy that insisted that differences of opinion over such matters as quality or timely delivery, including all litigation, had to be settled inside the Soviet Union.

"But let's keep discussing this," Serovski urged. "Perhaps we can work out some kind of exchange. Rather than sending us your dollars, you might be able to send us Zimbabwean products we haven't yet considered."

"I'm always glad to explore the issues with you, Vladimir."

"But please excuse me now," Serovski said. "I see another of my guests has arrived. I must attend to my duties. Do enjoy yourself."

Quimby mingled, moving at the edge of the little crowd into a second large room where displays of the Eastern Bloc's goods for export were set up. He watched earnest Russians and East Germans explaining terms and products with some of the passersby; he read printed placards pushing the East Bloc's manufactured goods; and he smiled and spoke from time to time with one or another of his import-export competitors.

He stood back at the edge of the tightest pack, studying the crowd: African women in their colorful shawls and beads and ankle-length cottons; German ladies in cool nylons and high heels, their blond and black hair done up in European fashion; Russian women—stocky, thick, and dowdy, dressed like farm women, several with their hair dyed an identical, unnatural red; black and light men dressed in black and light-colored suits, everyone chattering and laughing too loudly, pretending more interest in the displays than they could possibly feel.

He looked out through the broad doorway into the other room and saw that the ambassador had left the reception line and was standing with John Kado. The two of them appeared to be enjoying the funniest joke in the world, laughing boisterously, nodding and patting each other on the back; then Kado moved away, accompanied by another man.

Although he had never met him, Quimby knew who the man with Kado was: Colonel Heinz Seifert of the GDR's security organization, East Germany's version of the Soviet KGB. *The Herald* had reported that Seifert was in Zimbabwe with a small cadre of "advisers" to help Mugabe's government reform its security police organization, adding some finishing touches to the work the British had done.

Dressed in a formal dark suit, Seifert did not look at all like what he was—the surrogate of the Soviet KGB. He carried his shoulders high, his back very straight, but he had too much belly, a fat neck, a red face, carefully waved graying hair, and an air of pampered self-indulgence. The image he projected was that of an overfed Bavarian businessman rather than a director of secret police.

The German colonel put a hand on John Kado's shoulder and guided him into a corner, where they turned to watch the crowd. They accepted champagne from a waiter and stood talking, and Quimby guessed from the way they put their heads together that their talk was not idle. Kado's face grew drawn and tense as he listened to Seifert's words; he looked out over the crowd with a preoccupied gaze, and his free hand clenched and unclenched at his side.

After listening for several minutes, Kado put up a hand in front of Seifert's face, interrupting, making a reply. His famous profile was turned for Quimby to see, and his head and jaw thrust forward belligerently as he made his points, emphasizing them with sharp, chopping gestures of his left hand.

Quimby wondered what Kado was doing. Begging for more weapons? Explaining why he wasn't ready to move the revolution into South Africa more rapidly? Trying to get more of Seifert's help for his effort to wipe out the ANC's non-Communist leadership? Seifert and his policemen were supposed to be here to train Mugabe's cadres and shape up his secret police unit, but was he also the Soviet's liaison with the SACP? Was he standing over there giving Kado his marching orders from the Soviet Union? Raising hell because the assassinations weren't going fast enough?

Or were those two hatching their own private schemes, plotting how Kado would take over the ANC, how Seifert would arm him and help him, how one day soon they would be the two most powerful men in Africa? Kado would be Africa's Lenin. And Seifert? Maybe he wanted to be South Africa's Dzerzhinsky, Lenin's secret police chief.

He was making all this up, letting his imagination go, Quimby told himself. He had no evidence at all that connected Kado and Seifert to those commandos, nothing but the presence of those Czech Skorpions. Chitepo's first idea—that the killings were being carried out by the Communists—was just plain wrong.

But it had to be the Communists. If the killers were SAs, why the hell weren't the Communist leaders in the ANC National Executive Council getting knocked off?

A third man joined Kado and Seifert, and Quimby felt his face suddenly go stiff and the muscles in his shoulders and the back of his neck knot up. He had not seen this man come in. He had not seen that big-shouldered brute for six years, not since he'd tracked him up to the top of a granite peak in the Vumba Mountains in late 1978 hoping to kill him.

Quimby's mind ran back swiftly, putting him in those hills again. . . .

THAT big bastard was running a team of the Selous Scouts, working for the Rhodesians. Near the very end of the fighting, he got in behind the ZANLA camps, killing as he went, and Quimby tracked his movements for days, trying to catch up with him, determined to destroy him and his whole murderous crew. Muzingi—Victor Muzingi, that was his name—blasted his way through three big ZANLA camps. He cased their locations on the ground, called in the helicopters for the firing teams—the "sticks" of Rhodesian fighters who jumped by parachute to surround the camps, and the result was a thirty-mile-long path of dead ZANLA people, more than two hundred at least. And when that job was done he rampaged on down the valley, slaughtering innocent people in the villages, punishing them for hiding ZANLA fighters.

When Quimby finally closed in on Muzingi's trail, it was raining—a steady, soddening downfall. He and his four men were sick with anger, stinking filthy, exhausted; they had been in the bush for nearly two weeks, moving almost every minute, reading the tracks, eating whatever they could find in the forests, sleeping in the muck when they dared, arriving with infuriating regularity at Muzingi's killing centers too late to help. They walked past the gutted, hideous corpses of their comrades when they came to each of the wrecked camps, saw the pitiful, butchered bodies of women and children, shuffled past burned huts and scattered household goods, and went on, driven by their obsessive rage to catch and destroy Muzingi and his team.

Wounded survivors told Quimby about Muzingi, the huge wild man who came into the bivouacs after the paratroopers and heavy guns had done their work. With three or four others he charged in with his RPD, the submachine gun that was one of the best weapons for this kind of slaughter; he gave no mercy, killed everything that moved, laughing and screaming like a wounded hyena as he shot women and children and the helpless wounded.

Those who had somehow lived through his attacks insisted that Muzingi was the ngozi, the evil spirit of these mountains. They said that no bullets could reach him. He was the awful power of death and destruction, come back to punish the earth; they said his pleasure was killing, and his laugh was like the howl of the spent typhoons that swept up from the Indian Ocean and died in the mountains.

Quimby and his group finally caught up with the killers camped near a small earthen dam at the edge of a little pool nestled between three hills. He reconnoitered the area swiftly, placing his men at different points on the high ground so that no one could escape, and at his signal they fired into the little camp, running down two of the hills as they fired, killing all of Muzingi's five men as they huddled around a tiny fire.

But Muzingi made his way like a black leopard across the stream above the pond and up the side of the hill, and there he turned and cut loose with the RPD. He stood up there laughing with that shrill high voice of his, chopping up Quimby's team—two of them killed by the first burst, the others staggering to their deaths as Muzingi's bullets caught them. And when the men were dead, he screamed, "Hey you! Quimby! Muparadzi! Come get me!"

Quimby slipped into the bush, fought his way upstream, and moved recklessly toward Muzingi's position, out of his mind with the lust to have the man dead, but Muzingi was gone, leaving his tracks everywhere in the soft wet soil and the heavy grass until they disappeared over bare granite rocks. Quimby guessed which way the killer would move and went after him, wet and exhausted, dirty and hungry—crazy to finish the chase.

He persuaded himself that Muzingi was as far gone as he was—the man had been in ZANLA territory for weeks; he couldn't keep going forever. But he did, until early in the morning two days later when Quimby, slipping and sliding up a mountain of great granite boulders, caught sight of the powerful black body, bare from the hips up, the RPD slung over its back, climbing ahead of him some two hundred yards away.

Quimby strained every muscle to catch up, knowing that at the top of the hill he would kill this man. Swearing and grunting and tearing at roots and shrubs for support, he shortened the distance only a little, for Muzingi was moving like a mountain goat, almost running, as if he had to get to the peak by a certain time.

And long before Quimby was close enough for a clear shot at the figure moving through the rocks above him, he knew that Muzingi was indeed racing to make an appointment. He heard the damnable phut-phut-phut of a helicopter and knew that he had lost.

The helicopter came down out of sight beyond the peak, and he knew that Muzingi was going aboard; then the throbbing Allouette was over his head falling forward and upward into the sky, and he did not fire because he was out in the open and not yet ready to commit suicide. And all the anger and frustration had burst out of him at once; he had been like a madman pounding the rocks and bawling with fury. . . .

* * *

IN the trade center, Quimby watched Muzingi turn away from Kado and Seifert, and gaze slowly around the room. As that gaze passed him he knew without any doubt that Muzingi had seen and recognized him, although no expression showed on that heavy, black face.

Muzingi turned and said something to Kado and moved slowly through the crowd. Quimby guessed that the man was coming to him, and he felt again the old sensation of being locked in a vicious fight that had to be finished. He struggled to quell the old hatred and the surging desire to kill this man who had murdered so many good fighting men, so many innocent villagers. Muzingi had no right to be alive, no right to be walking free among civilized people.

Quimby clenched his hands and breathed deeply, aware that his heart was pounding furiously, trying to tell himself that the days he remembered were long gone, that other men had forgotten, recalling Mugabe's efforts since 1980 to persuade old enemies to forget their differences, his patient efforts to soothe implacable factions into living together in peace. No peace with this man, Quimby told himself. No amnesty for Muzingi. Not ever. But he knew that here in this trade center he had to be calm; he had to hide his hostility.

Muzingi came through the crowd as he had moved through the forests, as if the obstacles were not there, and, Quimby felt certain, Muzingi knew exactly where his enemy stood. The big man moved around women who could have no idea what he had been, what he was; they turned and smiled at him and moved to let him pass and went on with their talking. Men saw the brute size of him and quickly stepped aside.

Muzingi halted in front of him, and Quimby had to look up; the man was at least six-feet-four, deep chest, broad shoulders. His head and face looked bigger than life, partly because he sported a bushy, black Castro beard. His nose was wide and wide-nostriled, the whites of his eyes were yellowish, and Quimby saw the meanness and craziness in those eyes that he had imagined was there years ago.

"Until yesterday, I didn't know you were still in Zimbabwe." The high tenor voice, without resonance, hinted at the crazy laughter Quimby remembered.

"I'm in the import business here in Harare. Pharmaceuticals. And you?"

Muzingi registered surprise that anyone had to ask about him. "I am now deputy commander of Umkhonto We Sizwe, responsible for our operations in South Africa and for the organization of our combat units. Most of my time I am in Botswana or Namibia or Mozambique, on whatever borders I can reach that lead into South Africa."

Quimby's mind rocked with the effort to absorb the change in Muzingi's status. Umkhonto We Sizwe—the Spear of the Nation—the armed force of the ANC. That made Muzingi number two or three in the ANC's military organization. He had gone from being a mercenary for the Rhodesians, killing blacks as if they were troublesome ants, to become one of the leaders of the ANC's military arm, fighting South Africa for black justice. The leap was too great to swallow.

Parrying for time, Quimby said, "Then I suppose you're a member of the SACP. I've heard that Umkhonto We Sizwe is the stronghold of the Communists."

The big shoulders raised a little, and Muzingi's smile was tolerant. "Oh, yes. We are the best fighters. We have the fire in our hearts, the training and the discipline. Those who are not

Communist talk forever but are never certain that we must make the Afrikaners bleed. The Spear of the Nation demands that we be hard as steel, but of course *you* know that I am. . . ."

The challenge was flat out. Quimby returned Muzingi's stare but said nothing.

Muzingi added, deliberately provoking, but sounding almost nostalgic. "Many times, you know, I have found myself wishing that we had met again back there. It would have given me joy to kill the famous Muparadzi. Even now . . ."

Quimby understood that this giant still felt as he did; he sensed the force of Muzingi's hostility, the irrational murder-wish inside his brain—a hundred times more threatening than that cop in the Detroit alley had been. He felt again the driving madness of his hunt for Muzingi, and for a moment he was ready to start that hunt all over again, to finish it this time. Then he thought of Herbert Nkala's stubborn struggle to win justice for South Africa's people; he remembered the threat of destruction that confronted the ANC leadership and knew that this was not the moment to settle an old feud. He shook his shoulders, loosening painfully tight muscles, and managed a stiff smile.

Muzingi was looking at him curiously. "I have heard that you would like to join Umkhonto We Sizwe, that you would even want to join the SACP."

Quimby was confused. He had not expected his application to be acted upon so quickly at such a high level. "I may have mentioned my interest to someone," he said.

Muzingi frowned. "Let the thought die, Muparadzi." He mouthed the name scornfully. "Go play in your drugstore and leave serious fighting to men who are committed."

"That is probably best," Quimby agreed mildly, suppressing the anger that was suddenly choking him. "I am a man of peace, a businessman."

He nodded amiably into disbelieving eyes and turned away from the huge hairy face, feeling like a coward, wanting to get away and reflect on what he had learned.

NEAR midnight, he sat under a piece of canvas tied between two trees in a squatters' camp near the railway station, drinking African beer with Mungu and Mutota and Wally Panebondo, a slim man with the face of a dark Arab who had helped him kill Selous Scouts in the Chimanimani Hills.

Quimby spoke quietly, defining the problem, explaining that someone—either the Communists of Russia and the South African Communist Party, or the rulers of South Africa—was trying to wipe out the ANC leadership. And he described in detail what the consequences of the ANC's direct involvement might be.

He knew these men well. The agony of being oppressed for most of their lives had compelled them to turn themselves into warriors and fight in the bush for years. They had hated that role, but they had also loved it; it had marked the high point of their lives, and they hungered for that rare excitement again. They understood the importance to the ANC of having bases outside the country where it fought, for they had fought from similar bases in Mozambique; they understood, too, that Zimbabwe's freedom would never be certain until the apartheid rule to the south was destroyed. And they were, like him, still wanting to do something useful with their lives.

Mungu passed the beer carton to Panebondo. He lifted his heavy arms and rubbed his hands together thoughtfully, and he asked, "You have a plan, Muparadzi?"

"The ANC has asked for our help. Secretly, you understand; we must never admit to anyone—not even to our women—that it is involved. These killers have been shooting the non-Communist

ANC leaders when they hold meetings. They will do this again, and soon. We will know ahead of time when the next meeting is held, and we will kill the killers."

They pondered that for several minutes, and Quimby waited, knowing they could not be hurried. Then Wally Panebondo pushed the beer carton on to Mutota and put his question sharply. "Kill them with what? We cannot kill well-armed white soldiers with our hands. We learned that all too well—"

Quimby interrupted. "With AKs and Uzis, with RPDs and RPGs. The weapons are ready for us here."

Again the silence while they considered. Around them there were quiet murmurings of men and women moving by in the darkness, of someone snuffling loudly in his sleep, autos passing thirty yards away on Manica Road, a woman singing to her baby, men talking loudly by the railway station. Then Mutota, The Wet One, leaned forward, holding up four fingers, with the thumb lying across his palm. "The last time there were four commandos. They were strong and well-trained men, with dangerous guns. I felt their power with my hands. How many will come next time?"

"I will telephone the President of South Africa and the Secretary General of the Soviet Communist Party and ask them how many commandos are being sent," Quimby said, laughing quietly. He waited while the others chuckled. Then, serious again, he said, "I think more will come next time. If each of you would talk to old friends who fought with us before, men who are not afraid of fighting . . . If each of you would bring in four other men, we would have a force of sixteen. During the war we had only a few more when we won our greatest victories."

Mungu belched sonorously and reached to open another beer carton.

"I will pay for our expenses and food," Quimby added. "And

when this work is completed I will give each man two hundred dollars. This is only to compensate for their time. It is not possible to compensate them for their commitment to freedom."

Keeping their voices down, they discussed his proposal at great length, examining every possibility. How would they travel? How could they keep a military action secret enough to escape the government's notice? What would they do if the commandos arrived in helicopters? If the Zimbabwean police discovered what they were doing? How would they organize their little units?

Mutota observed that peace and native beer had made some of their old comrades fat. They would need training, weapons practice, drills in the field—until they became as tough as they had been during the war.

Quimby replied that he did not see how they could go into the field to train openly as they had during the war, and he pointed out what they all knew—there was a penalty of five years imprisonment for possessing a military weapon. Mugabe had repeatedly offered amnesty to ex-soldiers of every color, provided they came in and gave up their weapons, but now men with arms in their hands were called bandits and were hunted down.

He urged that only the toughest men should be selected since there would be little time for getting them into good physical condition, and he promised that one way or another he would get them into the field for whatever training was possible.

The others fell back from their first lines of thinking and began to discuss what could be done.

In the past, when the Rhodesians' airpower and heavy guns and helicopter-delivered troops had made resistance impossible, they had discussed ways and means to persist and found them; they had devised plans and tactics no one had ever tried before, and many of their innovations had worked. Here under the shelter, they settled into that effort again. Quimby listened to the flow of suggestions, made some himself, and knew that he would win the support he needed.

Ultimately, Mungu summed up their conclusions. "Four for each man is too many. Let each of us bring in two men we trust absolutely. Let each of us meet with these men. Each group will take a weapon, and we will practice without shooting to recall the operations and the misfunctions and how to repair them. If the wait is long, we will exchange with another group and practice in our houses with another kind of weapon. We will put our men through forced marches around Lake McIlwaine, or beyond the Ewanrigg Gardens, away from the roads. We will do running and other exercises, as Muparadzi taught us to do in the past, and we will study again how to make an ambush, how to attack a group of men on a farm, or on a hill, or in city streets. Muparadzi will come and tell us how our attacks are to be made—as in the old days, but each of us will train our men because we must establish discipline that will hold them in place when there is fighting."

They settled it; they worked out a system of communicating with one another; they decided how Quimby would deliver weapons and ammunition to them, the ammunition not to be used until they were actually firing at the commandos.

They agreed to another meeting on the following night at a beerdrink near a squatters' camp behind the Parktown shopping center; then Mutota and Panebondo pulled away into the darkness as if they were going to relieve themselves, but they did not return.

Mungu reached out with both his huge hands, putting them up on Quimby's shoulders, and although Quimby could not see his face clearly in the darkness, he knew that Mungu was following a ritual he had practiced in the past, pledging his faith to the death.

* * *

AT one-thirty in the morning, Peter Chitepo sat at the table in Quimby's kitchen, bent over a large map of Zimbabwe. He held one of Quimby's massive coffee cups in one hand and a homemade roast beef sandwich in the other. He nodded emphatically when Quimby pointed at the Caprivi Strip, the erected-penis-shaped sliver of Namibia on Zimbabwe's northwestern corner where Zambia and Namibia and Botswana all came together to touch Zimbabwe.

Chitepo gulped down a bite of the sandwich and spoke quickly. "The SAs have military airbases and at least fifty thousand men there, but it's nine hundred kilometers to Harare, too much for a small plane, far too much for helicopters. Beitbridge is six hundred kilometers. But over here in the east, Mutare is only two-sixty. The SAs are helping the resistance movement in Mozambique, so the resistance will help them; that means it's easiest to bring in people from the east with fixed-wing planes or helicopters and get them back out."

Quimby's finger moved to South Africa's military airport near Phalabarwa, close to Zimbabwe's southern border, and Chitepo shook his head again. "Too far."

Quimby measured the distance from Zimbabwe's several borders with his eyes. During the civil war, when Rhodesian forces had attacked the headquarters of Joshua Nkomo's Zimbabwe People's Revolutionary Army (ZIPRA) outside Lusaka, they had taken off from Rhodesia's northern boundaries, with the target less than a hundred and fifty kilometers away.

When the South Africans had attacked ANC quarters outside Maputo in Mozambique in the fall of 1985, their helicopters had been practically next door, and their armor had come through Swaziland less than fifty miles away. In May 1986, they had attacked ANC installations in three of the Front Line States all on the same night: Botswana by helicopter, Zambia with fighter planes; the men who hit the ANC transient facility in Harare had flown from South Africa into Hwange and driven rental cars into Harare."

"And if the commandos are Communists or mercenaries working for Heinz Seifert or the SACP?" Quimby asked.

"They'll be stationed in Masuku Barracks out east of town, or working in the automobile plant, or on a farm outside the city."

"Have you got any kind of line on Heinz Seifert? Are you watching his men?"

Chitepo shook his head moodily, wrinkling up his nose. "They're quartered with the Second Brigade behind barbed wire and dogs and sentries. Seifert prohibits them from coming into town. He wants them to be invisible."

"Where do they do their drinking?"

"In their own canteen, at Masuku Barracks."

"I keep wondering if their team is four men short."

Chitepo wheezed with exasperation. "It's impossible to get in there, Taylor. They'll shoot you on sight."

Next time the commandos hit, Quimby reflected, he had to come away with a prisoner.

Chitepo put two fingers on the eastern edge of the map, in Mozambique, north of Mutare. "South African commandos could fly from any number of fields over here and come in low without anyone being the wiser. They could walk in through the hills, and trucks could pick them up inside the country and drive them into Harare. They could have weapons cached here, and they could take their trucks back out the same way. If our boyos are from South Africa, I say they'll come up the Mutare Road."

Quimby poured coffee for himself and Peter from the thermos he used and put the container back on the kitchen counter. When he returned to the table, Chitepo had moved one of Quimby's ebony heads in from the bedroom and had it standing on the map. He was studying the elongated black face, the almond-shaped eyes, the tight ears. His long, spatulate fingers caressed the curving line of the throat and the smoothness of the lips. He looked up with a smile, and said, "Beautiful work. Old. I wish I could do as well."

"You do, Peter. Your 'Hunter and the Lion' is my favorite." Quimby gestured at the table in the bedroom, where the hunter stood waiting eternally with his little spear. He went into the bedroom and came back with the carving, set it on the kitchen table, and stood looking at it. "Right now, I see us as the guy with the spear, only we don't know whether we're facing lions or crocodiles."

Chitepo leaned back in his chair with his eyes closed and nagged away at his own line of thought: "For that matter, the South Africans could be here already."

"Maybe," Quimby replied. "But I think you should spot people at the airports here and at Bulawayo. Look for men with short hair who wear military boots with their civies. We need to have people watching the auto traffic near the customs posts at Beitbridge and Mutare and Plumtree and up at Chirundu. If the people who want our ANC leaders dead aren't here now, they've got to come in, and they've got to do that on planes or trucks, or sneak in pretending to be someone else."

Chitepo frowned hopelessly. "Taylor, for Christ's sake! I don't have a whole army of watchers."

"Enough to save your leaders?"

"We're doing everything we can."

"You have the weapons I asked for?"

"For twelve men. In three different places. Only six rounds for the RPG; it's old stuff; we don't even know if it will fire."

Chitepo told him where the caches were, how they could be

89

loaded into a car or van without attracting attention, and he handed over keys to a van and a garage.

Quimby took a turn around the kitchen, stopped at his refrigerator, and got out a bottle of cold water. He poured a glass, looked at Chitepo and poured a second glass for him. "What's with the surveillance on the SACP?"

"A lot of people go in and out of those offices; so far we haven't discovered anything useful."

"And Florence Mubaka?"

"She's in bed every night at ten-thirty. Alone. One of my men saw her pass Kado in a hallway without even a nod. Do you think you spooked her?"

Quimby shrugged his shoulders, indicating that he didn't know. "Maybe Kado keeps all the lights out when she's in bed with him so she doesn't know what he looks like."

"Shit." Chitepo sat looking frustrated.

Quimby changed the direction of his thought again. "You know, in ZANLA during the war we had one great weakness, and we kept it afterward because by that time we had developed the wrong habits. We used mujibas to carry messages; we wrote everything out. The Rhodesians had radios and codes and military telephone systems that covered the whole country, but we didn't. The result was that every time they captured one of our camps, they collected mountains of paper—all our messages and maps, and they learned exactly what our plans were, who we were, where we were living, what weapons we had—everything."

"We still use the mujibas," Chitepo said. "We use couriers into South Africa, primarily because we know that the South African authorities monitor certain telephone numbers here and certain numbers in South Africa. They do the same with our mail."

"And you use the courier system for your interoffice communications in Zimbabwe, because the security police bug your phones?"

"Yes."

"And they read your mail?"

"Yes."

"All right, you see what I'm getting at?"

Chitepo looked puzzled. "No."

Quimby grinned. "The informer we're looking for is probably tied up the same way. Doesn't dare use the telephone or the post. Doesn't dare be seen with the person he sends his messages to. Mujibas—couriers. You've got to watch the mujibas Florence uses, and watch her everywhere. If they're delivering to some intermediate drop, like a shop or a post office box downtown, or an office somewhere, find out who picks up the message and where it goes. . . ."

"Taylor," Chitepo said, sounding desperate again. "I just don't have the people."

Quimby turned sharply away and stepped across the kitchen, telling himself to hold his temper. He turned and looked back at Chitepo and saw the deep lines of weariness in Chitepo's thin face, the slumping, gangly figure, the way Peter's head hung forward, the pointed chin almost touching his chest, and he understood that his friend was exhausted. He said, "Please, Peter. Even if you have to watch them yourself. If you follow one of the mujibas, and if he leaves a message somewhere you think is suspicious—call me, let me take it from there."

"It's like looking for one special minnow in the bottom of Lake Kariba."

"You're tired. Listen, we're going to spear a big lion before we're through. Right through his pisser. Believe it, we'll make him scream."

* * *

FROM the late afternoon until the early evening of the fifth of November, Quimby lay hidden behind piles of maps and boxes in a closet at the back of a classroom of the secondary school in Mufakosa Township, west of Harare. At seven-thirty, he stood up and stretched. He put on a pair of aviator-style dark glasses and unfolded a bushy black wig from his pocket and pulled it over his head, moving its forward edge low on his forehead. Then he moved cautiously to the door of the storeroom to look out through the wide bank of windows across the room. It was getting a little darker outside.

In the breast pocket of his dark blue leisure suit he carried a forged SACP membership card, and his intent was to slip into John Kado's meeting with SACP district party organizers, which Peter had learned was being held in the assembly hall of this building at eight o'clock.

He listened to the sounds of cars parking along Mutamba Drive and Mupani Avenue. A train growled its way along the track behind the school, and when it had passed, he heard the buzz of conversation close by in the building. He cracked the doorway open, looked into the dark hallway, and saw no one. He stepped into the corridor and walked along it toward the front of the building until he was able to view the broad foyer near the entrance of the building. Crowded with people—serious men and women coming to a party meeting, businesslike, sober, proving their zealousness to one another.

Only one of the outside doors was unlocked and he saw that two men at that door were carefully checking each person against a list before permitting them to enter. As he pondered on how he would cross the empty space between this corridor and the crowd, three men detached themselves from a larger group and walked toward him, and he ducked behind a row of lockers, trying to think up some reason he could give for his presence here. Was he a guard? An official responsible for keeping this corridor clear? That would have to do.

The men turned into the corridor but did not pass him where he stood hidden. He risked another look, realizing that they had turned into the men's room by the corner. He walked quickly to that door and ducked inside. A glance in the mirror over the lavatories told him that the wig was placed well, changing the shape of his head, its bushiness altering the look of his face. He exchanged nods with three serious-faced men, relieved himself at a urinal, washed his hands in unison with the others, and managed to be a part of the group as it left the toilet and moved toward the entrance to the assembly room.

He saw that the others held up their membership cards as they moved into the assembly hall, and that the ushers or guards at the door glanced at the cards and faces of the members as they passed. He held up his card, gave the guard the same sober look everyone else seemed to be wearing, and went through the door into a large, bleak room with rows of chairs placed in three sections.

He had not known how many people would be present, but had hoped that a big crowd would help him hide himself. Instead, the hall was capable of holding at least five hundred people, but there were not even half that many present, and the ushers were compelling everyone to move down toward the front. He had hoped that the lighting would be fairly dark, but this room was the students' assembly hall—blank white walls, well-lighted, not a shadowed corner anywhere. Every face was clearly recognizable, and he began to wish that he'd done something more to disguise himself than wearing dark glasses and this sweaty damned wig.

An usher pointed him to the middle of a half-filled row of loose chairs where Quimby saw that he would be boxed in from both sides. He mumbled that he was waiting for a friend, asking if it would be all right to sit for a moment in the seat on the aisle, and he sat down quickly, looking stolidly at the stage at the front of the hall, discouraging further discussion. The burly usher hesitated at his side for a moment, then moved away.

Up on the stage, John Kado, wearing a well-pressed gray leisure suit, with a collar that could have been designed for Nehru, stood with three colleagues, greeting men and women who came up to meet him. Tall, handsome, brown-skinned, with smooth gray hair, he smiled with a great show of interest in each person who approached him, talking pleasantly to all of them, exuding vigor and enthusiasm. A ham actor putting on a show, Quimby thought dourly.

A hugely fat woman in a billowing red-and-black-and-yellow African smock bustled up to Kado, all smiles and bows and gracious hand gestures, and Kado and his three colleagues sat themselves behind a table, facing the audience. Latecomers scurried down the aisles and found seats, as self-conscious as tardy students.

The compact little man sitting at Kado's left called the meeting to order and explained briefly that the distinguished Secretary-General of the South African Communist Party was present to discuss the duties of district party organizers during this week before the international conference at Lusaka.

Kado stood up smiling to loud and prolonged applause. Then his face grew stern, and he cut off the applause with a bold and peremptory sweep of both hands, commanding silence.

Curious to know how this audience reacted to Kado's theatrical gesture, Quimby looked along the front rows of the audience and saw Victor Muzingi sitting uncomfortably huge in the aisle seat of the second row. He got up and moved quickly to another seat, placing himself behind two large men who might screen him a little if Muzingi turned around, and he sat low in his seat and began to listen to Kado's words.

Kado had a strong, melodious, baritone voice. It rolled out of his chest and throat with an almost incredibly persuasive authority, as if every word he spoke had the force of law.

"Comrades," he said, as if he were the Pope blessing the world, "we have picked up the spear in South Africa. We will engulf the apartheid system in the fire and thunder of people's war. I tell you tonight that the time of crisis has arrived. Lenin advised us that he who delays or hesitates when the moment to act is at hand betrays the revolution and the working class. He betrays history. We are the party of the working class, and I say to you: *The crucial moment has arrived! The warlords of South Africa will be overthrown! We are moving, and we will prevail!*"

Convincing, Quimby thought. The guy's got charisma. Magic.

The audience broke into applause as if it had been suddenly shocked awake. Someone shouted, "Forward to victory!" Then others began to yell, "Victory! Victory!"

Everyone in the room stood up, and men and women began to call out Kado's words: "We will prevail! We will prevail!" They repeated the phrase in unison, making it a chant, and in a moment they were timing the chant to their hand clapping and foot stamping, making a solid rhythm of sound, and Kado stood quietly on the stage letting it happen.

Quimby had been through too many ZANLA political sessions not to recognize the pattern. He did not particularly dislike Marxism-Leninism. He recognized that its powerful and simple explanation of how history worked was incredibly useful to men and women trying to make a revolution. For the Zimbabwean fighters, and for himself, it had provided a driving faith as well as precise and practical instructions about how to organize and fight, how to politicize the people in the villages and win their support, and how to inspire in them the belief that they could win. He settled down for a long and repetitive spiel from the platform.

But Kado did not conform to the pattern. He made that sweeping gesture with his hands again. The chanting stopped and the men and women standing around the floor scurried back to their seats.

Kado came forward to the edge of the stage, looking aggressive. "This is a tactical session," he declared. "You know our strategic goals, and I have just said that we are moving now to achieve them without delay. But to move effectively we must eliminate the rot that exists in the ANC alliance of which we are a part. Our greatest problem is not the imbalance of arms between our armies, between Umkhonto We Sizwe and the South African Defense Forces. Our greatest enemy is internal. It is embodied in the many people in our alliance against apartheid who hesitate, who say, 'Let us protract the preparation forever.' Who say, 'It's not time yet.' Or who say, 'It's dangerous to move against the powerful armies of the white supremacists.' Our worst enemies are those who say that we should turn the other cheek and forgive, or that we should try to negotiate reforms."

He raised his voice: "Our party, the vanguard of the people, declares the exact opposite!" He brandished his fists high over his head and roared: "NOW IS THE TIME FOR MASS CONFRONTATION! THE FLAME OF RESISTANCE WILL BURN THE WHITE OPPRESSORS OUT OF THEIR OFFICES AND FACTORIES AND HOMES. OUR PEOPLE HAVE SUFFERED TENS OF THOUSANDS OF LASHES: NOW IT IS TIME FOR REVOLUTIONARY VIOLENCE, AND WE WILL LEAD IT!"

He had his arms up and out, reaching to his audience, and he held that position while the applause and shouting ran on. Everyone stood and cheered and applauded for several minutes, while Kado stood stiffly, not smiling. Then he dropped his arms, and waited, making it obvious that he wanted to continue.

Here and there, individual men and women began to sit down; others followed, and pulled at those who were still standing. The hall became silent again.

Kado spoke into the silence with a forceful conversational tone, like a military commander issuing orders to his battalions:

"This week and next, and all through the days of the international conference itself, you must attack the internal enemy. These are the anti-Communist members of the ANC and perhaps some of our own party members who counsel delay.

"Denounce them!

"They are agents of the apartheid monsters!

"They are agents of the United States CIA, which aids and abets the apartheid beasts at every step!

"Drive the foot draggers out of the alliance. Force them to accept the fact that the time has come for action! Expose them for what they are—traitors, toadies of the CIA, petty bourgeois democrats, capitalists who want to preserve their wealth and privilege!

"Whoever does not recognize that the ANC must lead the revolution *now* is a coward, a fawning hyena of the oppressors, a running dog of the imperialists! See to it that all members of our party stand up and denounce these counterrevolutionary reactionaries!"

The audience sat completely silent, as if it were cowed by Kado's demands. Wondering if Kado's words were routine rhetoric, something these people had heard many times before, Quimby examined the faces around him and saw that every man and woman in the audience looked fearful and intense; eyes were fixed on Kado, brows were furrowed, lips were pursed or teeth were bared, and hands were clasped tight; excitement and total concentration were everywhere. These people were receiving orders for battle; their adrenalin was up; they were going into a fight.

"We can no longer afford endless discussion of all the pros and cons," Kado went on. "Our party leads the most powerful and angry revolutionary force in South Africa, the workers. We do not flinch from declaring: 'If other classes and individuals are not with us they are against us!' The people in your area who resist you are anti-Communist, antirevolutionary. They are corrupting from within the struggle for freedom; they must be purged, torn out of our alliance. They must be ruthlessly driven out. You will carry out this work at once."

He paused, looking somberly at his audience. Then his voice rolled out again, sounding like the voice of a prophet: "If we fail to move now, we may lose our right to a place in history. The opportunity of this moment may never return. Lenin's advice cannot be ignored. We will neutralize the apartheid army; we will activate the peasantry; we will mobilize the masses NOW! AND WE WILL SEIZE POWER IN SOUTH AFRICA!"

Kado scowled with what looked like real anger, and he sounded as angry as he looked. "But we cannot be successful while we still have Judases and traitors and CIA agents in our midst. They will be purged this week when you return to your districts."

He paused to look threateningly across the audience as if he were seeing Judases and traitors in its midst; then he added, letting the words roll out with solemn thunder: "And I promise you. I PROMISE YOU! YOUR LEADERS WILL COMPLETE THIS TASK AT THE END OF NEXT WEEK AT THE INTERNATIONAL CONFERENCE!"

Again, the members of the audience rose to their feet cheering and applauding, calling for struggle and victory.

Kado stood still and straight, eyes down, giving his listeners time to let his words sink in. The applause went on and on, until, finally, he shook his head disapprovingly and put up his hands, calling for silence. Then he paced slowly to the right edge of the stage.

His tone now was quiet, businesslike: "Our district leaders will now be divided into seven groups, as they are listed on the sheets that are being passed out. Each group will meet in one of the rooms of this building to discuss the concrete steps you must take during the next nine days. Your action must be swift and ruthless, as, I assure you, the steps taken by your leaders will be. Now, before we break up, are there questions of general interest?"

He waited through a long silence. No one, it appeared, dared to question the Secretary-General. Two or three people coughed. A woman's nervous giggle was cut off abruptly. Everyone seemed to sit very still under Kado's fierce eyes. Then, slowly, a tall, fat man who appeared to be in his early forties stood in the center of the audience, and Quimby saw the man's thick fingers moving in a kind of frenzy along the side of his leg.

The man's voice was high and thin, lacking resonance, seeming almost to quiver. "The Secretary-General has undoubtedly not forgotten the mandate that every member of our party must involve himself in the criticism of policy during the early stages of discussion. I want to say that I regard it as very dangerous for the party to move in the way the Secretary-General has directed. This can only result in a profoundly dangerous split, a destruction of the mass support enjoyed by the ANC in South Africa. In my humble opinion this represents an unfortunate effort—"

Kado roared, "NO, NO, NO!" The fuzzy, gray eyebrows were down over his eyes. He waved a hand impatiently in front of his face as if a bee were buzzing there; then he pointed a finger down at the first rows of the audience, giving a signal to someone.

Voices in the audience began to hoot and jeer. The chairman of the meeting sitting next to Kado shook his head emphatically and pounded on the table with the flat of his hand. Three big men, obviously the party's bully boys, came hurrying back from the front rows and forced their way into the row where the dissenter stood. By the time they reached him, men close to him were jerking at his arms, trying to pull him down. Then a fist hit him on the side of the head, and he stood crouching forward, his arms raised to protect his head.

The bully boys, with many hands helping them, wrestled the dissenter into the aisle, and he began to resist them, kicking and screaming. His shrill voice called out for the right to be heard, quoting lines from the party's rules, repeating them several times, yelling that he was only doing his duty, and his eyes desperately glared in all directions, searching for help.

A fist smashed his nose; another struck him on the forehead, but he continued to struggle and scream his complaints. The bully boys and two other men hustled him up the aisle, wrestling with him all the way, and when he was out of the hall his high voice could still be heard, arguing, defending his right to speak.

For several minutes the room buzzed with excited talk. Then as people realized that Kado had not moved, that he was standing at the center of the stage, waiting for their attention, they quieted, and he said, very loudly: "This policy is not to be debated. The treatment you have seen meted out to that vacillator and dissenter is the treatment you must mete out to the ANC anti-Communists and weaklings in your midst. This meeting will now be divided into the district groups, and you will go to the designated rooms for specific instructions."

Quimby stood when the others stood, intending to move with some convenient group to the back of the assembly hall. He made his way into the aisle, and was suddenly aware that Victor Muzingi, his body half out of his chair, his head twisted around, was staring at him with a strange look of concentration and perplexity.

Quimby thought: *Time to git.*

He pushed his way up the center aisle and out of the building, hearing Muzingi's high voice squealing commands. He sprinted the length of the building to a corner and ran toward the railway line. The high fence around the playground delayed him only an instant; he was over it and across Mupani Avenue, away and running easily, not hearing any pursuit.

He crossed the railway, and when he was beyond the embankment, he knelt and looked back, searching the fence-line and the ground between the fence and the school. He watched four men come out of the building and spread out over the playground, searching all its corners, and he saw them come to the fence and stare in his direction and point at Mupani Avenue and the railway line, but none of them climbed the fence, and in a few minutes they went back into the school.

He jerked the dank wig from his head and wiped away some of the sweat that had soaked his own hair; then he jogged eastward, following Marimba Road to get to the place where he had left his car, and he drove off pondering what he had seen.

5

TWO-THIRTY in the afternoon, a phone call. Peter Chitepo spoke quickly. "Get to Cecil Square. A man called Safirio by the fountain, looking for Chifamba. Right now!"

Quimby told his assistant he had to go downtown, and left his office half-running. He walked as fast as he dared up the First Street mall, went right at Stanley Avenue, entered the leaf-shadowed square, and approached a well-built man about his own age who stood watching the fountain.

"Safirio?"

The man turned toward him, dark eyes watchful, his right fist clenched for fighting.

Quimby said, "I'm Chifamba."

Safirio nodded and his eyes went back to the fountain. He put his hand over his nose so that it also covered his lips, and he spoke from behind that cover without looking at Quimby. "Florence Mubaka went into the Anglican Cathedral to make a drop. I saw her do it. You follow me in, but carefully. I'll go in and sit exactly where she sat; then I'll leave."

Quimby turned away and looked at the facade of the Meikles Hotel. Over his head violet jacaranda blossoms and yellow cassias made an unbelievable canopy of color. Around him dark purple bougainvillea flowered. He thought what a beautiful city this was, and back of that thought was the other: So Florence *was* the informer.

His mind worked swiftly to sort out what he must do. He had to be sure he understood the connections; he wanted to see what Florence's message said, but he couldn't just dash into the cathedral and look for it because he also wanted to know where it was going. That could mean having a talk with whoever came to collect it, or tailing the collector. He turned and drifted northward toward the parliament building, seeing that Safario was well ahead of him on Second Street, moving toward the cathedral.

He crossed the square to Baker Avenue, dawdling there for a moment; then walked down Baker and into the cathedral. Safirio was moving into a pew eight rows from the front. Quimby went to the right aisle and walked forward quietly, partly hidden from the main hall by rough-hewn granite arches and the shadows they cast.

As well as he could tell, there were very few people in the cathedral. Three black women knelt before a chapel across the way; a white woman in a light woolen suit sat up straight at the very center of the third row, looking forward at the altar. He studied the choir, the organ, the side entrances to the apse, and decided that Florence had selected an excellent spot for leaving messages. Who would suspect that a beautiful woman would use the church for her hollowed-out tree?

He stopped at the archway just back of where Safirio sat, and as Safirio rose and walked away along another aisle, Quimby focused on the paraphernalia on the little wooden shelf fastened to the back of the pew ahead of where Safirio had been sitting. He supposed Florence would have left her message in one of those books: prayer books, hymnals, little envelopes the churchgoers used for making a folding-money contribution when the collection plate came by. Probably he could find the message if he moved over there, but that wasn't the main purpose of this exercise. Besides, the collector might be in the church somewhere watching that pew; he could have been spooked already by seeing Safirio sit there.

Quimby inspected the interior of the church more carefully, looking for the best place to hide himself, knowing that he might be in for a long wait, and beginning to plan what he would do if the person who unloaded this drop was a man, a woman, or a fast-footed mujiba.

Standing in the dark corridor at the side of the main hall, he made a show of examining the displays on the walls—the crosses and stonework, the names of the dead. When there was nothing more he could look at, he went into the choir area and inspected the church from there, staying back in the shadows of an archway and staring out at the front of the church.

An hour later, worried by the thought that the collector might get away from him, he went down and took a seat two rows behind where Safirio had sat, some twenty feet to the right. From there, he would be able to see whoever came to empty the drop.

He was too close, but this was a church. He leaned forward and put his forearms on the back of the pew in front of him, clasping his hands as if he were praying. He put his head down on his arms, hoping that he gave a good picture of a man asking the Lord to wipe away his debts, or forgive him for something, or find him a better-looking woman than the one he had married, or keep his refrigerator filled with good German beer. He was pleased that whoever came to the pew he watched would not be able to see his face.

Another twenty minutes.

A small, slender black man dressed in a light leisure suit and wearing steel-rimmed glasses came down the aisle at Quimby's back, hesitated by a pillar, then sidled into the pew and sat where Florence had sat.

Quimby saw thin black arms, a soft, weak-looking face wearing an expression of fretful worry. The man looked like one of the neat and fussy government boys—a clerk, an accountant. Thick-lenses flashed as he looked around the cathedral and then, more surreptitiously, to his right and left, and back again to his right at Quimby. He craned further around to look behind Quimby, then turned about and watched an old white woman who came down the aisle nearest him and sat in the first pew, almost under the pulpit.

Quimby maintained his prayerful position and watched the man reach rather hesitantly for one of the soft-covered books on the shelf in front of him and riffle through the pages. He put that one back and looked to the right and left again, and Quimby chose the moment when the man's head turned away from him to rise and step over into the aisle behind the heavy arches and begin to walk away. He stopped beyond the second pillar and turned to watch the collector reach for another book, flip it open, and slip a very small piece of paper from its back pages into the left breast pocket of his pale blue leisure suit.

Quimby moved forward silently to the pillar nearest that row of pews, hoping the collector would enter as he had come in, along the right aisle.

The collector went to his knees and appeared to be praying for several minutes, although Quimby guessed that the praying man was also checking the aisle to be sure it was clear. When his prayers were finished, the collector rose and slipped along the pew toward the pillar where Quimby hid, and as he rounded that pillar, Quimby hit him—neatly and precisely, not too hard but hard enough—on the point of his chin.

The collector's head went back as if his neck had suddenly turned to soft butter, and he crumpled almost too fast for Quimby to catch him and ease his fall.

Quimby pulled the unconscious man up and pushed him into a pew, holding him upright, although the head lolled forward as if he were asleep, or, possibly—praying again. Quimby climbed over the inert body, and sat at its left, wedging the man's other shoulder against the end of the pew. He reached into the breast pocket of the leisure suit and found the slip of paper—about an inch wide and two inches long—with a single penciled line of gobbledygook, a meaningless strip of letters and numbers. Code . . . Quimby flattened the paper, got out his notepad, and copied everything on the page:

$$NVS2M2-0100-1/8/1988-3276-M2T52OC2-(4)$$

The collector wasn't going to remain unconscious forever; the important thing now was to learn where his message was supposed to go. Quimby stuffed it back into the breast pocket of the leisure suit and reached around to the collector's hip, looking for a wallet and finding it. He copied the collector's name and address from an identification card; then took all of the money out of the wallet and stuffed it into his own hip pocket. He scattered cards and folded bits of paper from the wallet on the floor, stole the man's wristwatch, and threw the open wallet on the seat of the pew. The scene looked right to him, and he stepped over bony knees to make his way toward the back of the church.

When the collector came to, Quimby guessed, his first thought would be for that message. Since it was in his pocket, he might believe it had not been seen. But his wallet was lying on the seat; his money and his watch were gone, and his papers were scattered on the floor. Hopefully, he would assume that he had been the victim of a mugging by someone wanting money for kachasu or heroin or marijuana badly enough to make an attack in the cathedral. And since his main concern would probably be to deliver his message, the chances seemed good that he wouldn't run to the police.

Quimby returned to Cecil Square and stood in shadows, watching the cathedral entrance. And while he waited, he studied the lines of letters and numbers he had copied, trying to guess the system of cryptography that had been used.

It seemed to him that he might have a useful lead because he had an idea what the message could be saying. If he and Chitepo were right, Florence Mubaka was telling someone when and where a meeting of the ANC leaders was about to take place. If that was the gist of it, she would be giving the time and the place, references to a map or map coordinates, a building or a street number, perhaps the names of the men who would be meeting. It wouldn't be the simplest code in the world because these people were working at a dangerous task; at the same time, they didn't appear to be aware that anyone suspected them.

He concentrated first on the numbers. One of them had to refer to a time of day: 0100, and the other, a date 1/8/88.

What was going to happen at one o'clock on the eighth of

January 1988 that was so important that Florence was dropping her message into a songbook in the Anglican Cathedral in the middle of the day? The answer to that had to be: *nothing*.

Florence was interested in right now, 1986. He subtracted two from the last 8, and two from the 8 between the slashes, and using the twelve months of the year as his base, he subtracted two from the one. So: 11/6/86. He thought about that and grinned with triumph, feeling like a brilliant breaker of codes. That was today, by God! And 0100? Did they do the same subtractions of two? So was it happening (whatever it was) at eleven? He decided to hold off on that decision.

He pored over the other numbers, not knowing if he should go on subtracting twos. 3276 could be 1054, or if he added, 5498, and (4) could be (2), or the parentheses could mean "hold," which would make it 4, or "add," which would make it six. He had no way of knowing which way to go.

The longer strings of letters and numbers hung him up. Some type of substitution code, he guessed. He was beginning to write out parallel lists of ABCs and numbers in his notebook to try to decipher the message using different combinations from the Vigenere matrix, but he was interrupted. The collector came to the entrance of the cathedral holding his jaw, looked along Baker Avenue both ways, stared over at the square for a moment, then tottered slowly down the steps.

QUIMBY picked Chitepo up at about five-thirty. He drove southeast on Mutare Road, outside of Harare, and neither of them was in a mood to pull his punches. Peter Chitepo protested that he knew nothing about a meeting of ANC leaders that night in Lusaka, and Quimby's question was roared.

"Well, why the hell don't you know?"

"Lusaka's out of my jurisdiction. I'm responsible for the leaders when they're in Zimbabwe."

"You mean you don't care if they get killed in Zambia? For Christ's sake, don't you guys ever talk to each other?"

"You're not even sure," Chitepo said defensively. "You worked some kind of message out of some kind of code. 'Lusaka—twenty-three hundred tonight.' How do you know you're right?"

"At 1054 Kashamba Road, and two or four or six of your leaders will be there. That's the way I read it. The number two is A; then with the next six letters of the alphabet you go two letters down—"

"Don't tell me. I'll work it out myself."

"Go ahead, work it out. Tell me what *you* think it says. But better yet, why don't you call Lusaka and find out?" Quimby pounded the back of the seat with his free hand. "And while you're at it, tell whoever you talk to up there I'll want a weapon, a handgun of some kind, and twenty rounds of ammunition, and a car. . . . My secretary reserved a seat for me on the eight o'clock flight, the only thing available. . . . I'll be lucky to be out on Kashamba Road in time."

"What in hell can you do?" Chitepo demanded. "You'll be on your own—"

"I'll stop your goddamned assassins. That's what you wanted—"

"I haven't even had a chance to check this message," Chitepo complained. "I don't even know—"

"Keep farting around, Peter—your chiefs are going down the drain—"

"Ah, shit! Muparadzi, you're going off half-cocked. Let me think—"

"The least you can do is check with Lusaka headquarters," Quimby insisted. "I need to know if my reading of that message is correct. Find out where the meeting is, when it is, how many people will be there."

"I don't even know if this *is* a report of a meeting."

"It's not a grocery list. Peter, I followed this courier back to the Altron Company on Kaunda Avenue. I watched him go straight into the boss' office. Altron is a South African Company, for Christ's sake. What more do you want? Why would Florence Mubaka be sending a coded message by secret courier to Altron? I place the answer before you on a silver platter: because she's working for the people who are killing your leaders."

Chitepo beat on the top of the front seat himself, and declaimed resentfully: "The great Quimby knows fucking all! Why don't we make Florence tell us who she's working for? When we know that, we'll just get her transferred to a job where she can't do any more damage while we go after her bosses."

"Maybe we'll do that—tomorrow. Or maybe we'll decide to let her run so we can monitor her messages and catch the bastards in the act. Right now I've got to get to Lusaka and stop the commandos *tonight*."

"You won't even try the peaceful way; you're determined to go up there and kill somebody."

"That's what you wanted me for, buddy."

Chitepo shook his head furiously, his face carved deeply with lines of anger. "Taylor, I tell you frankly: You go too fast. I'm beginning to be sorry I talked Nkala into bringing you into this."

"Well I *am* in and I *am* going to Lusaka. If there's some way you can do it, find out if there really is a meeting up there. Let me know if I've got the time and the address right before I get on my plane."

Quimby glanced into his rearview mirror and saw that Peter was still frowning, shaking his head.

Peter repeated himself. "You're so damned anxious to get up there and kill somebody."

"I'm trying to do my job. Nkala and you asked me to stop these people. Are you going to help?"

While Quimby watched, Peter went on shaking his head in frustration.

"There's no one in Harare I dare to ask about the meeting," Peter said. "Nkala's in Mozambique somewhere. I can't call just anybody in our headquarters at Lusaka and say, 'I need a gun for a friend who intends to kill some people tonight.' You heard Nkala. He insisted that we had to keep what you're doing separate from the ANC. Besides me, he was to be the only one who knew."

They drove in silence for a mile or two until Quimby found a place where he could turn around and head back toward Harare. He was thinking what poor, unorganized, chaotic things refugee parties were. They never had enough money, never developed the disciplined organization they needed. The leaders always talked well but endlessly, and involved themselves in feuds and schisms and closet conspiracies; they were driven by passionate eagerness to suffer for their goals, but they were just plain impractical, disorganized, incompetent. . . .

The damned ANC was supported by millions of people wanting freedom and equality, but they followed leaders who didn't know zilch when it came to practical knowledge about how to make something happen in the real world. . . . The leaders couldn't pound sand down a rathole, couldn't tell shit from Shinola, couldn't decide whether to run or fight, couldn't even keep themselves from getting killed like helpless chickens. How the hell could they ever dream that—

Chitepo came forward on the edge of his seat, his hands up on the back of the front seat, his narrow head up close where Quimby could see it in the mirror and out of the corner of his eye at the same time. Chitepo gripped Quimby's right shoulder with both hands and glared into the mirror, meeting Quimby's eyes. "Muparadzi, listen! If I can get a seat on that plane I'll go with you. I'll check in at headquarters and find a gun for you. I'll try to find a way to warn the leaders to stay away from that place, if there really is a meeting scheduled, and I'll get a car for you. Okay?"

But the people always come up with solutions that work, Quimby thought, suddenly and profoundly ashamed of his impatience. They keep going and they win. The followers don't just follow; they think, and they keep on thinking; and they take action instead of waiting around for the leaders to solve all the problems. Democracy, by God. The way it's supposed to be. Nothing messier; nothing more wonderful. He reached back to touch Chitepo's fingers and said, "I'll drop you at the air terminal in town."

QUIMBY came off the plane at the Lusaka Airport, carrying a small traveling bag, and followed a crowd of tourists through customs, where one of the officers knew him well enough to smile and call him by name. He showed his ticket on to Malawi for early the next morning, displayed traveler's checks and cash to prove he was capable of paying his way in Zambia, showed his passport and received a transient visa, paid the airport tax and got through the "Arriving Passengers" line without trouble. Ten minutes after nine. He had to be out on Kashamba Road and ready for whatever action was set up by eleven.

Just inside the main airport entrance, he stood for a moment, glancing back, seeing Peter Chitepo, his long head showing above the heads around him, smiling and nodding at one of the customs inspectors. They had planned to meet in Quimby's room at the Inter-Continental Hotel as soon as Peter made his arrangements.

Peter came away from the customs lines, cleared, and Quimby went on alone. A boy looking for a fat tip whistled up a battered Mercedes cab.

The driver went toward Lusaka at breakneck speed. Enjoying the warm wind from the open windows against his face, Quimby tried to guess how things would go.

For the moment, everything depended upon Chitepo. Reliable but cautious Chitepo, dedicated to the revolution but in permanent shock from the tactics of the people who hated his beloved party. Terrified by their violence, Quimby thought. And by mine. A good man working for a good cause, but he just couldn't believe the world was the way it was. In the next hour or so, he had to locate the people who ran things up here; without explaining why, he had to get that meeting canceled and warn away the leaders, and he had to get hold of a pistol and a car without making whoever provided them accomplices to what was going to happen tonight. Chitepo—loyal, conscientious, too hard-pressed.

There wasn't enough time. He didn't believe Peter could get all his tasks completed, and he began to consider what could be done. . . .

The clerk on duty at the hotel knew him from his past visits. The room was ready. A fifty-year-old black "boy" was assigned to carry his light bag and show him to his room. When the "boy" had gone, Quimby changed quickly, putting on dark clothing and running shoes; then he sat looking down on the swimming pool, counting minutes, trying to plan for contingencies he couldn't even imagine.

* * *

PETER came through the unlocked door at ten-fifteen, harassed-looking, his face shining with perspiration, the front of his shirt clinging wetly against his chest, showing the blackness through the white cotton fabric. His eyes took in at a glance the elegant furnishings, the two double beds; he walked to the window and looked down at the swimming pool off to his left three floors below, and he began talking hurriedly. "You were right about the meeting, but you should have subtracted your twos from the address. It's not Fifty-four Ninety-eight Kashamba Road; there isn't anything in that block but a ravine; it's 1054. We've warned three of the leaders not to be there, but we couldn't find the fourth one, Stephen Shamu. He may be out there already, or on his way. . . ."

Chitepo put his hands up on the flat sides of his head, wagging it back and forth with his hands, grimacing unpleasantly. "I've got a car outside, Taylor, but I couldn't get you a gun. The men responsible for them are out of contact; we couldn't find them. I can't just walk up to anybody in the ANC and say, 'Can you let me have a handgun for a few hours.' I'm sorry . . . I'm terribly sorry. . . . Listen, the meeting is canceled. If someone is sending commandos, we can't stop them. We ought to get out there and warn Shamu to stay clear. Then we ought to get out of Zambia. The commandos can't hurt anything if we keep Shamu away—"

Quimby looked at himself in the full-length mirror on the wall across from the beds. In dark trousers, a dark blue-and-maroon knit shirt and blue joggers, he was almost invisible in the dim light of the room. He had not come to Lusaka to let even one of the ANC leaders be attacked. Not only that—the commandos, whoever they were, had to learn that every effort they made to harm the ANC was going to be punished. His job was to destroy their assumption that they could kill ANC people without danger to themselves. He had to hurt them enough to make them stop trying.

He said, "Peter, tell me where the car is, where you want it left when I'm through with it."

"You can't go out there without a weapon."

"I'll find something."

"Taylor, you can't!" Peter's face hardened with fearful resolution. He rubbed his hands together tensely, like a woman washing disgusting filth from her hands; then he put his hands flat on his stomach as if something hurt down there, and he said, "I'll go with you."

"Calm down." Quimby motioned Peter over to the table where he had a map of Lusaka laid out under a lamp. "Look, if I go across on Independence Avenue and out Lumumba Road, will that put me where I want to be?"

Peter seemed unable to concentrate. His finger traced the route Quimby had described. He stepped backward and rubbed the knuckles of both hands across the top of his head. "I . . . Yes."

"All right. Give me the keys. Where's the car? Where do you want me to leave it?"

Peter gave him the details quickly, looking at him with frightened eyes, looking as if he had been ill for a long time. He said again. "I'll go with you."

"No. Get on your plane tonight. Get back to Harare, no fuss, no trouble. I'll see you tomorrow afternoon."

IN a distant corner of the hotel parking lot, Quimby opened the trunk of the old blue Honda Accord and found the tool kit in its special package. He stared at the array for a moment, hefted a wrench, decided it was too light, and selected the socket wrench designed to take off the wheel lugs. Ten inches long. Heavy. He held the Phillips screwdriver in his hand wishing it were sharper and wondering if he would have time to hone it to a better point on a rock somewhere. He put the wrench inside his belt and trousers, with the head at the top, the screwdriver on the other side.

When he attempted to sit inside the Honda, he had to adjust the screwdriver to avoid puncturing parts of his anatomy he very much wanted to preserve.

He drove west, first on Haile Selassie Avenue, then on Independence Avenue, across Cairo Road at the foot of the business section, then north on Lumumba Avenue.

The business districts in these Southern African cities never ceased to jar him with a feeling of unreality. They seemed too modern, foreign, and out-of-step with the rest of the land, like tight little mid-Western cities from the United States set down in a sea of black people who were often as backward and ignorant of the city as their ancestors had been hundreds of years ago.

Out in the veld, up in the hills, down along the rivers, there were strange and dangerous wild animals, deadly snakes and insects of all the kinds anyone could imagine, man-eating crocodiles and horrible diseases and people who believed in spirits that sometimes helped and sometimes killed but were always there. And every so often—one of these misplaced mid-Western cities with its steel-and-plastic facades and ornate government buildings.

Africa was changing too fast. In a car the transition across centuries was made in minutes, but the lands and the peoples had ten thousand struggles to go before they caught up with the cities. Given the famines and the wars, even God himself couldn't possibly know how things would turn out. . . .

It was dark in the Lusaka suburbs, and he drove slowly across the railroad track just short of Malambo, across the second set of tracks on the other side of Malambo. He slowed still more and passed the crossroads at Sheki-Sheki and Twatotela, and went on to the street he wanted—Kashamba.

At Kashamba he turned left, off Lumumba, stopped the car and sat with his lights out trying to get a sense of the terrain, wondering how close he was to his target, how many people were still awake in these houses on each side of him and how many of them kept dogs.

He could not guess which block he was in, and he got out of the car to walk along the street, trying to see if there were numbers on the houses.

This was another of those half-developed neighborhoods—uncurbed streets, shanties clustered between well-built, one-story houses, small bushes and young trees growing out of bare soil, low fences here and there. A power line on posts ran on the north side of the street, but most of the houses on the south side were in complete darkness, making him wonder if they had electricity at all.

A man's courteous voice startled him: "You're looking for anyone special?"

Quimby saw a dark figure standing in front of a house on the north side and assumed that it was the owner. He realized that he had gone into a crouch, and he straightened up quickly and said, "The fourteen hundred block. Am I close?"

"Further down. Eight blocks. This is six hundred."

"Many thanks. Pretty dark out here."

"Yo."

Quimby returned to his car, and drove on, turned his lights off in the third block, and pulled the car over. He was too tense; that voice in the darkness had shaken him; the man back there would never know how close he'd come to getting himself killed.

Quimby found himself hoping there weren't a lot of other

117

sleepless citizens standing around in front of their houses; then he realized abruptly that if the guy was still standing back there he would be wondering why this car had stopped three blocks away. He swore aloud, irritated because he had outfoxed himself, started the car again, drove on three more blocks, pulled off the road, and jogged back to the ten hundred block.

He stood against a bush, studying what he could see, wishing that he had been able to reconnoiter the area in the daytime. On the north side of the street, the even-numbered side, there were only two houses. Lights showed in both of them. No numbers were visible. A small car was parked in the driveway at the front of the house closest to him. He wondered if it belonged to the people who lived there or to the one ANC leader who had not been warned off, and he felt relief that the others had been warned in time.

It seemed probable that the first house was his target, but he had to make certain. He moved forward reluctantly, thinking what a helluva note it would be if he got shot out here by somebody who took him for a thief, and he wondered why the ANC didn't post its own guards for a meeting like this. After the assassinations of the past few weeks it stood to reason there would be other attacks. Surely it was legitimate for an organization like the ANC to defend itself? Then he remembered that Chitepo had got this meeting canceled; guards weren't needed. But shouldn't they have sent someone out here to warn Shamu off? Maybe they had. Or if Shamu was already here maybe there were guards lurking around somewhere. Too damned many dangerous maybes.

He approached the front of the first house and saw numbers on the door but could not read them. He crept to the door and traced them with his fingers: 1–0–5–4. This was it.

The light came from the back.

He walked down the east side of the house, and stopped before he came to the lighted window. A shade had been drawn; he could see nothing inside, and had no idea who lived here, how many people were inside. If Stephen Shamu was here, he must be getting impatient. . . .

In the light from the window, he looked at his wristwatch. Ten minutes after eleven.

If the commandos were coming, they were about due. Would they hit from the front or the back? He wished that Mungu and Mutota were with him; he couldn't be in both places at the same time. He needed someone at his flank, someone protecting his back. He wished that there was some way he could warn the man who was inside or maybe still coming, either to get the hell out or keep going.

He went back toward the front of the house, but stayed at the side. If Shamu wasn't here yet, he'd be driving up the road with his lights blazing. That could get both of them killed.

Quimby went to the car in the driveway and felt its hood. Hot. Shamu must be inside.

The tactic then had to be to fight these killer-types off, if and when they came. Drive them away . . .

There was little cover along the street; runty trees, few bushes, hip-level fences, flat yards that ran back from the street; nothing much around the houses, a shed in back of this one, but he wasn't sure he wanted to be in back. He had to be mobile. Mutota had asked how many would come the next time. How the hell did he know? His job was to drive them off. . . .

Between the two houses there was a slight dip; someone had plowed a line to mark the boundaries of the two properties, leaving a shallow ditch no more than ten or fifteen inches deep. He checked it up close, knelt and felt it with his hands, then backed away and saw that at one point the ground on the next lot rose a little. He could lie there and raise his head and see both ways; the rise in the ground behind him would hide the shape of his head. He went back and stretched himself out in the shallow ditch, resting his chin on the heel of his hand, trying to watch both the front and the back of the house.

THE solid growl of a powerful motor in a heavy car touched his ears and died. Around the corner, he guessed. South. Off to the left. Better there than here in front of this house. He rose and ran across the street, knelt just behind an outbuilding and saw something squarish at the edge of the road—half a block away. A van or a closed truck.

He moved back a little and tried to see between two houses on this side of the street, decided it was worth a try, and moved between the first and second houses toward where that truck had parked. No dogs barked and he went on between the houses facing the next parallel street until he was near that street. He had got himself behind the vehicle.

He moved to the back corner of the house flanking the road and squatted against its back wall, no more than six or seven yards away from a dark, windowless van. Whoever had moved up was sitting quietly inside, waiting. He wondered if he was wasting his time reconnoitering a van with a couple of lovers in it, somebody without a home and a woman he wanted to love. What a helluva note if he was piddling around here while commandos were climbing into the house half a block behind him. If that damn van started rocking he was going to clear out.

The door of the front passenger seat cracked open and a man stepped to the ground. Someone inside whispered, and the man turned and walked rapidly away from the van toward the corner at Kashamba Road.

Another man stepped down from the same door and stood watching his companion, who by that time was twenty paces away. Quimby saw the telltale long and thick barrel of the silenced Skorpion, pointing upward, the same profile he had seen fourteen days ago in Harare.

When the man walking toward the ANC meeting place was almost out of sight, Quimby stood up and ran toward the van with all the speed he could throw into a sprint of six yards. As he came closer to the van, he saw the man standing there swing around to face him, starting to bring the barrel of the Skorpion downward.

Holding the screwdriver handle with both hands, the point well out in front of his body, Quimby came face to face with the commando, his impetus giving him great force. The screwdriver, six inches of narrow steel, entered just below the rib cage, stabbing upward, Quimby intending that it would go all the way to the heart. At the same time his shoulder caught the man in the chest and slapped him hard back against the van. The man cursed aloud and began to scream, and Quimby grabbed at the gun, got his hands on it—the screwdriver still in the man's chest, and yanked it away.

The Skorpions, he remembered, had magazines that carried twenty rounds. He had to make them count. At least he had a gun. He stepped forward and put three shots into the driver who sat leaning sideways, peering out at him.

Behind him the man he had stuck was still screaming, which meant he'd missed the heart. The man was hurt but not dying, not dying fast enough.

Quimby heard the hard scuffling sounds of other men trying to move fast inside the van, the opening of the door at the back, boots landing on the ground. The man who had moved out toward the corner of Kashamba was running back.

Quimby retreated to the house from which he had launched his attack, and watched the running man stop and bend over the man with the screwdriver in his chest. From the back of the van a man came running flat out toward the house, and Quimby shot him and watched him tumble forward on his face. He threw a burst toward the side door of the van, hoping to hit the man standing over the other on the ground, and he tried to remember how many bullets he had used. Half of them?

Someone at the back of the van was shooting at him; bullets cracked near his head, smashing into the mud-brick wall of the house. Two men had thrown themselves flat on the road, one lying behind a rear wheel; he saw the little spits of flame coming from their guns, and he turned and ran back between the houses toward Kashamba Road.

As he ran the first man he had hit went on screaming. Someone else was giving orders in English, not yelling but speaking harshly, the sound of his voice carrying clearly through the air.

Breathing hard, Quimby reached the corner of the house on Kashamba where he had first moved when he'd heard the sound of that motor, and he turned to look back. He could see the square shape of the van, a form moving at its side. The scream was cut off suddenly, as if someone had put a hand over the screamer's mouth.

He searched the ground between himself and the van for those men who had been shooting at him; he turned himself so that if they appeared between the houses he had just left he would be ready, and he tried again to remember how many rounds he had fired.

They had to be reconsidering now, he thought. They had to be realizing they had driven into an ambush, wondering how many people were hiding around them; they would be thinking that at any moment now people would be turning on lights, coming out of their houses to see what had caused the screaming. If he had any sense, the commander of that bunch in the van would be trying to decide whether to go ahead with the planned attack or get the hell out of here. . . .

He waited silently, aware that his back was unprotected. He had no idea how many men had been in the van; it could probably carry ten or twelve. He had killed or wounded three, maybe four. If the others were coming on now, determined to finish their job, he was in a lousy position; he ought to move.

He twisted his head so that he could see the road off to his left. They would have to cross that to get to the house. He would need cover while he fired. He ran back across Kashamba and fell into the shallow ditch where he had waited earlier. Then, thinking about it, he began to believe that he had done enough to scare them away.

They had lost the element of surprise; they didn't know who they were fighting, but they knew damn well this was not going to be the quick and secret slaughter they had planned; they were in the middle of a country where they had no right to be, and they'd come to perform murder. The guy in command should be thinking about hauling ass.

Even as he had those thoughts, he heard the squeal of the starter, and the answering rumble of the motor. The motor growled into low gear and he heard the van moving; it went into reverse, then into low gear again and purred away.

Smart boyos, he thought. Shagging their little white asses out of here in a hurry, which is what I should be doing with my black one.

He considered going across the street to warn the ANC man that he should disappear too, but that didn't seem necessary. Shamu had no idea what had happened out here in the street. He was innocent. He was safe.

Quimby crossed the street again and scanned the surface of the road where the van had been, trying to see if his little friends had left the men he believed he had killed. He couldn't be certain, but the ground down there looked smooth; they must have taken their wounded and dead with them. He felt relieved, not just because the evidence of the fighting was erased, but because another worry had been nagging at his mind. He had left the screwdriver back there in that man's chest. Some smart cop could have tied it to the Honda he was driving, and sooner or later some innocent ANC Honda owner would have got the stick.

Carrying the gun with its barrel along his leg, Quimby returned to the Honda. He took the wrench out of his belt, laid it on the passenger's seat, and held the machine-pistol on his lap.

In Detroit and a lot of other places—he had learned not to trust anyone, not anyone. Those bastards in the van could be waiting down the road with their lights off, hoping that whoever had shot them up would come along and let them clobber him. Maybe, maybe not.

He drove with his lights off over to Sheki-Sheki Road, and turned east and drove all the way to Great North Road. He thought about throwing the Skorpion away, but decided that the ANC could probably find good use for a silenced gun. He stopped the car and put the gun in the trunk; then he drove south, straight down Cairo Road through the center of the business district and turned east at Church Road.

6

QUIMBY was back in Harare just before noon. He drove directly to the Voorman Hotel and went upstairs to the fourth floor. He found Tandy pulling the sheets from a bed, and as he entered the room, she turned, threw out her arms, and embraced him as if he had been gone for months.

"Peter told me where you were," she said. "I've been out of my mind."

He was tired and let down, and a little dismayed by how much he had to get done today, but her warm welcome, the firm pressure of breasts and belly and thighs against him was comforting and exciting. He pulled her tight, enjoying the clean smell of her, the touch of her hair on his face, and the strong hands flat against his back, and he thought about that rain check she had given him the other night.

"It worked out all right," he said. "I'm back, but we're not through. I want to give you a report for Peter and tell him what I'm going to do next. Can you get away?"

She nodded eagerly. "I'll find the supervisor and take an early lunch."

She pulled back, and he admired her smile, the quick intelligence of her eyes that made her whole face so attractive, and the starchy yellow uniform that was meant to make her look like a bulky "thing," but actually emphasized her feminine gracefulness.

"My car is in the lot downstairs," he told her. "I'll be down there. Has anyone ever told you you're the finest good-looking woman he's ever seen?"

She grinned broadly, her eyes flirting at him, and went out the door with a flounce of her skirt and a smooth swing of her hips.

THEY sat in his car in the parking lot, and he told her what had happened in Lusaka. He ended by saying: "And tell Peter how much I appreciated his effort last night, Tandy. I couldn't have operated at all without his help."

Tandy held his hand and pressed it hard. "You could have got yourself killed. You should have had more help. I worry—you're holding a rain check on me and I'm afraid you won't live to collect it. . . ." She giggled comfortably, and moved closer, a hand on his upper arm.

"Tonight," he said. "I'm not going to wait any longer. I'll come to your place after your dance and take you home with me."

The tip of her tongue appeared between her teeth. She looked at him boldly, but the smile on her face was suddenly hesitant and withdrawn, thoughtful calculation in her eyes. "We'll see," she said. "Peter didn't tell me I was supposed to sleep with my partner."

He put an arm over her shoulders. "Part of the deal. The rules say that all partners must be in bed together by midnight whenever they're both in town."

They grinned and moved closer together, and he explained what he wanted her to tell Chitepo about his new plan.

It was too complicated; the details weren't all worked out; but he was going to go ahead with it, and he wanted Peter to know. As soon as he left Tandy he intended to pick up that courier whose chin he had whacked in the cathedral. He was going over to the Altron Company and when that courier came out to go to lunch they would have a little talk. It was obvious that when Kado and Florence Mubaka learned about the ambush in Lusaka, they would guess that their communication system had been penetrated, and if they put a little pressure on their courier they would find out what had happened. Quimby wanted to move before they did.

On the plane to Harare this morning, he had worked out a message written in the code that had sent him to Lusaka. His message announced another meeting of ANC leaders outside Harare, the day after tomorrow, the ninth. The place was an abandoned farm he knew off the Chinoyi Road, a perfect spot for what he had in mind.

He explained to Tandy that the farmhouse was set in a little hollow forty yards from a wide ravine that served as the farm's western boundary. Anyone approaching the place had to come across open fields. With his men closing in behind them they would have no chance to get away unless they fled into the house or ran to the ravine. But he would put some of his men inside the house, and the sides of that ravine were too steep and dangerous to descend. He would have the commandos boxed in, and he meant to kill enough of them to persuade their bosses, once and for all, that the cost of murdering ANC leaders was more than they could pay.

He wasn't sure yet just how he would run his ambush. Mungu and the others were almost ready; he would probably make the attack with them, but he was also thinking that he might notify the Zimbabwe military forces that a group of commandos was coming in, bent on murder. If he could get Zimbabwean troops involved, the hullabaloo, the international scandal, might be enough to quash the murder squads long enough for the ANC to get through its conference. He wanted Peter's opinion about using Zimbabwean troops.

Tandy listened thoughtfully, shaking her head at Quimby's audacity. She interrupted to say, "You can't have any idea how many they'll send."

"More now, I think. They know now that they may run into opposition whenever they come in. After last night, they'll be looking for revenge again."

"But you're faking this," she protested. "You're deliberately luring these people into a trap so you can kill them."

He said, defensively, "They're trying every way they know to kill the ANC leaders."

"I know, but it's always seemed to me that it's wrong to stoop to your enemy's level of evil. There ought to be some other way to stop these men, some way that doesn't involve killing."

He had been through this argument a thousand times and he knew where he stood. She was right, of course, but being right didn't help when people were trying to kill you. He said, "I agree. There ought to be a better way, but there isn't. Tell Peter I'm going ahead."

"God! I worry about you." She looked lonely and frightened.

"How can you hope to beat these people? If you're fighting the Soviets or South Africa . . . They have thousands of soldiers and guns. Killing a few of their soldiers can only be . . . you know . . . just a minor irritation. You may be a real Gaboon viper, but you're only one. They'll just keep coming."

He thought he knew better. Good commandos were costly to train. From his experience in the Green Berets and the Delta Force he knew how hard it was to recruit and hold fighters who would go wherever they were sent, who would shoot instantly at almost anyone the commander pointed to. Even in the U.S. and England and Germany, the numbers of men who could be found and who qualified for the special service units were limited; there just weren't that many motivated men with the brains and bodies and guts the work demanded.

Not only that: He was convinced that every time he hit back he was affronting one of the white governments that was probably involved. He was tweaking the great white rulers' tails, cutting bloody little notches in them, hurting their pride, telling all the arrogant, pink-cheeked horses' asses in their diplomatic suits and elaborate uniforms that the best they could do wasn't good enough. He was telling them there were some black people in Africa who could make their best men look silly and were damned glad to do so.

He twisted toward Tandy in the seat and leaned forward to look into her eyes. He put his hands on her shoulders, then lifted his left hand and touched her soft cheek and the hair above her ear. He brushed one of her dark eyebrows with his forefinger, marveling at its glossy beauty, and he smiled into her eyes, wanting her to understand. "It's the work I do, Tandy. It's the only way I know that lets me help. May I come by tonight?"

She tipped her head forward, and he saw tears starting up in her eyes. She moved to him and laid her head on his shoulder, and she sat there close to him, a warm, human, loving thing giving him a promise of softness and peace, of luxurious pleasures and profound happiness. She roused in him a great hunger, not just to bed with her, but to live the kind of life where he could totally love and trust another person, the kind of life she seemed to promise.

She moved closer and kissed his cheek. She pulled back and said, "Dammit, I want you to stay alive." Then she twisted away quickly, pushed the car door open, and hurried off to the hotel, and he sat with the hunger throbbing in his mind and body for something he was sure he would never have.

THE courier's name was Jason Sindsa.

When Quimby reached the Altron Company's offices, it was a few minutes after twelve. The place looked deserted but for a young white woman who had been left to answer the phone during the noon hour. Quimby found a mujiba and sent him in to ask for Sindsa, and the boy came back with information that a friend had come in this morning saying Sindsa was sick. He was staying home.

Quimby had Sindsa's address in Glen View, a few miles out of the city, and he drove out Willowvale Road to that government-issue, straight-lined town where concrete bases had been laid out by the municipality when the Rhodesian government was still running things. For a down payment and a monthly rental, a family got the concrete base and its water closet and agreed to build a house that conformed to the municipality's specifications. One room had to be completed within three years, the house within ten, and if those steps were taken successfully, the land became the family's. War and new government and unemployment and thousands of people flooding into the area had complicated the process. Many of the houses were still being built while the families lived in what was already completed.

Quimby drove past Jason Sindsa's house, went on another block, and turned the corner. He parked the car in the street and started to walk back, aware that behind him women and children were drifting into the street to stand and look at his shiny white car. It had been stupid to drive it out here, he realized. He needed transportation, but an expensive new car in these townships stood out like a neon sign over a whorehouse; he should put it into dry dock and ask Peter to find him a less visible hack.

All things considered, he decided, it would make sense to have Sindsa disappear for a few days. Mungu could probably find a place for him to stay, for his own good. What did they call it in the States? Preventive arrest? Protective custody? Something like that.

The houses in the geometrically drawn streets of Glen View were several cuts above the slums of Chitungwiza, but the place was like an army camp with permanent squad-sized barracks— each house almost exactly like all the others, with square, small windows and low, corrugated iron roofs, each one the same distance from the next, from the road, and from the house behind it in the next row.

The differences were small—brightly colored curtains in some windows, women growing different kinds of flowers in their front yards, wire fences and stick fences and wattle fences, and no fences at all, and everywhere piles of sand and lumber, concrete blocks, unburned bricks, and boxes for making mortar—the ugly mess of construction work that had been going on for years.

A barefooted man wearing only a pair of soiled brown trousers was working in Sindsa's yard, moving concrete blocks from a covered pile to a hip-high, half-finished wall of a new room he was building. Not very tall, with thin, frail-looking arms and undeveloped shoulders, his chest almost hollow, tufts of gray hair around the nipples of his breasts and under his arms. Quimby saw that the whole left side of the man's face was swollen, realized that he was looking at Sindsa, and regretted what he had done to him.

Sindsa looked up as Quimby came through the little gate, and by the quick flickering of the man's eyes, Quimby guessed that Sindsa had recognized him.

Holding the concrete block against his belly, Sindsa turned toward the house, as if looking for a way out, saw none or decided that he could not escape, and turned back, and Quimby smiled carefully for the benefit of the neighbors and the wife and children who might be looking out of their windows. He said, "You know you're in trouble, Jason? You know the commandos who went to the address in the message you collected yesterday were ambushed? They're dead."

On Sindsa's dark face there was no change of expression, but every inch of it tightened and grew more wrinkled. The light of hope seemed to go out of his eyes; he looked down and shuffled his bare feet, and Quimby felt a sudden pang of pity for this man with his skinny, bony rib cage, the arms without strength, the soft, suffering eyes. Here was one of the victims of apartheid, living in a foreign land, trying to fight back but lacking the strength to do it well.

"Who are you?" Sindsa whispered.

"I'm the man who killed the commandos. I'm the man who's going to kill your family, every member of it, unless you do exactly what I tell you."

Sindsa's whole face squeezed into a frightened scowl, and he stretched his mouth wide as if to relieve a painful cramp in his facial muscles. He was still holding the concrete block in his arms. He looked down at it, then shuffled forward to set it on top of the wall. He turned back and gazed passively at Quimby, believing the threat, fearing it, waiting for whatever was to happen next.

"Your family is inside?"

Sindsa's Adam's apple rose and fell. "My wife, the baby, my old mother. The children are at school."

"Let me return these to you." Quimby handed Sindsa the wristwatch and the folded bills he had taken from him in the cathedral, and Sindsa took them quickly, a quick gleam of gladness in his eyes.

"We will go inside and you will dress for the city," Quimby said. "I want you to carry one more message for me. That is all I will ask you to do. When that is done you will be in trouble with your party, but of course you are already in trouble with it because of what happened yesterday. If you do what I ask, I will help you avoid its punishment; otherwise, there will be no mercy for you and your family, from me or from the party."

Sindsa turned to the water faucet standing upright on a pipe coming out of the ground and began to wash himself, and Quimby, standing close, added: "For your wife: Say that I came from the city. You are needed at the Altron Company. You will return soon."

They went inside, and Sindsa spoke in low tones to his wife, ignoring the wrinkled, pipe-smoking granny who sat in a little alcove.

The room they stood in was clean but cluttered. Pale gray linoleum on the floor, a few unpainted chairs around an oblong table, three bunks, one above another against one wall. Something with onions and meat in it simmered in a pot on the woodburning stove, mixing good smells with the tobacco smoke. From one wall a black-and-white, framed picture of Robert Mugabe stared into the room, and over by the front door a baby slept in a box someone had supplied with metal rockers.

Quimby stood near the crib, facing the open door of the second room where Sindsa carefully unfolded a white shirt and put it on, then worked with a narrow black tie, dressed himself in a black suit, socks and shoes, and fitted on his shiny, steel-rimmed glasses.

They walked outside and along the street and turned to advance on the gang of children staring at the Toyota, and Quimby asked, "How do you know when there is a message for you to pick up at the church?"

Sindsa answered carefully: "Someone calls me on the telephone. A voice says, 'Thirty,' nothing more. Then I go to the cathedral."

"And you give the message to someone in the Altron office?"

"Mr. Jameson. Charles Jameson."

"White? South African?"

"Yes, both."

"Why do you do this?"

"I was informed that this advances the cause of the party."

"Who told you that?"

"I swore never to tell."

"You will tell me," Quimby said, looking hard at him.

Sindsa studied Quimby's face an instant and stumbled. He whispered the name, "John Kado."

"But you are a member of the ANC."

"And also the SACP."

So Kado *is* the kingpin, Quimby thought. He said, "Now another kind of question. Does the code of those messages you deliver change from day to day?"

"I . . . I don't think so. I don't really know, but when we started, I deciphered one of the messages because I was curious.

Another time I tried the same method and it still worked. Please . . . tell me what I have done wrong."

"You are an accomplice in the murder of ANC leaders, and you're in trouble with the SACP because I read your message yesterday. I can help you, but we will talk about this later. Can you take this message in to Mr. Jameson, as if you were just bringing it from the cathedral?"

Sindsa took the slip of paper Quimby handed him. He held it close to his eyes and studied the letters and numbers as he walked. He nodded his head.

"That is what you will do," Quimby told him. "After that, I will bring you home, and we'll work out a plan for keeping you safe from your party."

QUIMBY parked off Kenneth Kaunda Avenue between other cars, so that he had a fairly clear view of the front of the Altron Company building. He sat behind the wheel as Sindsa got out, and he watched Sindsa walking along Kaunda where it turned up toward Forbes Avenue, wondering if Sindsa had the strength and self-control to carry out his assignment.

He was not concerned that Sindsa would double-cross him once he was out of sight. He had told the man he would kill his family unless he performed properly, and he had seen Sindsa look at him and believe him. The man was terrified, ready to do anything to protect his family and that house of his, and also, he had seemed to take it for granted that what Quimby had told him about his party's involvement in murder was true.

He knows his only hope is getting back here after he delivers that message, Quimby thought. I promised I'd protect him. I will.

Despite all that, he got out of the car and followed Sindsa, who was more than half a block away, walking slowly on the other side of the street, sixty yards from the front door of the Altron entrance. Quimby stepped forward to a setback between two buildings, moved into the shadow, and halted to watch. If Sindsa did double-cross him, if men came pouring out of Altron's looking for a man in a white Toyota, he wanted an escape route.

Sindsa had studied the message and said he thought it would pass, but he was so weak and frightened, so obviously unused to being in any kind of trouble, that he had been trembling when he got out of the car. Even now, as he pottered down the street, his thin legs and the way he seemed to bend forward from the waist as if his stomach hurt made Quimby wonder if the man would ever reach Altron's front door. He watched as Sindsa paused on the sidewalk, then moved away from the street to rest his shoulder against a building.

What was he doing? Having a heart attack? Was he going to pass out? Quimby moved back to the sidewalk and began walking toward Sindsa, meaning to march him right up to the front of the Altron offices if he had to. That message had to get to Jameson.

As he came to the edge of the street, a Datsun land rover passed him, slowed, and halted close to where Sindsa leaned against the building. Two black men got out and hurried over to Sindsa and spoke to him, as if they had realized he was ill and needed help.

Quimby began to run toward them; he didn't want some goddamn Good Samaritan screwing up his scenario. He had set this thing up and it had to work.

He was still half a block away when Sindsa pulled himself away from those men and started a shuffling run toward the Altron building. The two Good Samaritans ran after him, and the biggest of them pulled ahead of him, turned, and stood in his path. Quimby saw the big man step close, putting out one arm as if to embrace Sindsa, and he saw the other arm pump forward, delivering a short punch into Sindsa's belly.

136

The ineffectual little man began to fold forward, but the two men held him up, each one grasping him by an arm, and they trotted him back to the car and tumbled him into the backseat. The big man got into the driver's seat; the other into the back. The car pulled out fast, going away from Quimby, and Quimby saw the man in the back hammer a fist into the side of Sindsa's head.

Quimby stood frustrated and angry—as furious as he had been back in that Detroit alley when the cop was popping away at him with his stupid shotgun. Sindsa would talk of course; he would tell those bully boys everything. Those had to be Kado's people, and they would know about the fake message within minutes. The plan to ambush the commandos was ruined. Sindsa had seen him and his car, had probably taken the trouble to memorize his license number. Kado would know within the hour who Taylor Quimby was and where he could be found, and Kado would send his allies around—the sweet boyos with the silenced guns—to pay off a debt.

From being a bright boy with a hot idea about how to bring in more commandos and chop them down, Quimby suddenly saw himself on the other side, running. He'd blown it; they knew who he was; it was time to start looking for deep cover.

He would have to go underground, inform his people. . . . He would call his office and tell them he would be in Mozambique for the next week, tell them where to pick up his car, where to put it. He should get to Tandy somehow without compromising her or Peter; they would need a new system for communicating. He wasn't quitting, but he was hot; the whole situation had changed. Kado's thugs would be hunting him.

He wondered if it would be possible to get out to his house. He needed money, clothes for rough travel, the kind of shoes he could wear in the bush. He should get to the bank and pick up some cash. He'd go to the squatters' camps, or find a berth in one of the outlying townships; Mungu or Mutota could hide him until he figured out what to do next.

He needed transportation. He couldn't walk the streets, not and get done what he had to do. The buses? Not a chance. His bicycle was locked up at the house. Morning and evening there were thousands of bicycles on the streets, out on the road eight or ten abreast, people getting to and from the townships—transportation for Africans. He'd have to pick up his bicycle, or buy one.

HE drove to his office on Manica Road at Second Street, just three blocks from where Sindsa had been kidnapped. He cleaned out his cash box: almost three thousand Zimbabwean dollars, and told his assistant, who was used to the boss' quick comings and goings, that he expected to be in Maputo for at least a week. He also explained that he would leave his car in a parking lot down the street by midafternoon, and asked his assistant to drive it out to the house later in the day.

At home, knowing that the bicycle would not fit into the backseat or the trunk, he found a wrench, took off its front wheel, and fitted the two parts into the backseat.

Inside the house, he moved swiftly, collecting the knife he had used so often in the past, the leather sap that fitted his hand so well.

He changed his clothes, putting on heavy but worn denim jeans, a dark blue, long-sleeved Rugby shirt, and a black nylon jacket that was so large it made his shoulders and chest and hips look shapeless. He donned a set of old combat boots, the kind with the leather flap that fastens above the ankles, with heavy, lugged composition soles. Every man in the country who had been in the war on one side or the other had a couple pair of boots like his, although by now many had cut most of the leather away to make them into sandals. He put on a pair of dark glasses, looked on a shelf, found an old fatigue hat, dull green, with a low brim all around, and he pulled it on well down over his forehead.

He stood before his mirror a moment, slouching, hunching his shoulders, turning his head down, making himself look a few inches shorter than he actually was. He resembled, more or less, some three hundred thousand other black workers and young unemployed men who lived in and around the city. He looked poor, unthreatening, young enough to be active but not the kind of man who ever hoped to climb very high. The glasses didn't help all that much, but he would let his beard grow. If he lasted a couple of days the fuzz would blur the shape of his jaw line.

He put a strong military belt through the loops of the jeans and slipped the sap and the knife in its sheath into a pocket of the nylon jacket.

He went into the bathroom and put a toothbrush and a tube of toothpaste inside a green plastic grocery bag, grabbed a heavy gray sweater, socks, and shorts from a drawer in the bedroom, and added them to the bag. Then he took off the hat and the jacket, so that curious neighbors wouldn't think some stranger was trashing the house if they saw him leaving. Carrying these things, he locked up the house, went out to his car, and drove off, watching his rearview mirrors until he was sure that he was not being followed.

In the city, he parked the Toyota where he had told his assistant he would, and he sat for a moment looking out over Manica Road. People walked by, thirty yards away, but he saw no one standing still or sitting in an automobile, or even inside the windows of surrounding buildings, who seemed to be paying any attention to him.

He put on his hat and glasses, got out of the car and put on the jacket. He got the bicycle out of the backseat and reassembled it.

He tied the plastic bag on the carrier behind the seat, left the keys where he had promised, and pedaled down to Kenneth Kaunda Avenue, on his way to visit Mungu in Highfield.

THE rest of that afternoon and early evening, until about eight o'clock, Quimby spent in the field near Lake McIlwaine. He met the men Mungu and Mutota and Wally Panebondo had recruited—six of them, all five or six years younger than he was. Four he had known during the war, and they were men he trusted. The other two had worked with Mutota across the border in Mozambique.

Quimby started by talking with them together under a tree, letting them get acquainted with him, letting them understand the kind of authority he intended to exercise, trying to judge them.

The judging, he knew, was always the most difficult part. Men who were bright and conscientious in training could forget everything they ever knew the instant bullets started flying. Judging how men would fight by watching them perform a training exercise, was like trying to guess how women would make love by watching them work in their kitchens.

Just the same, training and discipline were essential. And leadership. Those were the keys to any really effective unit, but they were based—first, last, and always—on having good men who knew why they were fighting.

Mutota's new recruits were thin wiry men, and Quimby studied them as carefully as they were studying him. The wiry ones, he believed, were usually the toughest; they tired less easily, kept going longer. Time and time again he'd seen the quiet, thin little guys no one really expected to shine in a fight, out in front and plowing ahead while the big boys with muscles and too much beef were dragging their tails.

He reviewed his methods of moving in the bush, the hand

signals and the night sounds they had to see and hear, and the way he wanted them to move when they received his signals. Through the afternoon, he worked them in the forest, one team of three men at a time, dispersing them, hiding them, assembling them in a clump of brush, behind a few trees, between carefully designated boulders, moving them through eight-foot-high buffalo grass flat on their bellies.

When the separate teams had been drilled, he worked all three together, pointing in the direction each team must move, indicating with his hand signs how the "enemy" hill must be flanked or taken head-on, switching a team back into a reserve that could push past a pocket of the opposition to take it in the flank or rear, or simply move on by undetected.

He was not kind to the men who failed to see his signals, who were not thinking ahead about what would come next, and he was cruel when Mutota complained that his men were too tired to run anymore. He ran with all of them and kept them running all-out until he had given them good reason to believe that he was tireless, reason to fear and hate him. He wanted them to know that Muparadzi was back, that no matter how their bodies felt they would move as he ordered and think as a team because only in that way could they be effective against Kado's bullies or the fighters the South Africans or the East Germans would be sending. . . .

It was nearly dark when he called the teams in, and he was well satisfied with this first session. He told them so, and they looked at him with proud eyes. All of them had sweated through their clothing, red dust had caked dark on their faces; they were exhausted, but they looked at him with little smiles, knowing they were tough, knowing he would make them tougher, and he saw that they would stay with him when the time came.

He told them something about the kind of men he and Mungu

and Mutota had found the enemy to be and why these white men had no business trying to decide how South Africa would rule itself, and they interrupted him with a variety of obscene comments about white baboons, making it clear that political spiels were not required.

In the darkness, he followed Mungu along an almost empty road back to Mungu's junkshop of a house and yard in Highfield. They washed themselves and drank a little beer, and they ate a feast of cornbread and vegetables. Then Mungu found an old windup alarm clock and helped Quimby set it for 11:05 so that he could keep his appointment with Tandy. For two hours Quimby slept.

BECAUSE it would have been stupid to hang around outside Tandy's quarters in the center of the city, Quimby waited for her in the shadows across the street from The Chief's Den. But when she came out she went off in such a hurry that he had to follow without announcing his presence to her, irritated because she pedaled her bicycle so damned fast. He was tired.

She dismounted at her door and fumbled with a key, holding her bicycle against her hip with one hand. As he came up and dismounted behind her, she glanced backward at him briefly, uttered a sharply threatening, "Take off, you!" and went on with the process of moving her bicycle inside.

Quimby nosed his bicycle forward, trying to follow her, and she swung around in fury, her voice low but hard, "You son of a bitch, get out of here!"

Quimby said, "Even if I'm Ole Chifamba?"

Tandy suppressed a quick screech of laughter and recognition. "You fool! Come in!"

She pushed her bicycle against a wall and came back to hold the door and help him to move his inside, and when that was done, she took hold of him, and they hugged each other as if he had just come home from three years on the moon.

"You look like a goddamn bum," she told him. "I thought you were making a play for me."

"I am."

He felt her fingers discover the knife in its sheath at his back, and move on to his shoulders. She pressed her body against him. "So how did your plan go?"

"A catastrophe." His hands were on her hips, caressing the great curves. They rose to her firm back with its deep dorsal ridges of strong muscle. His face was in the hollow between her throat and shoulder—a comfortable, warm place he had no wish to leave.

Tandy arched her body against his, kissing his cheek. "And now you want to report to me so I can tell Chitepo?"

She was a warm, wonderful thing in his arms, making him hotly aware of her thighs and belly, her breasts and lips, the way her hands held his arms, the way she seemed to curve into his body as if she had been made to fit him just this way. "First things, first," he said. "I came to make love to you."

"But you smell like a farmhand." She giggled hilariously but suppressed the sound at once, and she leaned her torso back, hips against him, her eyes questioning.

"I've been in the field all afternoon with my fighters. If you let me use your shower, I'll come out smelling like a rose."

After he had been in the shower a few minutes, Tandy came in and watched him and washed his back. She had undressed herself, and she was all that her dance had promised. Her stomach moulded smoothly with thighs and the dark V of her mons veneris, her breasts stood out firmly the way he thought plastic surgeons and their clients must dream about, and the aureoles around the nipples were large and dark and exciting. The curve of her hips seemed to go on forever in a kind of miracle of curvings that moved to thigh and buttocks, belly and torso in a way his preacher-father would have considered the work of the devil.

She turned him about and exclaimed about the size of his penis, flattering him, grinning wickedly when she took hold of him, wondering aloud where they would be able to put "such a big thing."

She stood back, still holding him there, and admiring him. "Oh, you are a good-looking man, Ole Chifamba," she told him. "Since that time I came to your house, and you showed me the chest wounds that go out through your back, I've thought you are the most beautiful man I've ever seen. Look at you." She pressed his muscled belly, his chest, the hard shoulders.

She placed both her hands on his throat and pulled him close to kiss him, pressing his erected penis with her belly, and he, as his father would have said, "nothing wroth," put his hands on the curves of her buttocks with the feeling that he was being rewarded with infinite kindness for having a hunger he could barely control.

Because she insisted that the bed would make too much noise, they pulled the mattress onto the floor. They played with each other; they invented ways to please each other; they fondled and handled and caressed and pushed and pulled and kissed each other, exploring each other's bodies for many minutes until both knew that their bodies were screaming for an end to play.

He rose to his knees then, entering her slowly and carefully, feeling her respond, feeling the incredibly soft, warm, moving touch of her over every inch, not just inside her, but everywhere they touched. They made love then—carefully, judiciously, sensitively, thoughtfully, passionately. They moved softly and less softly; they pressed hard and they rocked together and laughed into each other's faces, and he wanted to sing with this pleasure of giving and receiving such pleasure. He turned her and himself, and she was on top of him, in the stance that had roused him so at the end of her dance, and in that position she was dark flame and perpetual motion.

They mounted a high curve of glittering dark space into bright light, moving together, but moving in rhythm against one another like the cross-patterns of that Shona melody and the drums that pounded out the complex rhythms of her dance. They rose to the peak of the curve with no way of coming down, and they rose higher, and he, with a growing sense of exultation, held her frantically moving hips and moved them faster, driving upward and upward with a sense of impending perfection. Then he exploded within her, and her thrusting hips hammered down on him, going on and on, her breathing a tight groan of pleasure, her hands pressing hard and flat on his chest. They roared down a long slide, and rocked on, breathing hard, slowing into softness and appreciation, and a feeling like grinning at everything. She bent forward to kiss him and their wet bodies slid smoothly together.

Later, she snuggled against him, a kind of miracle that had known what he needed and had rushed exuberantly to provide it, and he had the good feeling that he had served her pleasure well. For him, it had been the way it was supposed to be; they had come together and were completed. The hesitancy and distrust, the hiding and deceiving that sometimes almost seemed to be the whole game in his relations with other women, disappeared with Tandy.

He lay half-drugged by the sense of her incredible curves, her warmth, her friendliness, her passionate giving of herself to him, and his own satiation. He held her quietly and in a few minutes heard her breath slip into the quiet purr that meant she was asleep.

He lay thinking about her—her quick sympathy, the strong spirit of independence, the courage that had made her insist on partnership with him. She had a powerful love of life, an ability to enjoy that he felt he lacked. She laughed easily, and expressed her thoughts directly and clearly without the defensive tricks other women he had known seemed to play every minute of their lives. She liked music and colors and the world she lived in, welcomed every experience as if it had been designed to please her, came at everything face-to-face, seemed not to fear what she saw, and her laughter had a lusty joy that made him want to shout.

He had been too long without a woman. And Tandy had made him feel as if he had never been with a woman before. She was magic. He began to speculate about what might be possible, if they got through this mess with the commandos, if the two of them could be together. . . . He did not think out for how long and under what conditions, but he knew he wanted to consider this idea seriously.

He felt self-conscious, watching himself beginning to dream of a life with two people in it. . . . It had never been possible to think like this before; he had never met a woman with intelligence and courage wrapped up in a sense of humor and Tandy's eager willingness to run at life straight on.

The idea of actually living closely with a woman, which he had tried once and failed at miserably, made him draw back, and he found that strangely amusing. He might be tough in the field, but with this woman, even after the lovemaking they had just enjoyed, he felt hesitant, almost worshipful. I'm shy, by God, he thought, and realized that he had some thinking to do; things had to change around in his mind. . . . She had all of the characteristics he had been looking for in a woman all his life; she knew when to laugh at him, when to be serious; she had more courage than most men he knew; she was beautiful and intelligent. . . .

He moved his arm, beginning to free himself from her, wanting to get into her bathroom and shower and dress; and as he moved, she came awake, understood at once what he was up to, and sat up on the mattress. "You go ahead," she said. "I'll come in when you've finished."

He showered and toweled himself on a Voorman towel, and gave the bathroom over to her. Because she had commented on his filthy clothes, he did not dress, and when she came out in her short green nightgown, with a man's long denim shirt over her shoulders, he still wore nothing but the towel around his middle. He had put the mattress back on the bed and remade it, military fashion, with the top sheets pulled tight and cornered at the foot with good GI corners.

She looked at him in the light of the lamp and grinned at him as if to say, "Didn't we have a time?"

He returned her grin, moving his head from side to side, feeling like a well-fed diner.

"So now to the second order of business," Tandy said.

"Stay with the first for a moment. D'you know I like you one hell of a lot?"

She looked at the floor. "I hope you do. We go well together."

"If we get through this mess—"

"I know that, too, Quimby. I may not want to let you go. Not ever."

"You won't be able to get away from me," he said. "I've never seen anyone like you before. Never, no place, not ever."

"Maybe we'd better wait and see how we get through this commando business."

He was amazed at how their minds ran to the same conclusions. "Probably." He sat at the foot of her bed. "All right, now—the next order of business."

He told her in detail what had happened with Sindsa, about the men who had taken Sindsa away, and who he thought they were. He pointed out that Sindsa had received his orders from Kado; so the killers were working for the SACP, but they were white men—Kado's mercenaries, or, possibly, people provided by the East Germans. The other important point was that Sindsa had said that he turned over his messages in the Altron Corporation to a Mr. Jameson who was white and South African.

"Ask Chitepo to get me everything he can on Jameson," Quimby said. "The sooner the better."

Blaming himself, he admitted that he had blown his attempt to get a fake message through to the commandos, and in the process he had let Kado know who had penetrated his message system, who was killing the commandos. So now the situation was changed.

"I'll be hiding out in the boondocks," Quimby told her. "But we've got to keep our communication lines open because we're going to finish this thing."

Tandy was sitting cross-legged on her bed, looking worried and tantalizing. He moved to sit closer to her and touched her cheek. "So here is the new plan," he said. "Tell this to Peter, and do everything you can to make him agree to make it work."

She grinned fiercely and flipped her hand in a vigorous twisting gesture. "I'll twist his tail."

He smoothed her hair, admiring the way it moved up from her brow. "They'll change their system of passing messages, but they're not going to quit trying. They have only eight days to create the vacancies they need for their Communist replacements on the National Executive Council, and that means they can't afford to fail again. They need to get a whole bunch of ANC leaders out of the way in a hurry. Tell Peter I want him to fake a sort of preparatory conference, here in Harare. It ought to be billed as a meeting where the ANC leaders will make their final preparations before the international conference on the fifteenth. You know—someone can say that the leaders need to cross the t's on the political platform, or plan how they're going to pass their new resolutions, or resist the infighting at the regional levels."

His hand smoothed the curve of her bare hip. He moved it across her belly, fingers enjoying the feel of her, but his mind was tracking on his plans. He said, "Peter's got to see that whoever in the leadership normally advises Florence Mubaka of the meeting does it this time too. Nkala may have to help. The point is, I want Florence Mubaka to send out that information so that the commandos take it seriously. We'll cancel that meeting at the last moment, and if the assassins come in we'll chop up enough of them to put an end to their efforts. Tell Peter I think they'll come in force prepared to win no matter what kind of resistance we put up."

Tandy put her head on his thigh. "You don't ever give up, do you?"

"Be sure to tell him about Jameson."

"Right. How do I get in touch with you, and you with me?"

"I thought we were doing pretty well a little while ago."

She pretended to bite his leg. "Stop being silly."

"I'll find you at the hotel or the market or The Chief's Den. Tomorrow I'll catch you at the market."

"Someone will recognize you. Kado's men will kill you."

"You know about omelettes?"

She nodded, grinning somberly. "Someone has to break the eggs."

"Right." He leaned over to kiss the back of her neck. "I'd better get my smelly clothes on and get out of here. Tandy, thank you."

7

IN the morning Quimby and Mungu refreshed their memories and began to run through a drill with the Soviet light machine gun, the RPD, until Mutota and his men drifted in one by one. Then, each man went through the steps of the gun's operation—connecting the ammunition drum with its hundred rounds to the receiver, pulling down the lock on the underside of the receiver so that the drum would stay in place when the gun was fired, pushing the tab of the blank-bullet-laden metal belt into the left side of the receiver to seat the first cartridge against the cartridge-stop so that the gun was ready to fire.

While the others watched, the man at the gun pulled back the cocking handle, moving the slide and bolt back, then let the slide push the bolt forward so that the first bullet would be driven out of the belt and up into the chamber. Then he moved the right thumb so that the safety catch would rotate back and free the gun for the only kind of fire it knew—full automatic.

Ordinarily, Quimby knew, these men would have worked noisily, laughing and joking, celebrating each successful run with little bursts of encouragement and formal Shona hand clapping, but in this low room of Mungu's house with its patched-tin walls, the watchers sat on the floor or squatted around the gun, soberly checking every motion made by the man working with it. All of them understood that it was not enough to be able to name its various parts and know how it operated. They had worked with this kind of gun before, but their memories were old, their fingers awkward, and they knew that the next time they pulled the trigger in the field, the gun had to fire true.

The trick was to be able to make the RPD function when their minds were frozen with fear, when they were being shot at, or when they had been hit and had to shoot accurately to stay alive. Mind and muscles and gun had to be melded into one instrument; hands and fingers and eyes had to function so well together that all the separate movements became one fluid action that set the gun to firing at its target almost before the mind made its decision. To achieve that degree of competence, they needed to work until hands and fingers moved automatically, instinctively. The gun had to become part of the man.

Quimby fashioned a blindfold from a rag, and each man went through the process of loading and firing and correcting malfunctions without being able to see. It was dull, tense work, with someone's humiliating fingers stopping the hand each time it was about to take the wrong step.

From time to time Mungu walked past his windows, looking out across the junk in his yard, keeping watch. They were all aware of his vigil and they relaxed a little each time he returned to the group to touch a man who had done well or grumble at one who persisted in making mistakes.

The smell of sweated clothing, tobacco smoke, and gun oil built up strong in the room, but Quimby would not let Mungu open the door or the window, for though the men concentrated silently on their work, the moving parts of the gun made the smooth clicking and slapping of milled steel against milled steel. On a quiet night that sound carried more than a hundred yards. There were men walking along the street who had heard it in the bush during the war for freedom. He feared they might recognize the sound, and talk about it, or report it to the police.

"We could open the window and turn the radio up low," Mutota suggested.

"And have the police think we're running a shebeen?" Quimby asked. "No. Concentrate on the gun."

Each man, including Quimby, practiced blind, as they would have to do at night, with a second man releasing the drum and fastening another for the gunner, and tapping the gunner's shoulder to tell him that the drum was attached, the tab in the receiver. Then the cocking and firing—over and over and over again.

When each of them had performed the ritual perfectly many times, Mungu looked for approval at Quimby, and received it, and put the RPD away under a part of the floor. He pulled his bed away from one side of the room and brought another kind of gun forward, the Israeli Uzi. Eighteen inches long with its metal-framework stock folded, with straight twenty-five-round magazines that fitted neatly up inside the pistol grip. Mutota, who said that he had fired the Rhodesian model, the Rhuzi, during the civil war, pointed out the principal parts they needed to understand: the cocking handle, the change lever that could move the gun from automatic to single shot and to safety, and the grip safety. Then he demonstrated the way to hold the gun for close-up fighting, clamped under the armpit or down hard against the hip.

Each of them disassembled and reassembled the Uzi several times, learning how the parts went together to make the weapon fire; then they practiced loading and cocking and firing, but with empty cartridges in the chamber. And again, when the flow of those processes was understood, Quimby put on the blindfold, and they practiced until their motions were almost as automatic as the gun's.

The effort they gave this work was inadequate, Quimby knew. They needed more practice; they needed live firing exercises, with quick-rising silhouette targets to shoot at, the repetition of firing many times until mind and body were trained perfectly to respond without hesitation and hit every target dead on, until no one had to think or decide but simply fired.

They would do more tomorrow, Quimby assured them, and they would work with the rocket launcher. They drifted away then, with Mutota agreeing to send along Wally Panebondo and his men and Mungu's two for their drill.

AT eleven-thirty, Quimby sat at a table on the outer rim of the beer garden where he had met Tandy before. They listened for a few minutes to the loud talk and laughter in the beer garden proper just beyond the low wooden partition where they sat, and when Tandy was settled, sitting on a bench facing him, her back to the beer garden, he asked, "Is it going to work?"

She handed him a piece of folded paper, showing a line that was lettered *Salisbury Drive,* a road beyond Salisbury Drive that traveled northward from *Mutare Road,* an *X* on the east side of that unnamed road with an arrow pointing at it, and a square by the *X* marked *Victoria Farm*. At the bottom of the page, he read: *November 11, 2330.*

"Good for Peter," he said with satisfaction.

"He said that a real meeting has been called, but that he will see that the meeting is canceled no later than ten o'clock that evening."

Quimby nodded that he had heard her, but he was already thinking how he must prepare for this fight four nights from now. He asked, "Can you drive a car?"

She looked at him proudly. "Of course."

"Driver's license?"

"Yes."

"Tell Peter we need an old car, not a rented job. We'll want to have a look at this farm and we can't do it in a van full of guns. Tell him, if we get the car in trouble, we'll let him know in time for him to report it stolen so he can't be held responsible. . . . *Wait!*" He stretched out a hand and touched Tandy's knee, pressing hard, his eyes looking past her into the beer garden.

He knew the pattern well enough: Zimbabwean beer gardens were supposed to be places where friends could go for beer and noisy relaxation. This one was a bare floor forty feet square, with loose, rough, movable benches and a few randomly scattered tables, the whole covered by a flat corrugated iron roof and open to the elements on three sides except for a low partition that rose from the floor to a height of about four feet. On the fourth side, at the "servery," people lined up to buy and pay for their beer, which they took back to the benches in half-gallon-sized plastic steins, waxed cartons, or quart bottles. At the benches and tables, groups passed the big plastic steins and cartons from hand to hand, carrying on a tradition born in the villages, where at almost every ceremony or celebration it was part of the ritual to pass around a big gourd of home brew or several smaller gourds from the common pot.

An opening in the low partitioning next to the servery led outside to the bus terminal toilets, and the opening at Quimby's back gave access to the buses. The men who had just come in from the toilets, one still fiddling with his fly, had caught Quimby's attention. Big, thick-shouldered, wearing black suits and felt hats, they stood just inside the door in the shade of the roof, looking very carefully about the room.

Their inspection lasted too long. One thing people didn't do in a Shona beer garden was stare at their neighbors, or act like policemen. This was a place to talk, to make friends, to find a woman, or if a man wanted to mind his own business it was a place where his wish was respected.

But these men . . . They separated, one moving around the far edge of the crowd, the other coming toward this back wall, sweeping the crowd with his eyes. Policemen, Quimby thought at first, but he changed that opinion at once. His memory brought up the scene in that school where Kado was having his meeting with the SACP leaders: that party man objecting, voice squeaking with fear but speaking his piece, the bully boys charging back, going after him, pulling him out of the rows of seats where the audience stood watching, wrestling him up the aisle while he screamed his protests. Quimby recognized the face of the man coming toward him. One of the bullies who had carried that guy out . . . He was also the man who had caught Sindsa yesterday and thumped him in the belly.

Hunting for me, Quimby decided. He watched the two men come together and start across the room toward this back section, and he knew that it would be impossible to get up and leave without attracting their instant attention. He bent his head forward, the fatigue cap covering most of his face, and he said to

Tandy, "Don't look around, I repeat, don't move your head. Look at me. Do you have your bicycle in the market?"

She held her frightened, puzzled face steady, her eyes searching his, trying to understand the reason for his question. "Yes. I—"

"Go get it. Pedal out Beatrice Road. Not too fast. Let me catch up with you."

"I . . . what's wrong?"

"Kado's bullies are coming this way." He looked up and saw the man, closer now, twelve feet away. "I think one of them has recognized me. I'll take care of him, but you—keep your head down, get out of here as fast as you can, and go out Beatrice Road. *Move!*"

She rose and started to walk by Quimby to get outside by the back way. She hesitated as a man came toward her from the bus station, and the man Quimby was watching vaulted over the partition and caught her by the arm, swinging her around, trying to see into her face.

Tandy reacted with instant fury. She tried to pull away. She brought her free arm up and drove her fingers toward the man's eyes, making him turn his face away from her and duck.

Quimby, still bent over, coming to his feet, saw that he had to take advantage of the diversion she had given him. The man's back was half-turned, and Quimby hit him over the right kidney, harder than that policeman in Detroit had ever hit anything. He saw the man's back arch and the shoulders jerk back, and he hit the same spot again, knowing the man would be down and howling for minutes to come.

The second man was coming over the barrier, not vaulting it as the first man had, but climbing, one leg over the top of it. Quimby hit him on the side of the head with a beer bottle from the table where they had been sitting and saw the man's eyes glaze and the body begin to slip back across the wall.

He took Tandy's hand, rushed her out of the back edge of the place, and hurried her between the buses and across the crowded pavement of the terminal. "I'll catch up with you on Beatrice Road," he told her. "He got a good look at you and he knows you were with me. You can't stay in town. You're going underground, too."

WHEN Quimby introduced Tandy to Mungu and told him briefly what had happened, Mungu offered his tin-walled shack for her home with all the graciousness of a village chief. Tandy bowed and smiled into Mungu's homely-handsome face, brought her hands together to make a little sound of clapping, and said, "It will be a great honor to remain here."

Mungu smiled modestly, bowed his own head, and clapped his hands together. He ushered her into the house, turned his blaring radio off, and found a chair for her. He went back outside and brought both their bicycles into the already-crowded room and covered them with an old blue blanket; then he sat quietly in a chair, watching them with a look of thoughtful patience as they sat catching their breath.

Quimby said to Mungu, "The ANC meeting will be out on Mutare Road on the eleventh, four nights from now. Do you know anyone out east, in Mavbuku or Tafara, or close by? We should move closer to our field of operations and get our weapons out there."

He realized as he spoke that what he had taken for patience and modesty on Mungu's face was something else. Mungu was looking at him with sorrow, his face expressing pity or sympathy mixed with what seemed to be fear, and Quimby guessed at once that something terrible had happened. Mungu sat half-turned away from him, big hands clenched together on his knees. Sorrowing. Mourning.

Quimby demanded, "What is it?"

Mungu would not look at him. He twisted his head away, his thick lips pressed so tightly together that the whole lower part of his face was wrinkled like an old man's.

Tandy looked up quickly at the sharpness in Quimby's voice, then turned to Mungu; she rose and went to Mungu and touched the side of his face with gentle fingers. She knelt by him and took one of his big hands in hers, looking up at him with concern and sympathy in her eyes.

"Mungu?" Quimby asked again. "What is it?"

"The radio a few minutes ago," Mungu replied. "It said that Herbert Nkala has been killed in Maputo."

Tandy bowed low where she knelt, and exclaimed, "Nkala? Oh, no!"

Quimby felt as if someone had hit him in the solar plexus. His heart bumped and his stomach cramped and the skin of his face suddenly felt as if it were crisscrossed with wires. He pushed out a question, "How? How was it done?"

"The radio said he was going into the city from the airport. Two white men in a car drove by and shot him three times. The radio said the driver did not hear the shots but heard Nkala cry out to stop."

"Ah, the bloody sons of bitches!" Tandy said fervently. She turned her head, looking anxiously at Quimby.

Quimby got up and walked out of the house. He had not expected this. He felt violently ill; his breathing was strange; his bowels were jerking, cramping. He crouched forward at the side of piled scrap-iron because of the sickness in his belly, grasped a metal bar sticking out from a pile of rusty metal for support, and vomited, thinking what a man Nkala had been, what courage and dedication he had shown. A quiet little man, but a powerful leader against the Afrikaners, refusing ever to compromise or back away, determined that his people would be treated like human beings. Dead now. Dead at the hands of these fucking whites and their fucking Skorpions.

He realized that his body was shaking as if he were cold. He stared at his trembling hands and thought: I should have guessed they would go to a different method. I should have known. I was supposed to prevent this, and I failed, and they got Nkala. They're going to kill the ANC leaders one at a time. Good Christ, how do I stop them?"

He had seen Nkala only that one time at Chitepo's house, but he had been hearing and reading about him for nearly a decade. A prisoner along with Nelson Mandela, then a fighter out in the open, showing his people how to be principled and fearless. For the black people of South Africa he had been what Malcolm X might have become in the United States if his rivals had let him live. He had been the leader, the man in the field, the fighter who stood for equality and democracy without compromise or fear. He had understood what had to be done, he'd had the guts, the talent, the intelligence, and the inner fire it took to make things happen. In terrible times he had kept his balance, his modesty, his respect for others, his certainty that victory would come, but he had never let up the pressure on the rulers of South Africa. *Dead.*

Quimby's stomach went on contracting, forcing him to retch and cough. For many minutes he was unable to control the spasms. He felt cold, desolate, sorrowing as he never had before. Like a son who has lost a beloved father, he wanted to sob aloud at the injustice of Nkala's death, not only in sorrow but in anger at the killers, and at himself for having failed that little man. Instead he retched and swore out his fury, built quick feverish dreams of violent revenge, and steadied himself by holding onto the rusty iron bar with both hands.

Finally, his stomach grew quieter. He stood up straight and breathed deeply for several minutes, his eyes picking out Mungu's orderly stacks of petrol cans and old lumber, the jars of bolts and nuts, the odd metal brackets, the rusty surfaces of the walls of Mungu's house, and he had the thought that regret and sorrow would change nothing. What was needed was rational planning and careful preparation, the methodical ruthlessness it was going to take to stop these bastards. He would destroy them.

He went back inside the house, where Mungu and Tandy looked at him silently but with curiosity and compassion.

He found his toothbrush and toothpaste and went outside where the water tap rose out of the ground, and he washed his teeth several times, trying to get the sharp, bilious taste of vomit out of his mouth.

He washed his face and hands. He went inside the house again, poured coffee for himself, and sat drinking it, looking soberly at Tandy, trying to think how he would revenge Nkala's death, how he would put a halt to this murderous plague of white killers.

To Tandy he said, "The unfairness is what gets you. These white men believed they can kill our leaders and get away with it. I should go to Pretoria and kill the President and his ministers and his military commanders. I should go to East Berlin or Moscow and kill their leaders. That would be fair. Instead we kill only their soldiers."

"It has always been that way," Tandy said. "If you were to do what you say, it wouldn't help. If you killed the Afrikaner leaders the whole white nation would go to war and destroy many innocent people. They would consider that you had given them good reason for killing us."

"But it's so goddamned one-sided," he objected. "How can they believe that what's fair for them isn't fair for us?"

Tandy pulled her chair over to his, facing him. She reached out her hands and grasped his shoulders. "None of us understand," she said. And after a moment, she added: "Taylor, we don't even know who these killers are."

He realized that she was trying to calm him, that he was whining like a baby, wallowing in self-pity, railing against the injustice of it all. He had heard ten million words of that in Detroit and a lot of other places, and he had sworn he would never fall into the whining habit. Tandy was right, of course: It had always been this way. Black people were always opposed to some white power that called itself a nation, and opposing the white nation was always a crime. But the ANC was fighting to change that in South Africa, and he had promised to help.

He pulled away from Tandy but not sharply, and he sat straight and threw Mungu a hard glance that advised him not to begin thinking that Muparadzi was getting soft.

He asked Mungu, "What about it? D'you know anyone in Tafara or Mavbuku? Can we find a place to stay over there?"

"I will go in the evening and look for kinfolk or someone from my village. But I should not leave you and your woman unprotected."

"I won't be here tonight for a while," Quimby told him. "Can we get Panebondo to guard Tandy?"

"I will go to him."

Tandy was sitting back staring at him, looking less worried than she had earlier. She asked, "What are you up to now?"

He grinned at her. The coffee gurgled in his stomach; he was feeling better. He answered her question with a question of his own. "We had to get out of that beer garden in such a hurry I didn't get to ask you: Did Peter find out anything about Charles Jameson?"

"Who? Oh. Yes. He's Rhodesian, not South African. Went to the university here and in South Africa and studied mining engineering. Peter says he's a man who works hard and keeps to himself. His only social activity seems to be his membership in a gun club, The Jameson Sports Club, named after what's-his-name, Leander Starr Jameson, the guy who helped found this city. Sir Leander Starr Jameson; he was a prime minister in South Africa later. This one, Charles, is apparently a nut about shooting and a fanatic about Rhodesia. He spends his weekends at this shooting club—out north of the city."

"I'll look him up, him and his club," Quimby said. "We've got to find out who's fighting us. If I knew that I'd know how to break them up or guess what they're going to do next. I'd know how much strength it's going to take to beat them. We've got to find out who they are."

A MILE down the road from Masuku Barracks, the three bars stood along the road, settled in dumpy concrete buildings, each of them with a little set of outbuildings where the girls slept in the daytime and plied their trade with the soldiers at night. It was dark now and the cribs were busy.

During two hours of drifting from one bar to the next, Quimby had witnessed a major brawl involving eight men, a scuffle between four men that was ended quickly by one man's karate kicks, and a screaming girl who stabbed a soldier in the leg because he refused to pay her the money she said he owed.

He had also heard too much loud laughter and canned music. He had talked with several men he had known in his army days, and had been surprised at how many new faces there were and how much older his friends who had stayed in the service seemed to be.

He drank his friends' beer and bought more for them; he laughed at the stories they recounted about the "old days," talked a little about what they were doing now and what he was doing, and when he felt certain they could not help him or that he could not ask more important questions without making them suspicious, he walked down the road to the next bar and started again.

It was time to move on. He left the grimy "Funhouse," walked behind the "Paris Bistro" to relieve himself, and headed for the first building, "The Dreamhouse." He ducked through the canvas-curtained doorway, stepping down into a low-ceilinged smoky room, intending to get over to the bar, and someone yelled through the noise, "Hey, Quimby! Quimby, by God! Come over here!"

Past the dim lights at the center of the room and through the smoke and the people who thought they were dancing, Quimby located the source of the voice, a stocky dark man with the big eyes and nostrils of a bull, who was smiling and waving both hands over his head.

Quimby remembered where they had served together but his brain was slow to dredge up the name. Dibby, Dabby . . . Dabenga. Joe Dabenga. They had been in the One Parachute Battalion after the war. He pushed his way through the crowd, grinning, playing a little drunk.

The stocky man rose and pounded his back, lips pulled into a broad smile that displayed yellowed teeth, his big eyes looking a little fuzzy from drinking. "Where the hell you been, boy? Ain't seen you for years!"

He pulled Quimby down to the table and turned to a lean, youthful soldier sitting across from him. "Meet Taylor Quimby!

Fastest man in Africa with a barrel of nails." He laughed uproariously and pounded Quimby's back again. "Me and him, we were on that sweep through Bulawayo four years ago. We went through the whole town, by God. Four thousand of the ZIPRAs deserted and a bunch of them started their own war. The government sent us in there—the One Paratroop Battalion, all of us tough as batshit, and we did all right. He and I chased a couple of ZIPRAs inside a hardware store, and I ran right in after them, and here they were pointing their guns at me ready to cut me in half. Brother Quimby came through a window on the second floor and dumped a whole keg of nails over their heads. Christ, there were nails everywhere! Scared the hell out of them; they thought they'd been hit with a new kind of heavy artillery and ducked, and I shot 'em. Saved my life, by God! Son of a bitch! Quimby, old buddy, how are you?"

Dabenga stopped talking and held out his carton of Chibuku beer. "Drink it down, old buddy!"

Quimby sat and drank and laughed and talked, and went after more beer. He came back and they explored each other's recent lives, getting themselves up to date, and he began to believe that in Dabby he had somebody who might be able to help him. He turned the talk to what Dabby was doing, and Dabby wiped the sweat from his face with the back of his sleeve, and said, "Jesus! It's too damn hot in here. Let's go outside."

Quimby bought a fresh carton of beer. They walked outside along the road, and Dabenga talked more quietly. "You know, three years ago, I was in that new Fifth Brigade the government put together. They brought in the North Koreans to train us and kept us out in a camp in Inyanga. We had everything; we were the only mechanized outfit in the country, and the training made us the toughest in the country. Then they transferred us to Gweru, and I got bored and hit one of them North Koreans in the ass with a shovel. So how come you left the One Battalion?"

"I was bored too. And I had a chance to get a job in the city."

"Yeah . . . I wish I'd done that. Too late now." Dabenga kicked at the dusty ground as he walked. "Anyway, last year, I transferred to the Republic Police, into the Police Support Unit. We're stationed down at Gweru."

"You're a Blackboot?" Quimby said, using the nickname most people used for Zimbabwe's paramilitary police unit.

"Oh yeah. They use us against the bandits, and for riot control, for smugglers and poachers. It's good duty. Lots of action. You'd like it. Right now, I'm up here at Masuku helping these Germans train our new levies. . . . Real tough stuff, these Germans, like us in the old days; they've got everything figured out, don't move unless they know exactly what's going to happen, and demand the best we've got. If we don't do it right the first time, we keep doing it into the middle of the night until they're satisfied."

"I've heard about them," Quimby said. "The paper said that about twenty of them came out."

"Twenty-one. They rotate seven of them back to Germany every two months and send out new men. We just lost a bunch last week."

"Lost a bunch?"

"Rotated, man." Dabenga passed him the carton.

Quimby drank and probed again. "Did you see them go?"

"No. This German colonel, he's got orders to keep a low profile. They leave in the night, fly out in a Bulgarian plane."

"If they play so hard, don't they ever get hurt? In the old days, we were always having injuries and accidents."

"Nah! That colonel would bite their butts off if they did anything wrong. I'll tell you who the wild ones are, though."

165

"You mean your own men?"

"Nah. Listen." Dabenga leaned close, put an arm around Quimby's shoulder, and began to whisper. "I'm going to tell you a military secret. It's all right, though. The colonel says we're not to talk about this anywhere, but what the hell, you're one of us; you saved my life with a barrel of nails, eh? Best shot with a keg of nails in the whole One Battalion."

"I still don't know why I didn't use my gun in that store," Quimby said, walking on.

"What we're doing, see, besides the Blackboot recruits, we've got a platoon of ANC troops in there, from Umkhonto We Sizwe, you know? What we've got, it's a special assault platoon. Fifty men. Like we used to be, what they call an elite group."

"But they're not a part of Zimbabwe's armed forces," Quimby protested. "Why would Mugabe let the Germans train the ANC?"

"That's why it's secret, see? It's so secret somebody said even Mugabe himself probably doesn't know what's happening. The colonel says, "Not one word. The whole deal's *verboten*. That means we're supposed to keep our bloody mouths shut.""

"They're giving these ANC people the works? Teaching them how to go into buildings in the dark, shoot up a plane, demolitions, clandestine work?"

"Everything," Dabenga said solemnly. "And these Umkhonto We Sizwe boys—this is what I wanted to tell you. They're wild, tough; they want to fight; you can't stop them; they even scare the Germans. There's about twenty white men—"

"White men?"

"That's what I said. All Communists, see—Swedes and Bulgarians, Poles, a couple of South Africans, and a Jew. Wild men, ready to charge into South Africa all by themselves and cut up the country."

"They've got to be crazy."

"That's what I'm telling you. They are. This morning I asked this Pole, Mikulski, as polite as a little lady, 'Can't you put more of the bullets in the center?' And he says, 'I'll put them in the center of your head,' and he swung his gun on me and tried to bean me with the gun barrel. Tough and crazy. They're always fighting, everywhere they go. Always half a dozen of 'em in the infirmary."

"Do they ever kill anybody?"

Dabenga swung around scowling. "Wait a minute. . . . You're asking too many questions."

"I haven't asked anything," Quimby said, retreating quickly. "I just said, 'Do they ever kill anybody?' I meant you can act tough all you want to, but if you haven't been in a real fight, if you haven't been hurt, you're not tough yet."

Dabenga crushed the beer carton between his hands and threw it down on the road. He put a hand on Quimby's shoulder and brought his worried face up close to Quimby's. "Listen, old buddy, I been talking too much. Promise me you didn't hear me say nothin' about these Communists. Promise you won't tell nobody. They'll pull my arms off."

"I don't even remember what we were talking about," Quimby lied. "Let's get some beer."

8

THE apartment manager, Mrs. Boyington, took in Quimby's unshaven face and scruffy appearance and gave Tandy a skeptical stare.

With shy laughter and a sound of girlish confusion in her voice, Tandy said, "You'll just have to ignore the way we look. We were married last week, in town first, and then we had to go to my village and do it according to the tribal traditions. My parents insisted. We're just back from five days in the village and you know how it is out there. No bathrooms and no running water, and they kept us going all the time."

The woman was white, elderly, and jaundiced-looking, but Tandy's exuberance forced her to smile. "I had thought you educated blacks had put all that superstition behind you," she said, not knowing how many spirits and traditions she had just trampled.

"We have, of course," Tandy told her. "But the old folks live by them, and if you want to keep your friends and your ties with the village you must respect the traditions. My mother and grandmother would have died if I hadn't gone. And not only that. . . ." She turned to Quimby, putting her hand on his arm with a look of great pride. "My husband is from America, the United States. He's interested in anthropology. He wanted to see the village and the ceremonies."

Quimby did his part. "Very interesting," he told the rheumy, watchful eyes. "Have you ever seen a Shona village wedding ceremony?"

The woman made a sour movement of her lips and jaw that expressed her total lack of interest in such things. She stood in the doorway of her first-floor apartment, dressed in a worn but frilly linen dress, straggly white hair tied back in a knot behind her small head, studying them and making up her mind. "Well," she said, coming to a slow conclusion. "We do have two vacant apartments. One on the second floor, one on the third. One bedroom, and you have the bath and electricity."

"That would be fine," Tandy gushed, and Quimby nodded eagerly, trying to look like a lustful bridegroom.

"I would want a month in advance."

"Fine," Tandy told her. "We both have good jobs in the city."

The woman found her keys and trudged upstairs ahead of them, blue-veined, unstockinged feet slapping the steps in worn red velvet slippers.

She showed them the third-floor apartment first. Completely furnished, she insisted. Dishes and cooking utensils—water, heat, and electricity, all metered. A fridge in the kitchen. Fifty dollars cheaper than the second-floor apartment because the sun made it too hot up here.

They looked at the brown rug, the soiled, buff walls, the scuffed linoleum on the kitchen floor. They pretended to consider it, decided against it, and stood waiting for the woman to show them the other apartment, the one next to Florence Mubaka's.

In the second-floor apartment, Tandy was volubly pleased by the kitchen stove, the better linoleum, and the new daybed that opened into a full-sized bed in the main room.

They hemmed and hawed again, putting on a show of deciding, until Quimby told the woman they would like it and asked what papers needed to be signed; then they went back to Mrs. Boyington's apartment, where he produced his passport and city registration card, signed a printed agreement, and paid in cash for the first month.

When the formalities were completed, Quimby said, "We'll have to go back to Mufakose where we were going to sleep tonight at Tandy's brother's house. He has a little truck, and he'll help us bring our things in. . . ."

He paused and looked at Tandy, who was making a convincing show of looking exhausted. Quimby waggled his head and sighed, as if he too was weary, and he said, "I wonder, Mrs. Boyington, would it be all right if we just went back upstairs and rested awhile before we go out to Mufakose? We've really been tramping the streets. . . ."

It was all right, of course. Now that she had her money, Mrs. Boyington was all smiles and politeness. She nodded and bobbed them out of her place, assuring them that she would attend to the formalities of reporting their move to the city authorities tomorrow.

They took their keys, and Quimby put his arm around Tandy's waist as they went up the stairway, smiling into each other's eyes.

When they were inside the apartment next to Florence's they got down to business.

TANDY pulled Quimby to the tall French windows and stepped out on the balcony, showing him how it might be possible to climb down the bricks and the drainpipe to the ground if their way out through the hallway was blocked. Quimby agreed, and asked her to go into the hall after he was gone and unlock the doorway that opened to the outside stairway at the back of the apartment house. Advance planning. Escape routes in a hostile environment.

They pressed their ears to the wall next to Florence's apartment, listening. Tandy had called Florence at her office no more than thirty minutes before, asking her about a new ANC ruling on women as soldiers in Umkhonto We Sizwe. Florence had been at work thirty minutes ago; they hoped she was still there.

Armed with a lockpick and the key to the apartment they had just rented, Quimby went down the hall. Getting through locked doors was one of the skills he and other Delta Force men had been taught; they were supposed to be able to get into and out of everything but a bank vault. Bank vaults, the ex-con who taught them lock picking had liked to repeat, were easy to open only when you were there at the right time and had a pistol at the bank president's ear.

Quimby knelt close to the door, working carefully until the last tumbler fell away. He turned to look down the hallway where he knew Tandy was watching through the slightly opened doorway. He made the sign with his index finger and thumb that meant "Okay," and stepped inside.

Florence had spent a good deal of time and money refurbishing her apartment. Smooth, sand-colored carpet covered the floor. The heavy pieces of black, leather-covered furniture were low and elegant, the African figures on a bookshelf and the low ebony table were authentic and attractive. Pale yellow drapes were heavy enough to keep out the light, but with the sun making them glow translucently, they gave the room a golden cast. Prints by Degas and Dufy added a European look. Florence had taste.

Quimby moved quickly to the kitchen with its little breakfast alcove and mock-tile floor, to the bathroom, small and clean, and to the two closets—the first, a small room used as a pantry, lined with shelves of cans and glasses, cleaning materials, papers and recipe books on a shelf, a laundry bag, and brooms; the second was a walk-in space behind sliding doors along one wall of the main room. He looked into that and saw dresses and shoes, hatboxes on the shelf.

What the evidence he wanted would look like he wasn't certain. Something that proved she was a member of the SACP; letters, correspondence, codes, pictures—anything that might nail down the responsible chief of the assassins. He wanted to know who the commandos were, who was sending them, and where they stashed their Skorpions. He was on a fishing expedition and was prepared to settle for almost anything.

He started with the drawers of a mahogany lowboy on one side of the main room. Working swiftly, he pulled out the first drawer, pawed through sweaters and scarves, felt under it, looked at the back, pushed it in, and went to the next drawer, turning over lingerie, panties, brassiers, nylon slips, hosiery. She had a passion for sheer, peach-colored things.

He reached to the back of the second drawer and found a box with a pistol. He lifted it: Type 59, the Chinese copy of the Soviet Makarov SL. He wondered where she had obtained the Chinese version, and answered the question himself. Many of Mugabe's weapons had come from the Chinese and the North Koreans; these guns were hidden all over the country. But so were the

Soviet Makarovs. Was it significant that her gun was Chinese? He didn't think so.

He slid the pistol's loaded magazine out, looked inside the chamber to be sure it was empty, and put the magazine in his pocket. He let the slide move forward and put the pistol back. No sense in having a loaded pistol around if Florence rushed home and got mad about having a visitor. He checked the bottom side of the drawer and felt the back of it. Nothing.

In the bottom drawer: folded blankets, sheets, pillowcases—and a package of four notebooks, five inches by eight, held together by rubber bands.

He knelt on the floor, removed the rubber bands, and looked quickly through the first notebook. He put it down and paged through the others. Notes Florence had kept while she was in Russia, notes from lectures. He went back to the first, and examined the pages more carefully: how to prepare a Molotov cocktail, how to make explosives out of sulphur and potassium nitrate and charcoal, how to rig booby traps along forest paths. Squad maneuvers, crude drawings of how guerrilla camps should be set up, where sentries should be placed, instructions about sabotaging railways and power lines.

She had told him that she had studied management in the Soviet Union.

He turned the pages quickly: more of the same. Too much to examine here. He put that notebook down and picked up another: Marxism-Leninism, Organization of the Communist Party of the Soviet Union, Rules of the Party, definitions of democratic centralism, peaceful coexistence, world socialism, Lenin's theory of imperialism, international cooperation between Communist parties.

It would take hours to study all this, and all these pages might tell him nothing he didn't already know. He packed the notebooks together with the rubber bands around them and stuffed them inside his shirt. He stood up and looked around the room. Elegant but simple furnishings; not many obvious hiding places. He would come back in a moment to look behind the pictures and under the cushions of that big divan.

He went to the clothes closet and moved his hands along the shelf above the dresses, feeling behind hats and hatboxes. Nothing. He took the hatboxes down and looked inside them, seeing that Florence had succumbed to one of Moscow's special offerings. Bought herself a handsome mink hat. He fingered the thick lining, wondering where the hell she was going to wear mink in Zimbabwe or South Africa.

He felt through the dresses, touching seams that looked too wide, shoulder pads that might be hiding documents. Down on the floor again to look behind the shoe rack, inside the shoes. Nothing.

He went into the pantry, not looking for secret materials but for the kinds of papers anyone has to keep and store. On the shelves there were cookbooks, newspaper clippings of recipes stuffed into a looseleaf notebook, two long boxes with letters and bills, a packet of old Christmas cards people had sent her, an album of photographs.

There!

He pulled down the album and saw that its photographs were fastened to the pages with little plastic corners. He looked in the back first: Florence in the Harare Gardens with a handsome young black man dressed in a light suit that was much too tight for him; Florence standing with two other young black women, all of them wearing blue track suits, in front of that crazy church in Moscow's Red Square; Florence in a bathing suit by a pool, young-looking, standing with her knees together like a professional model, facing the camera obliquely with her hands placed low on her hips, obviously attempting to hide the heaviness there. A very tall and good-looking black man stood close behind her with his hands on her shoulders, both of them laughing.

He turned through the heavy pages, came to the earlier part of the album, and stopped at a page where one or two black-and-white pictures had fallen out of their frames or been removed. He searched down between the pages for the missing pictures, failed to find them, and turned the album upside down, brushing the loose pages. Nothing fell to the floor. He put the album down and raced through the recipes in the looseleaf notebook, considered the cookbook, but picked up the packet of old Christmas cards.

Some of the cards were in the envelopes they had been sent in, and he reached inside each envelope on each side of the card and separated the folded cards. He found two photographs in a blue airmail envelope that had been sent from Budapest, and he studied it hurriedly. One was a family picture: the father, a tall slim man with the face and straight black hair of an Indian; standing in front of him, clearly recognizable, Florence—probably about fifteen or sixteen; in front of Florence, sitting on a chair, a buxom black woman about the father's age, and sitting with the woman, a man—thirty or thirty-five years old, his face also clearly recognizable—*John Kado*.

Quimby guessed at once what he had. Florence was Kado's sister. He wondered how Kado could be so slim and Indian-like and Florence so obviously a black, with her heavy hips and protruding buttocks and broad nose. . . .

The truth stared out at him, and he put it into words. Kado's father had been married more than once. John Kado was obviously much older than Florence; he was the son of an earlier wife, and Florence was the daughter of the woman in the photograph. So she was Kado's half-sister. But she had said that she didn't know John Kado.

175

He studied the second photograph. Florence, wearing a dashiki and duka, smiling broadly, looking younger than she was now. Around her, three men in an ornate, old-fashioned office. The men . . . He didn't recognize two of them; the third was Heinz Seifert in a Red Army uniform, looking younger, much thinner than he was now, stern and ambitious.

A few feet from Quimby's head, the wall thumped at him, three quick raps, then a fourth. Florence was coming home. That fourth rap said she was already in the hallway.

Quimby stuffed the photographs into his shirt pocket and threw the Christmas cards back on the shelf, looking right and left for a place to hide. No place in the pantry or the kitchen. He hurried back to the main room, stepped into the clothes closet, stumbling a little on the shoes. He pulled the sliding doors almost shut, got himself to the back of the closet, no more than two feet from the doors, and pulled the dresses together in front of his body.

He heard Florence exclaim aloud as she came in the door and knew that he should have locked that door behind him when he came in. A man's voice answered her, and Quimby saw her flash by in a pink dress, going toward the kitchen. In a voice that shrilled with anger, reminding Quimby of the momma bear in the story, she called, "Someone has been looking at my album!"

Through the crack in the doorway, he saw the figure of a man come to a stop in front of the closet, and realized that this was a big one. He had to crouch a little to see the man's face, recognized Victor Muzingi, and felt the quick thrust of fear pound through his mind. His heart began to pump; he felt cold and hot all at once, knew the adrenalin glands were blowing their stimulants into his blood, and began to look for ways to fight.

He would not use the knife, he decided; he was not here to kill. If things went wrong and the police got into this he would look like a thief trying to murder his way out of a corner. All he wanted to do was hit Muzingi a good one to slow him down and get the hell out of here.

He slipped the blackjack from the pocket down on the side of his leg, and held it up at face level, thinking what he would have to do when Muzingi looked in here.

Florence declared loudly: "Someone has been searching this place, I think we should—"

Right across the nose, Quimby was thinking. No talk, just smash him and get out of here. Carry on our feud sometime when there's room to maneuver. He tried to push the dresses back, quietly and slowly. When Muzingi opened these sliding doors, there wasn't going to be more than a split second to move. That big bastard outweighed him sixty or seventy pounds. What the hell was Muzingi doing here?

Through the crack in the sliding doors, he saw Muzingi with his finger at his lips somewhere inside the heavy beard, shushing Florence. He saw Muzingi turn toward the closet, and he wished that he could see better. Things in here were awkward—the goddamn dresses were in his way, the rod they hung from crossed in front of his nose, the shelf over his head compelled him to crouch, Florence's goddamn shoes were all over the floor.

The doors slid back as though they had been thrown. Muzingi came in like a bull, his big arms up and out to push the dresses further back, seeing Quimby against the wall, reaching forward with his thick hands.

Quimby tried to swing upward at Muzingi's face, but the sap slapped harmlessly against the underside of Muzingi's forearm.

He didn't get a second chance. Muzingi's fingers clutched him around the throat and yanked him forward, out of the closet, twisting him off his feet, throwing him back and down, and the huge body came down on top of him, smothering him, powerful fingers tightening around his throat like steel cables.

Quimby dropped the sap and jabbed the fingers of both hands upward at Muzingi's eyes, missed them, caught at Muzingi's mouth and pulled at it, trying to tear the man's cheek enough to make him release his strangling grip. Muzingi jerked back his head and bit at Quimby's fingers, then butted his head forward, hitting Quimby's jaw with his forehead.

With that big head so close, Quimby reached for the man's ears, got them in his hands and yanked at them, pulling them down, doing his damnedest to tear them off.

Muzingi swore and let go of Quimby's throat with one hand and crashed a big fist into Quimby's jaw, and Quimby, with purple stars and green splotches whirling through his head, yanked again, felt the ear in his right hand tear away, and heard Muzingi's high-pitched squeal.

Quimby twisted his body, kicking, forcing his knees up, wriggling like a panicky fish to get himself out from under, while Muzingi battered with both fists on his cheeks and forehead. He was away at last, his head reeling, and he staggered to his feet, trying to turn in time to meet Muzingi's rush, thinking better of that as the giant came at him, belatedly trying to step aside far enough to pull at the man's outstretched arms and throw him against the wall.

None of that worked. Muzingi was all over him, like an octopus trained to crush rocks, beating him back, working knees and elbows and fists, stamping on Quimby's arch, butting his jaw, hammering at his throat.

Out of the corner of his eye, Quimby saw Florence standing by the door to the kitchen, both her fists up, watching not with fear but with hateful fascination. Really loved it, didn't she? he thought. Goddamn sadist! He stamped on Muzingi's arch, but his boots seemed to make no impression; he swung an elbow into Muzingi's face and the giant ignored it; he tried to get a fist up to slam into Muzingi's throat, but the huge arms smothered his effort. He brought his knee up to kick the man in the crotch, but couldn't reach it. The son of a bitch was just too high off the ground, too fast, too strong.

Muzingi's first groan when his ear was torn, was down now to a piercing, moan that sounded crazy mad.

Quimby backed away, wanting room for maneuver, trying to remember what loose things there were in the room. He needed a weapon; something to break this brute's head. He took a hard cut on the temple from the edge of Muzingi's hand, and he went down, grabbing at Muzingi's ankles, hoping to bring the man down with him.

An oversized black shoe lifted and kicked him in the ribs. His breath went out of his body, and he pulled the ankle to him and bit the huge calf, started to his knees with his arms around the ankle, thinking he would lift this leg high enough to drop Muzingi and get on top of him, but a fist clubbed the side of his head and the back of his neck. He fell over sideways on the floor, dazed but rolling, far enough away, he hoped, to get to his feet and grab that ebony head on the coffee table: He had to stop this bastard.

Muzingi was having none of that; he followed his punches with another kick in Quimby's ribs. Then Quimby, sobbing with pain and gasping for breath as he tried to get up, heard a peculiar bonging sound, like a half-filled metal oil barrel being hit with a dull mallet.

He turned his head to look up.

Tandy was behind Muzingi, bringing the flat side of an iron skillet down on Muzingi's head a second time. Again Quimby heard the bonging sound, and Muzingi was falling to his knees, eyes closed, his head leading his body, falling toward Quimby, hands and arms limp at his sides.

Quimby tried to roll away but the huge body fell on him. He

struggled away from it and came to a sitting position, trying to comprehend what had happened, and Tandy stood above him with the heavy skillet in her hand, looking scared and warlike and absolutely beautiful, scowling down at him.

Quimby tried to get to his feet, but reeled and fell. He tried again, the easy way, getting up on all fours, and was aware that Florence was running past him. She reached the drawer where she kept her lingerie, and turned with the pistol in her hand, her lips curled back showing teeth and pink gums, her face looking like a Greek mask of tragedy. She pulled back the slide and let it go forward; holding the gun with both hands she pointed it at Quimby and pulled the trigger. She looked surprised and fearful, waited, and pulled the trigger again. She cursed and pulled the slide back and pulled the trigger once more, and when nothing happened, she threw the gun at Quimby. It hit him on the shoulder and thumped down on the floor.

Tandy ran at Florence with her skillet raised.

Quimby meant to yell, but he only groaned: "Wait!" He saw Tandy halt before Florence, turning to look at him, and by that time he was upright—wobbly, but able to think. He took a pace backward, leaned against the wall, and looked down at Muzingi's unconscious form. He tried hard to get his breath, while Tandy and Florence watched each other warily, and when he was able to speak, his voice came out in a fuzzy squeak.

He said to Florence, "Unless you know how to sew ears back on, Muzingi needs a doctor as soon as you can get one." He coughed, and the excruciating pain in his throat brought tears to his eyes. He put both hands up to his throat, holding it, but that helped not at all. He got another breath into his chest, feeling a sharp pain in his ribs, and hoped the ribs weren't broken, and he went on: "I figure you aren't going to call the police. You'll have to clean up this mess and come after us later."

He saw his sap on the floor and squatted slowly to pick it up. With this guy a sap was useless; he'd needed a baseball bat. Because he was close, he put a hand on Muzingi's throat to feel for a pulse. "Your friend is alive," he told Florence; "You'd better get your needle and thread out and put his ear on. Seriously, you can probably save it. Why was he here?"

Florence's face and eyes hated him. "We know who you are; they thought you might come after me. He escorted me home to keep me safe. Ha!"

"Tell him, next time I'll kill him."

"Shit!" she said contemptuously. "Your woman saved you. You were going down the tube."

Quimby looked at Tandy and tried to smile his thanks, knowing that the swellings on his face must make him look pretty gruesome. He tasted blood in his mouth and on his lips, wiped it off with his hand, and said to Tandy, "Let's go."

They went. Into the hall and back to their apartment, and when he had washed the blood from his face and hands, they left the building by its back stairway.

AT Mungu's house Tandy taped Quimby's ribs and he held pads of cloth saturated with cold water against various parts of his face, trying to control the swelling. He felt a hundred years old and lucky to be alive, and he told Tandy more times than either of them could count that he had never heard such sweet music as the sound of her skillet on Muzingi's head.

Their study of the notebooks, which were made of coarse, gray Soviet paper, gave them one more piece of unexpected information. Florence had told Quimby that she had been in the Soviet Union from March 1981 until July of 1982. Her first notebook had a series of entries dating from January 1979, and the fourth one ended with an entry dated September 1982. She had been

181

nearly four years in the Soviet Union. Tandy studied the photograph of Heinz Seifert and Florence and expressed the opinion that Florence had to be far more important in the SACP than she had admitted.

Tandy told Mungu how to make contact with Chitepo, and just after dark, Peter wandered into the house. He was gloomy and depressed by Nkala's death, and his depression seemed to grow as Quimby told him what they had learned from Dabenga and the visit to Florence's apartment. "They've got us all sewn up," Peter complained disconsolately. "Wherever you look, they're already there, organized, taking our party away from us, subverting the Umkhonto We Sizwe, using every branch of the ANC as a cover for their dirty business. It's hopeless. Umkhonto We Sizwe even has its own counterintelligence group. Claims its business is military counterespionage, and doesn't talk to me, doesn't tell me anything. I've never heard a word about this assault platoon. Why? Because the Communists are keeping their damned secrets. D'you realize what Dabenga was saying? The ANC's own military organization may be trying to kill our leaders. The unit we should be able to trust most of all doesn't even belong to us."

Frowning, head down, he listened apathetically while Tandy spoke of the time she had heard Nkala speak in a township outside Johannesburg; then he hunched forward in his chair, gazing hesitantly into Quimby's eyes, and his words came out painfully. "I don't know if we should go on with this," he said. "With Nkala gone, I don't have the authority to risk drowning the ANC in blood. I don't have the right to take the responsibility."

Quimby looked at the floor to hide his anger, and he kept his voice low. "Nkala wanted the killings stopped," he said firmly. "We're going to complete the job he gave us. We have to if you want to save the ANC."

Peter glumly shook his narrow head, rubbing the palms of his calloused hands together, and worked his lips unpleasantly, as if he had something rotten in his mouth but couldn't spit it out or swallow it. He eyed Tandy, still shaking his head, and a tentative smile appeared on his face. His hands came up, and his fingers touched the line of her forehead, her cheekbones, her jaw and chin. "I've got to do you in the blackest ebony someday," he said, sounding quite hopeless. "Your face is a masterpiece. Ah God! How beautiful you are!"

He looked back at Quimby again, with a rueful half-smile, and said, apologetically, *"Damn this world!"* He balled his right hand into a fist and shook it vaguely at the ceiling. "They've killed the only man I've ever known who was a kind of saint. His whole life was devoted to the cause. Listen, Taylor, on the eleventh I want to be with you at Victoria Farm. I want to get some of those bastards personally."

"Peter," Quimby said mildly, "you're going to have your hands full that night. I've got bigger plans for you we'll talk about. D'you think the commandos will really come on the eleventh?"

Peter gave them the reasons why he felt it was certain they would come. He was working hard to make sure that anyone in the SACP who wanted to know about special meetings of the ANC leaders would learn about this one. He had sent people around to whisper how important it was—the leaders were writing up the resolutions to be approved, deciding on the selection of new members of the National Council, finalizing the agenda of the international conference.

And because he was now half-convinced that the South Africans were involved somehow, he had gone to great pains to persuade them too that this meeting was bona fide.

Letters had been sent to addresses in South Africa, to black townships outside Pretoria and Johannesburg. The addressees were ANC fighters, men who had recently and secretly left South Africa. The letters had been sent as if the ANC was not aware that those men had departed, and they mentioned the meeting on the eleventh. "Indirectly," Peter said. "Cryptically. The SAs will be congratulating themselves for their brilliance in ferreting out the messages."

Men working for Peter had made telephone calls to Durban, delivering cryptic messages in code the SA police were known to have broken, mentioning the place and time of the meeting to two men who were asked to be present. The men who received those calls fled from pay phones in the townships as soon as the call was completed, and the men whom they pretended to be were already out of the country and had no intention of going back soon. Peter believed the South African police had intercepted these messages and would take them seriously.

Quimby praised Peter for his efforts, and they worked out a series of logistics problems that concerned Quimby's plan to meet the commandos at Victoria Farm. Mungu had reconnoitered a squatters' camp outside Tafara, well to the east of the city, where they would move early the next morning. Peter would deliver a car he said he could borrow to the edge of Highfield, and Quimby and Tandy and the teams of Panebondo and Mufato and Mungo would be ferried over through the day and would settle at different locations in the camp.

Contact with Peter would be maintained through a man who worked in a beer garden in Tafara and who had access to a telephone for ordering beer. Also, Peter would swing through the camp two or three times a day in case either he or Quimby acquired information the other should have.

Peter stood up at last getting ready to leave, but Quimby said,

"We're not through yet, Peter. Did you case that gun club Charles Jameson is so interested in?"

"I did. It's not very impressive. A three-story lodge built into the side of a hill. Some firing ranges have been set up against the hill. Actually it's a sort of social club, I think. These Rhodesians get together to talk and drink and work off their frustrations by firing at paper targets."

"Can I get inside, do you think?"

"I'm not sure that would be wise; a caretaker sleeps out there."

"White?"

"An ex-lieutenant of the light infantry, no less."

"We'll need some rope then. And a small crowbar." Quimby realized that Tandy was staring at him resentfully. "And I'll want a lookout, probably someone with a skillet."

"You mean you're going out there now?" Peter demanded. "But you're all bunged up."

"Look, why does Florence run across to the cathedral and send messages to a fanatic little Rhodesian patriot with roots in South Africa? I want to know how the hell this little fella and his shooting club fit into this."

"But what if we run into trouble?"

Quimby was tired of explaining. "Maybe you'd better bring a skillet too."

A SMALL graveled driveway of the sport club led from the road to the front of the lodge, which seemed very modest, showing only a low-roofed, one-story facade from that direction. Chitepo had explained that the club was built down the slope of the hill, at least three stories of it.

Quimby and Tandy trudged up the road from where Chitepo had parked the car he was driving, and Tandy pushed at the bell, while Quimby flattened himself against the fieldstone wall by the door. Nothing happened for a long time, and Tandy pressed the bell more insistently, keeping her finger on it. In a few minutes they heard bars and bolts being shot and a key being turned in the lock, and a light turned on over the entrance.

A tall, sleepy, red-bearded man with touseled blond hair and orange pajamas carried a FAL rifle in his hands, and growled at Tandy.

"What you want, girl? Why're you banging on my door?"

"Please, mister, we've had an accident down the road," Tandy had herself sounding half-hysterical. "Two of my friends are hurt bad. They need help."

"Nothing I can do. I have to stay in the building."

"Do you have a telephone? Could I use your telephone to call an ambulance, a doctor? I'm afraid they're going to die. One of them's bleeding awful, and I can't get under the car to help them."

The guard pushed the screened door open a little and peered out, studying the driveway. "Oh well . . . come on."

Quimby caught him as he turned to let Tandy enter, when the gun was pointing upward at the Southern Cross. He took him by the hair with one hand, brought the point of his knife down in front of the guard's face so that he could see what it was, then laid it against his jugular. "Be very nice," Quimby said. "Hand her the gun. Lie down on the floor on your stomach. Carefully now, we don't want your blood all over the rug."

Tandy hurriedly stuffed some of Mungu's rags in the guard's mouth and tied another one around his mouth and neck to keep the gag in place. Quimby brought hands and arms together behind the guard, bound the legs and brought them up to tie them to the hands, making it impossible for the guard to struggle without hurting himself more than he would want to.

"You just lie still there a few minutes," Quimby told him. "When we come back, we'll untie you."

The guard's blue eyes were studying him and Tandy. He would be able to give someone an accurate description, down to the swelling over Quimby's left eye and under his right one. Quimby switched off the light at the entrance, and they went further into the building, lighting their way with flashlights.

On the first floor, the entryway opened on a lounge perhaps forty feet wide and twenty-five deep, with big picture windows revealing a splendid view of nighttime Harare to the south. At one end, an ornate bar was done in the style of frontier Rhodesia, with tall stools and mahogany furnishings, and in the center at the back of the bar, not a large reclining nude but an oil painting of Leonard Starr Jameson, flanked on the right by an only slightly smaller painting of Cecil Rhodes, and on the left, by Colonel Pennefather, the man who had led the military group of the British South African Police that founded the settlement of Salisbury.

The room was furnished with comfortable-looking leather chairs and divans and square dark tables, and wherever wall space permitted there were framed black-and-white photographs of military groups, looking fierce and drawn, or fresh and pompous, brandishing weapons and big mustachios and sticking out their chests.

At the east end of the room, next to a huge fireplace with a formidable lion's head mounted above it, was a door with a little sign that said "Office."

The door was locked. Quimby did not waste time with the lockpick; he forced the door open with his crowbar, and they played their flashlights around a disorderly room filled with a crowded desk, three sets of filing cabinets, and shelves overflowing with stacked papers.

"The files, first," Quimby said. "We want a list of members, a statement of what they think they're doing, what their purpose is."

He jimmied the locked file cabinets, and they searched hurriedly. In ten minutes they had a list of members, and the constitution of the club, which stated innocuously enough that its purpose was good fellowship, game hunting, marksmanship, and the preservation of effective security for Zimbabwe. Charles Jameson's signature as secretary followed the scrawls of the president and the treasurer. Quimby folded the lists and the constitution and put them in a pocket, looked further in the files for headings like arms, weapons, ammunition, handguns, but found only paid bills for clay pigeons and target loads for skeet shooting and for other mundane supplies like food and liquor.

The next level down was an exercise room, well-furnished with pulleyed weight lifts, barbells, treadmills, and several machines Quimby didn't recognize, apparently designed to torture muscles he didn't have. So the members were health nuts, a bunch of overage-in-grade Rhodesian officers, war buffs interested in Rhodesia's military history, keeping themselves in shape for the next one. No one could object to any of that.

He and Tandy took a quick turn around the room, blind on two sides because it was down in the ground, but with big windows on the south again; they went through the sweat-smelling locker room and the showers, left them, and filed downstairs to the third level.

This floor was different. Only about half as wide as the rooms above, it had been dug back into the hill for almost a hundred feet, and at the far end there was a row of four paper targets set up so they could be drawn forward by a rope-and-pulley arrangement for inspection. Quimby recognized what in the United States they called a "Thousand Inch Range," where men could fire fairly heavy infantry weapons fitted specially with .22-caliber barrels and have the benefit of seeming to be out on an outdoor range with full-scale guns.

The place was immaculate: smooth gray shellacked concrete walls and floor and ceiling, pads and gun stands and big earmuff protectors at each station, a line of chairs well back from the shooting positions marked by black-painted lines on the floor.

They moved down the narrow concrete walkway at one side of the range and came to a double door in the wall. Quimby pulled at it, saw that it was made of light steel, that it was cabinet-set into the wall, and he jimmied it open. Inside were piles of the targets used to teach men how to operate the traversing and elevating wheels on machine guns; there were big round targets for pistols, full-sized silhouette targets, even some tiny lions and kudus and birds for the hunters. But no weapons.

He left the cabinet and walked the full length of the room, inspecting both walls, and the wall in back, and all appeared to be absolutely seamless. He returned to the cabinet, and he and Tandy tugged at the metal shelving that held the targets and glue pots and ramrods and other gun-cleaning equipment and pails of empty shell casings. When they had a clear view of the back wall, he tapped it with his fingers and knew that he had discovered a false wall finished in concrete gray and shellacked, but soft, like hardboard or plywood.

At first they could see no way to remove the false wall, but Tandy's sharp eyes found a minute break in one of the seams, and when Quimby scraped along that seam, he discovered that a small square of metal had been fitted into the wall so meticulously that it was almost invisible. He pried open the square and found a small lever. He turned the lever and pulled hard, opening a door that he could not get wide open because of the shelves behind him, but they managed to squeeze through and walked into a dark, cool room. With Tandy behind him, he pulled the door almost shut and they searched the wall by the door for a wall switch, found it, and flooded the room with light.

They had found an armory. About thirty rifles were carefully locked in their racks, three machine guns sat on their tripods, burnished and clean. More than a hundred pistols of various makes were locked under glass. But these were not the most impressive displays: Piled high against the walls on two sides were the rifle crates. Quimby walked along them swiftly, counting. He estimated something like four hundred rifles. Boxes of 7.62-millimeter ammunition were piled above his head in the center of the room: enough to carry on a small war for several days. Twenty light machine guns and twenty 81-millimeter mortars were still in their crates, and thirty-eight rocket launchers with boxes of rockets were piled behind them. He found antipersonnel mines, explosives, and way in the back, in a separate cabinet, blasting caps and a blaster.

He poked with his flashlight into every corner, looking for a Skorpion, looking for a box of them. But he did not find any.

He led Tandy back to the range. "No Skorpions."

She seemed awed by the display of weaponry. "But what are they *doing* with all those things?"

"I think this is a revanchist group, getting ready to try a coup against Mugabe. Maybe only dreaming about it. Going to get rid of black rule and bring the White Rhodesian regime back."

"But Jameson is mixed up with Florence and Kado. I don't understand the connection."

"Neither do I." He added: "There's gelignite back there and blasting caps. I could blow this whole cache to hell."

Tandy shivered in the cold room. "Should we?"

"I'm not sure how it will help us. If I had found the Skorpions,

I would be wiring the place right now. Maybe there's a better way to get rid of these guys. Let's get out of here."

AT a pay telephone on the outskirts of Zengeza, Quimby studied the telephone numbers he kept in his wallet and put in a call to a man very high in government whom he had not seen for three years. It was nearly midnight, and a servant and a wife objected to waking the august official, but Quimby persisted. He needed to talk with the Minister of State Security, Enos Karwi, and at once, and he asked that they tell Karwi that Muparadzi was calling.

He had known Karwi through the war and they had worked closely during the police actions after the war. He believed that despite Karwi's rise to great authority they were still friends, and when at last, a heavy voice growled a doubtful hello into the telephone, Quimby said, "Kamba?" That had been Karwi's wartime nickname; it meant tortoise, and tortoise in ZANLA had signified "Slowpoke."

"An old joke I do not like anymore," Karwi said.

"I have something you must know," Quimby replied, and he talked swiftly, named the gun club, and told Karwi the size of the arms cache he had seen only a few minutes before.

When he had finished, he heard Karwi yawn, and say, "Ah, the blessed revanchists. Why don't they give up these crazy schemes? This is a fine discovery indeed, Muparadzi. I will move our troops in the morning."

"Kamba, Kamba. Morning will be too late. They know I saw their weapons tonight. Tomorrow you will find nothing but peaceful hunters and old men. I saw enough weapons in that room to carry out a successful coup in Harare tomorrow."

"O dear. Well . . . so you have ruined my sleep for this night. I do not thank you for that. We will move at once then,

191

Muparadzi, and I will see that you get proper credit for your service."

"Please, no," Quimby objected. "Take the credit for yourself. Let me be an unidentified informant. Please."

"Well then . . . yes, but come in and talk to me soon. I'll want to know what you were doing in this gun club. You say the members' lists are in the second cabinet."

"That is right."

"And don't expect to read about this in *The Herald* this week," Karwi added. "It will take time to run down these members and complete our investigation before we go into court. Good night then."

THE car Peter had promised was the Toyota truck Quimby had sat in the night he waited for Florence Mubaka to come out of John Kado's house. In Harare, such vehicles were seen everywhere, loaded with men and women and young children being transported between the city and the townships and out to the great farms still owned by white men. In three trips they moved everyone, along with pots and pans, blankets and sleeping pads and bags of vegetables and cornmeal. By midmorning, Quimby's little troop of fighters was settled into three different clusters of squatters' huts on the southern fringes of Tafara, the easternmost settlement of greater Harare.

Quimby discussed with Chitepo and Tandy the possible significance of the action he had taken with Karwi, and they agreed that the effect Karwi's raid would have was not clear. Except for the connection between Charles Jameson and Florence Mubaka, they had no evidence that the club was behind the commandos' efforts to destroy the ANC leadership. Having that armory wiped out might complicate or end the threat of new commando attacks, or it might have nothing to do with them.

"And the fact that we didn't find the Skorpions might mean nothing at all," Quimby reasoned. "The commandos doing the hard work could be keeping their guns somewhere else. We need to remember that Jameson and the other members look south and backward, to South Africa and Rhodesia. The guns in those crates came from South Africa, but does that mean these guys are trying to kill the ANC leaders, or that they've signed on to help the South Africans do it? We don't know, and since those members are likely to have other guns stashed around, I think we have to prepare for an all-out fight on the eleventh, no matter what Karwi has done."

Both Peter and Tandy regarded him with serious frowns, nodding their heads almost reluctantly, as though they regretted not being able to come up with some different suggestion.

He made his initial reconnaissance of Victoria Farm by driving the truck along Goromonzi Road, and he returned to the camp just before noon, indicating to Mungu that he wanted a meeting with his team leaders at once.

He sat on the ground outside an upside-down, bowl-shaped shelter made of canvas and black plastic sheeting pulled over long bent saplings. Tandy sat just inside the shelter, guarding their possessions, and all around them were similar shelters, some so close to each other that it was impossible to move between them.

Children were everywhere. Women—barefooted, dressed in ragged garments, with white or colored scarves over their heads—sat by open fires, with white-enameled cooking utensils and cups and dishes spread on the ground, nursing their babies, making *sadza*, the stiff cornmeal mush that was their staple food, or just sitting and watching the people around them.

Everywhere there were buckets and cans—buckets for water, gallon cans for cooking, five-gallon cans for sitting on, smaller tin cans for drinking cups or childrens' toys, and others rusting, used, and discarded, half-buried in the ground, lying between bundles of sticks for firewood, making the whole area resemble a garbage dump.

The smells of filth and food and smoke and human excrement hovered thick in the air, and through all this, children ran and played and quarreled and urinated on the ground, women scolded the children and ran after them, and men with no work dozed inside the shelters or drifted about on the slope that led downward to the sewage plant and the marshy stream beneath the camp.

It was not Quimby's idea of the perfect spot for a staff meeting, but as he sat smiling at two children fighting over a grimy-black piece of cooked meat, his team leaders drifted in and sat cross-legged around him, carefully avoiding the appearance of coming to a meeting, looking indifferent and lazy, as if they were dropping by to pass the time of day, fitting themselves into the environment.

Quimby showed them the sketch he had made. He pointed to the north, showing them how the sketch was oriented. He pointed out the road they had traveled to Tafara. He moved his finger slowly, so they could see how they would go back to the Mutare Road, east a bit until they were beyond Ruwa at the turnoff for Goromonzi; then north along the Goromonzi Road for about two miles.

"On the right side of the road," he said, showing them; "these are big tobacco farms. Here and here. Just beyond the Shaw Corporation farm—you will see its big green-and-white sign—there is a great tract of uncultivated land, and on that land, on the ridge, here, perhaps half a mile back from this front field, there is a farmhouse that is not really a farmhouse anymore. A white businessman from the city lives there with his family and servants. This is where the ANC meeting will take place on the eleventh, the day after tomorrow; this is what the enemy must attack."

He paused, letting them think about what he had said; then he added: "The nearest house is almost a mile and a half away."

Two little children in dirty white dresses stood behind Mungu, solemnly looking at the back of his head. Mungu turned and scowled fiercely, making a threatening gesture with his arms over his head, sending them shrieking away behind a shelter.

Wally Panebondo, his Arab-like face thin and intense, his dark eyes seeming to look into the future, leaned forward and asked, "How do you think the enemy will come?"

"By car or truck along the Goromonzi Road. By helicopter, perhaps, but where the grass on the uncultivated land has not burned away it is very high, well over our heads. I think the pilots would prefer to land up on the ridge at the farmhouse if there is space. If they come by car, they might choose to leave their transportation hidden off the highway, march across the fields, and hit the farmhouse from the rear."

Mungu took the sketch in his thick fingers and stared hard at it, as if he were trying to see the hills, the grass, and the rocks.

Quimby said, "I'm going to take you out there with your teams at different times this afternoon and drop you off at different places. I want you to walk the ground, get as close to the farmhouse as you can without making people curious. Move through the grass, look over the ridges, consider how twenty or thirty well-armed men will use the ground and how we will stop them. When you come back I will want to hear how each of you would plan the fight to stop these men."

He had complimented them by asking their advice, and he would get it. These friends had their own ideas about fighting, and he would have heard them even if he hadn't asked. They

195

nodded their understanding, and Mungu turned and made another terrible face at the two children who had come back to play the frightening new game they had discovered. This time when they ran, the leader tripped over a rope and began to bawl loudly.

A woman with a baby at her breast rose from her fire to comfort the howler. After he was quieted, she turned and stood glaring at Mungo until he turned to look at her; then she made a horrible face at him. He turned away, frowning and worried, looking into Quimby's eyes.

Quimby saw Mungu's lips form the silent word, "Witch," and knew that Mungu was thinking that the woman had cast an evil spell on him. During the war he had learned to respect the Shona people's deeply rooted belief that witches can enter another person's spirit and sicken or kill him. He lifted a hand to wave at the woman, smiling at her in his most friendly fashion, sharing her joke with her. She waved back and entered her shelter laughing aloud, and Mungu grinned sheepishly.

Panebondo was squinting excitedly, and remembering this land. He said, "There are rock outcroppings along the ridge? A great slope of valley away to the east?"

"Yes. The ridge narrows suddenly here to the southeast, then rises at the highway."

"I have been here before," Panebondo said. "Let me walk in from the highway to study the earth to the east and north. We should also know the trails that lead into the kraals."

"Good. And study how the house stands on the hill. Remember, we will be working in darkness."

Quimby sat looking at them for a moment, and when they asked no other questions, he said, "The enemy may be here already; he may be reconnoitering this place as we are. The white farmers will be hostile and suspicious. Do not advertise that you are in the area. I will be there with you, but you will not see me, and I do not want to see you. Between seven and eight o'clock, I will come for you along the Goromonzi Road in the truck."

"IT did not last long," Tandy said. "And it lasted forever. I heard the women shrilling, calling the children the way they do when a panther or a lion has been sighted, or a crocodile in the water. I saw the first man, then the second. They were walking slowly through the camp, dressed in dark suits like those two at the beer garden. I thought they must be the police, and I thanked God you and the others were in the hills, and then I saw the big man, Victor Muzingi, following the others, and I thanked God even more that you were not here. But I was so afraid that you would come walking in. . . ."

Quimby went into the shelter with her and held her in his arms, feeling how her whole body trembled, and he listened attentively as she told him what had happened.

She had hidden herself in the back of their shelter, pulled a white rag over her head, hunkered over a bowl, kneading at the sadza, hardly looking up when a man bent to look inside and ask her where her man was. She had mumbled something about "the city," and he had seemed satisfied and had gone away.

She had peered through a slit in the plastic wall, watching the men, six of them, she thought, as they moved from hut to hut down the slope and gathered only a few feet away to await Muzingi's orders.

Muzingi had come and questioned several of the squatters. She had seen him give them money. Then he had whistled and three more men came up the slope from the marsh and its high grass where they had been hiding. "If you and the men had been here," Tandy said, "you would have run off into the marsh, and they would have caught you."

She described how all the time that Muzingi and his men were in the camp the women kept their children in the shelters and how the children remained perfectly silent.

"It was as if a plague had struck," she said. "Muzingi—so big, so terrifying, with his head and the side of his face wrapped in a white bandage, with his great staring eyes—he looks like death."

Her hands shook and her eyes filled with tears, thinking back. "A little dog barked at him," she told Quimby. "Just a gangly little puppy. It came close to him and kept barking, and Muzingi reached down very quickly and grabbed it by the back of its neck. He swung it up in the air very hard so that it landed thirty feet away. It was hurt and it howled and howled, and he did not even look in that direction. He is a monster."

She went on to say that after Muzingi and his men had departed, walking slowly up toward Tafara, the children began to come outside the shelters, the women came out and blew on their fires, and the old men collected and discussed the raid and prophesied that the police would come now and move everyone to jail or to another camp.

While Quimby listened to Tandy telling what the searchers had said to others, he tried to decide whether Muzingi had learned from an informer in the camp that suspicious newcomers were in the area, or whether he was merely carrying out a systematic search of all important outlying settlements.

When Quimby's people had moved in during the morning hours, each group had gone its way, building its shelter apart from the others. At the same time, other people were coming in, and some were striking camp to leave. He knew that every squatters' camp was made up of a moving, shifting population that changed almost hour by hour, although, certainly, many people were permanent residents simply because they had no other place to go.

But squatters' camps were notorious for their informers and petty criminals, hungry people ready to do almost anything for a few dollars. Tandy had seen Muzingi giving certain people money. How safe was it to stay?

Quimby left Tandy and walked through the camp, his hat pulled low on his forehead to hide his half-closed eye and swollen cheek. It was about six-thirty. Cooking fires were burning and many families were already huddled around the fires, eating sadza and cooked vegetables or bits of meat with their fingers, babbling happily together.

He stood and listened to a group of old men who were still talking about the "police raid," and he wished that he had some safe place to move his little army. But his men were spread all over the hills, and when he picked them up, they would be exhausted. They needed a good night's sleep, and another tomorrow night. He considered how difficult it would be to move them out of this jungle of a squatters' camp in the dark, and he decided against it.

Instead, he would ask Mungu and Mutota to look around later tonight to learn what the other squatters were thinking, what they had heard, what kinds of questions Muzingi had asked. If Muzingi had asked only about a man and a woman, that would mean the others were safe. He and Tandy would take the truck somewhere else tonight and sleep in the back, and tomorrow, they would keep out of sight as well as they could. . . .

He told Tandy what he had decided and held her close again, seeing the terror in her eyes, and, because she trembled so in his arms, he asked her to come with him to pick up the men.

She said, "Oh, yes!" so quickly and gratefully that he had to laugh, and they walked into Tafara to the truck.

* * *

AT nine-thirty he did not want to travel the Goromonzi Road again tonight, because the little truck had been back and forth along that road seven times since early afternoon.

The trouble was, Mutota and one of his men had still not appeared.

Mungu and Panebondo were back in the squatters' camp with Tandy, waiting to give him their information and their ideas, but Quimby cruised the highway near the Goromonzi turnoff going over in his mind for the twentieth time where he had left Mutota and his team, trying to remember what Mutota had said about how he intended to approach his reconnaissance, wondering if Muzingi and his men had made a visit to Victoria Farm. The others hadn't mentioned seeing any other parties of men; he himself hadn't seen anyone but the workers in the fields. . . .

He parked the truck off the highway just short of the turnoff and stood in the dark, listening, hearing a freight train puffing a mile to the south, hoping to God nothing had happened to Mutota and his man.

Quimby's concern had him thinking like a panicky mother whose child has disappeared; his mind manufactured every possible form of mishap: Some arrogant white tobacco grower had called in the Republic Police to investigate the actions of two men skulking through the fields; Mutota and his man were in jail. The commandos were already in the area and they had taken Mutota and his man and were interrogating them. Mutota had stepped on a snake in the high grass, or come across unfriendly baboons in the rocks, or broken a leg. . . .

Quimby's impatience and worry had him ready to yell. Where the hell were they?

He deliberately turned his mind to what he had learned during his own four-hour walk around the farmhouse earlier in the day. Bright sun and clear blue sky, great patches of black where some of the grasslands had recently burned, other great patches, biscuit-colored, unburned; the long cultivated fields of the tobacco farms, scored with parallel lines in the orange soil, marched over curving hills and disappeared; dark red rocks stood straight up on the ridges like the rocks he'd seen in paintings of medieval Italy; and whenever he looked up it was to a new vista of the miles-long valley with violet and pale blue hills in the distance. He loved this high African country. He loved being out in it.

Scrounging along the ground past tall anthills and blue-green lizards with orange-and-gold heads, he'd seen the details he needed to see.

The road into that farmhouse was the only road in and out. If the commandos came in that way they would have to return the same way. But they didn't have to use the road; the slopes up to the ridge were fairly easy; his own men could move up on any side. Cover was best in the grass, of course, but in the dark the grass was dangerous; he'd been lost in stuff like that several times during the war. On a cloudy night it was like being under water. You needed to see the sky; you needed a reference point.

He would want someone down at the highway to tell him if and when suspicious vehicles turned into the Goromonzi turnoff. Tandy could do that; they would need to get hold of a couple of radios.

He thought about how he should set up the farmhouse meeting so that the trap would be properly baited. It would be useful to have men drive up to the house and go inside as if they were the leaders, then pull out in the dark and hide in the rocks until this thing was over.

After what had happened in Lusaka, he felt certain the commandos would have observers in place to protect them from ambush and make certain that the ANC leaders were inside the house before they hit. He considered it highly probable that observers were already hidden in the Shaw Corporation barns, or in the high grass, and if he was right, they were probably wondering what the hell this Toyota truck was doing tooting back and forth hour after hour on Goromonzi Road. Three nights from now, despite the observers (if they were there), he had to put men inside the farmhouse, get them out in a hurry, and put them into position for a fight. He sure as hell didn't want to give the game away tonight.

He was dog-tired; his legs were stiff from walking and climbing. Each time he took a deep breath his ribs caught with a sharp pain where Muzingi had kicked him. Parts of his face were stiff, one eye was still puffed half-closed, and the swelling on his cheek throbbed like a misplaced headache. He wanted some sleep.

It was nearly ten. Mutota and his man were almost two hours late. He started the truck and turned at the cutoff to make one more tour up the Goromonzi Road.

AT ten-forty, Quimby entered his makeshift hut in the squatters' camp and found Mutota seated with Panebondo and Mungu and Tandy, grinning like a dark Cheshire cat.

"We walked right up to the farmhouse," Mutota said in explanation. "We knocked at the back door and asked if there was any work we could do for a meal and a dollar, and the white lady—oh! She was so glad to see us! She was building a wall, down at the end of the grass, a wall in front of her vegetable garden. The men who were supposed to do this didn't come out this week, and her own people were off in the village. We worked all afternoon, and she fed us and gave us each two dollars and drove us to the highway where we got a ride on a truck back to Tafara. Very nice!"

Quimby suppressed the irrational fury that had him wanting to yell at Mutota for worrying him so. At the same time he was immensely glad to see his friend's face. He returned Mutota's grin and asked, "What did you learn?"

"Gawd! That my arms and back are weak. That stones are heavier now than they used to be."

Then Mutota laughed and quickly held up his hands to halt Quimby's retort, and he hurried to answer Quimby's question more soberly: "We learned—it is a big house with a long veranda on the back, looking out over the valley. The great lawn—smooth grass, cut very short—could land two or three helicopters. We learned—there is a ditch as you come up the road to the house, on the south side of the road, starting thirty meters from the house and leading away from it for another fifty meters. It is a ditch made for people like us to crawl along or hide in. You cannot see it from below. You cannot see it from the house because there are bushes and flowers and the ditch is lower than the house. And . . ."

Mutota paused, obviously trying to remember what else would be valuable. Then he said, "We learned about the wall we helped build. Ten men could hide behind it and their fire could keep other men away from the house. . . . And . . . there are trails behind the servants' huts and out into the grass. We learned that the servants went for a vacation back to their villages yesterday, that the family will be away in the city for two days beginning tomorrow afternoon, that the children are being sent to England—"

Quimby interrupted with a slow clapping of his hands, expressing his approval and respect. Mungu and Panebondo and Tandy joined in, and when they had thus signified their gratitude for Mutota's work, Quimby said, "You were possessed by the spirit of the hunter today. Your information is of great value."

Mutota ducked his head, embarrassed by the attention but smiling his pleasure.

Quimby waited until they were ready to hear him, and he said, "Now, this is what I want to do. We will prepare three alternatives, three options, three ways to stop the enemy who comes in to kill the people in the house. We will assume that the enemy has twenty men, well-trained and well-armed, who have been brought to this farmhouse by truck or by helicopter. I will start with Mungu."

He turned to Mungu, looking at him gravely, and explained. "We want to know how you think the enemy will attack, and the best way for us to stop him and drive him off. We want to know why you choose the tactics you choose, especially what features of the ground or the rocks or the house or the roads made you choose your tactics. Mungu, tell us."

Mungu said worriedly, "But *you* must lead us, Muparadzi."

"I *will* lead you, good friend. But tonight we want to hear your ideas."

9

A LITTLE after one o'clock in the afternoon on November tenth, Tandy came near the doorway of Mutota's hut so that her shadow fell on the men inside. Quimby had been rehearsing the tactical options that had been decided on, thrashing out the details of who would move when and where. He was on his knees before the battle plan he had drawn on the ground with a stick, and he turned his head quickly, thinking she had come to warn that Muzingi was back. His team leaders looked up at Tandy and waited silently.

Quimby got to his feet and stepped into the bright sun. Mutota's hut was set on the low edge of the slope some distance from the other squatters' huts: safer for meeting and planning than the hut he and Tandy had abandoned. Still, he was very conscious of the people who sat around their fires on the slope above them, and he covertly scanned their faces, wondering who among them were Muzingi's informants.

Tandy tipped her head down respectfully, as if she were speaking to someone senior to her, something she did very carefully when he was with his men. She said, "Chitepo's here."

"Good. Did he bring the two-way radios? And the food?"

"Yes."

Quimby leaned back into the gloom of the hut and explained that he needed to meet with Chitepo. He promised that he would be back to work with them on the radios and arranged that at ten-thirty in the evening they would run a practice exercise on the farmhouse hill. Meanwhile, he suggested, it would be well to work with their men to get the three plans straight in their minds. "Every man must know exactly how he will move tomorrow night and where the rest of us will be, especially if we have to change from one plan to another," he said. "Above all be sure each knows which directions he must *not* fire from each position. We will be there to kill the commandos, not each other."

Mungo solemnly nodded his head in agreement, Mutota grinned cynically, and Panebondo lifted his eyebrows as if to say that he hadn't needed to be told that. Then Quimby asked each of them to have a man with a food bag follow him discreetly as he walked up the footpath into Tafara. "Don't let anyone see the radios," he added. "We'll take them into the field tonight to see if they work."

Taking a roundabout route, he walked up the slope with Tandy, moving slowly, as everyone but the children did here, wanting no curious minds wondering why this beat-up man and his woman were in a hurry.

His face was still misshapen on the left side where Muzingi had hurt him worst; his eye was still swollen, but better; his jaw was covered with four days' growth of beard, and he wore the jeans and woven dark blue shirt he had put on four days ago. They were red with dust and wrinkled from last night's sleep in the back of the Toyota. He felt that he looked so much like the other men in this sad place, except for the welts on his face, that he was practically invisible.

Chitepo sat inside an old gray Peugeot 504, watching four naked children in the street who were playing soccer with bare feet and a ball too soft to bounce. He got out of the car when Quimby and Tandy arrived, his tall body unfolding slowly to tower over the Peugeot so that they looked at him over the top of the car, and Quimby saw that he was grinning triumphantly.

Quimby came around the car, bubbling with excitement. "You suggested I put people to watch the airports and the customs stations," he said.

"You've discovered commandos coming into the country?"

"Yah! Two white men drove into Mutare late yesterday and went on to Marondera. They registered at the Wedza Motel. My people got curious because they drove a rental car from Mozambique and had Mozambican passports but spoke English like Afrikaners. Only an hour ago, two others came into the same motel, also from Mozambique. My man said two are young, two are older; they're all tough-looking. And here's the rest. Karwi's raid last night must have set off a warning. My man saw Charles Jameson go into the motel early this morning. He's meeting with those men from Mozambique."

Quimby felt a quick surge of hopefulness. "I'd give a lot to know who Jameson's friends are. I think Tandy and I should drive down there and have a look."

"Wait," Chitepo said, "there's more." He grinned apologetically. "Understand now, I'm just giving you our suspicions.

". . . Yesterday evening a safari van operated by a company here in Harare picked up twelve men who came through customs at Beitbridge, all of them from South Africa. They're supposed to be on their way to Victoria Falls, and they'll be arriving in Harare later today. At Beitbridge they told the customs officer they were insurance salesmen on a safari the company paid for because of their high productivity, but the man who spotted them says they're too young and fit and . . . unsociable . . . to be insurance salesmen. He says they've got legs like soccer players."

Quimby started to speak again, but Chitepo held up his hands and rushed on. "And we've identified another pair of tough guys. A white man flew in from Malawi last night, rented a car at the airport, and checked in at the Hunyani Motel in Harare. British passport. Another man came in on the same plane, rented a second car, and also registered at the Hunyani. Another British passport. I saw them having breakfast together this morning: thirtyish, very hard boys, stiff-backed, sunburned. My guess is we'll have some more of the same tonight when that safari bus arrives. I'll give you another guess: Some of these jocks will be out looking at Victoria Farm tonight."

Quimby found himself grinning. Chitepo's surveillance had paid off royally. "Pretty damned good, Peter," he said. "Was that group going to Victoria Falls carrying hunting rifles?"

"No weapons. Hunting season is over up there."

"So where are their weapons? Were they expecting to use some of the stuff at the gun club?" Quimby reflected a moment, and then said, "If these are the men we think they are, we could probably stop them before they get started, but we don't want to. We've got to catch them in the chicken coop with feathers in their mouths. Is this my car?"

Peter nodded. "I'll drive the truck back."

Quimby got out his roll of money, peeled off several large bills, and passed them over. Money for food, money to pay someone for the use of the car.

While Quimby watched along the isolated street for Muzingi's informants, one of Mutota's scrawny little fighters sidled up carrying a green plastic garbage bag. Tandy and Chitepo dropped a sack of cornmeal, tins of canned meat, and batches of carrots and onions into the bag, being careful to hide what they were doing.

The two-way radio, with its characteristic square shape, was a more difficult problem. Mutota's man solved that by putting it in the bag with the food; he hefted the bag over his shoulder, and shambled away, looking like one more squatter carrying all his belongings on his back.

After several minutes, another fighter came along the street and stopped to talk with Quimby, waiting quietly while his two brown paper bags were filled.

The third man came from the opposite direction. Tandy and Chitepo filled that man's faded military duffel bag, and when he had drifted away, Quimby said to Chitepo, "Lock up the car and let's walk a little."

Chitepo locked the car and handed Quimby the keys, and the three of them sauntered along the dirty street.

Quimby said, "Our plans are getting complicated. You've both got important roles to play tomorrow, each of them at least as important as what the men and I will be doing. I know Nkala wanted the ANC connection to be kept secret, but after tomorrow night it's going to be clear to everyone that at least you two have been involved. When that happens, we've got to sound off loud and clear so that everyone understands that the commandos—whoever the hell they are—are bloody assassins trying their damnedest to cut off the ANC's head. The whole world has to see that; otherwise the ANC leaders will never be safe. Here's what I want you to do. . . ."

JUST after four o'clock they approached the town of Marondera and turned away from the highway to seek out the motel where Chitepo had said his "strange tourists" were staying. The Wedza Motel, at the southern edge of the town, on the road leading south to Wedza, was not the best Quimby had ever seen, and not the worst: an L-shaped, one-story, whitewashed concrete structure with the clear blue of a pool tucked inside the L.

Quimby went through the motel's driveway, turned back out to the road, and drove the car to the square at the center of the city. They found a clothing store where Tandy bought a salmon-colored, cotton-and-polyester dress, panties and brassiere, a slip, and a bathing suit. Quimby found new jeans for himself, a pair of jogging shoes, another dark-red polo shirt, and a pair of crimson-colored swimming trunks. He began to think about things Tandy would need tomorrow night, and insisted that she get herself some heavy jeans and dark, strong-laced jogging shoes.

To carry their new clothing, they bought two small canvas satchels, and packed their purchases inside them.

At the Wedza Motel they went to the registration desk, where a bright-eyed black man eyed them doubtfully.

Quimby said, explaining their appearance, "We've been camping up in the Vumba. Some thieves beat me up and stole our bags. We've been to the stores in town to get some clean clothes, and now we need a shower and a good bed."

"The thieves up there would steal your hair if they thought they could sell it," the clerk said sympathetically. "They stole an old pair of boots from me about three weeks ago. How many nights?"

"Just one. I'll be glad to pay for it now."

The clerk nodded his head, accepting that offer. He watched while Quimby filled out a registration card, and turned to select a key from its box. "Room nineteen."

"Does that open on the pool?"

"All our rooms do. If you wish you can drive your car down to your left about halfway and park in front of your room. Better lock your car and keep your room locked when you're out."

They reveled in the clean room. The shower was made of enameled sheet metal that reverberated like distant thunder when they bumped its surfaces, and the water came out of the showerhead in a reluctant stream. But it was sheer delight to get clean and they stood in the main room with its bed and toweled themselves, enjoying the cool darkness and the privacy.

Because she was there and beautiful to look at, Quimby put his arms around Tandy, enjoying the cool-warm feel of her body. She hugged him close for a moment, then pushed him away, laughing up at him. "Don't forget what we came here for."

"I was beginning to."

He put on his swimming trunks and his new polo shirt to hide the tape on his ribs, and he watched her pull and pack her body into the one-piece yellow bathing suit. When that show was over, he went to the glass sliding doors that opened on the pool and pulled the heavy drapes back a little to study the pool area. Not many people; no one in the deeper water; children playing at the far end in a wading pool. Mothers—several sizes and shapes of them, sat in a clump under a green-and-white beach parasol, gabbling comfortably, ignoring their kids. Two big women stood like wet, black hippos in the wading pool, watching the young to keep them from drowning.

Just outside his door, three slim teenage girls lay on their backs, wearing dark bikinis, their skins various shades of black and brown, oiled and glistening in the bright sun. Beyond them two black men in their fifties—potbellies and spindly legs—sat in lounge chairs under an umbrella reading newspapers.

At his right, near the end of the pool, thirty feet away, was the white enclave. A middle-aged, flabby-bodied white woman with perfectly waved, blue-gray hair lay back in a lounge chair, a book resting open on her stomach, her dark glasses probably hiding the fact that she was snoozing. Close to her a man who looked to be somewhere in his sixties sat upright in a chair—pale pink-and-white skin, sandy hair, thick-looking in the middle. He wore a light blue robe over his shoulders, and Quimby guessed that he was either sensitive to the sun or ashamed of his fat belly.

The men he and Tandy had come to see were sprawled on blue-and-white-striped towels several feet beyond the elderly white couple. Three of them. He looked around the pool again for the fourth.

They looked like Rhodesian whites—one blond, two brown hairs, skins tinted from yellow-gold to brownish red, two of them long-boys with long-muscled arms and narrow hips, the muscles of their backs standing out in hard ridges. The third man was older, slab-sided, the bridge of his nose flattened; plates of muscles over his chest and arms and legs made him look like a model for an Italian sculptor. He looked powerful and dangerous, but the younger, leaner men, Quimby guessed, would be quicker fighters.

They were soaking up the sun, each of them wearing dark glasses and colored shorts, the two younger men lying on their stomachs, the older man on his back, legs splayed out, the bottoms of his feet showing gray-white.

Quimby turned back into the room, and Tandy was standing there in her bathing suit, all the curves emphasized by the contrast of the hard yellow against her purple-black flesh. Her face was tight and her eyes frightened. "Are they out there?"

"Three of them. How do I do this? Just walk up and say, 'By Jove, aren't you the commando boys from Mozambique? Jolly good show!' I don't want to spook them. I just want to hear them talk and know where they're from."

Tandy took her turn at the window, and he stood admiring her from the rear—beautiful legs, beautiful bottom, strong shoulders, all her curving lines outlined sharply by the sun.

She turned and bobbed her head when she saw that he was admiring her. "Why don't we just go and sit fairly close to them?" she asked. "If they talk at all we'll hear them. Can I swim a little?"

He nodded. They collected towels and made their way to a spot on the hot concrete surrounding the pool that put them so close to the white men that Quimby could see the red-gold fuzz on their forearms and chests, the thin nostrils and sun-bleached eyelashes. The slender men were in their mid-twenties, college age, trained down to taut skin and muscle. He was going to kill them because they were here to kill the ANC leaders, because they thought there was something about being white that made them superior to black people, because they thought that being white gave them the right to harass and humiliate and kill blacks whenever and however they goddamn pleased.

For a moment he regretted coming to Marondera. If he was going to kill these men, it was better not to have to think about them as human beings. He had always believed that the business of war would be easier if he were in an airplane, or firing artillery at long range, or shelling a coast from a ship. His mind tossed up quick and bloody pictures of killing he'd had to do in the bush— men whose faces he'd seen in agony and death, and the memories knotted up his guts.

He studied the older man. Looked like a regular army noncom, the kind that knew army and fighting and nothing else. Another professional.

The troopies of the Rhodesian Light Infantry, which Quimby's unit had fought in the war, had looked like the younger men, but the Selous Scouts had been a different kind of package altogether. That gang had let their beards grow wild; they ate whatever they found in the bush, never washed or shaved or cut their hair so that they would look and smell like bushmen; they wore any kind of rags that suited them and did their damnedest to look like blacks—painted their faces and necks and hands black and wore floppy-brimmed hats that came down over their faces. But their straight hair and blue eyes, and the shape of their faces and heads and bodies gave them away. Black scouts like Muzingi were the most dangerous because they could creep into a bivouac area and no one knew they were there until the shooting started. The young guys on the blue-striped towels looked like neat Rhodesian troopies. The older guy was a no-holds-barred Selous Scout type.

Chitepo had said they carried Mozambican passports. Who was that supposed to fool?

Quimby wondered again where the fourth man was. Up the road having a look at Victoria Farm? Or behind one of the curtains here, watching, guarding these three? He suggested the latter possibility to Tandy, and she nodded and said, "So I won't stare at them."

Tandy walked to the end of the pool, a few feet past the three men; she made a perfect flat racing dive into the water, moved into a slow crawl, swimming like an otter, and kept at it for several lengths.

Quimby considered going into the water, remembering how he had learned to swim in the Detroit River, swimming in water littered with garbage. They'd taught him to do better in the Delta

Force, but he'd never taken well to the idea of being a frogman. He liked having his feet on solid ground.

Tandy's swimming was attracting attention. The men had seen the dive, and they were all watching her move through the water. The older commando raised himself on his elbows and said something Quimby did not hear to the younger man nearest to him, and that one snickered. The other young one turned around and sat up in order to see better. He pulled his dark glasses off, and the look of sun-drugged boredom left his face to be replaced by excitement and lust.

"Hey, that's what we need, Jack," the lustful one said. "Nice black ass. We can screw ourselves to death the rest of the day. I volunteer to go first."

The older man chuckled comfortably. "Senior man leads," he said. "I might be through with her by dark. Wait'll she comes up here. I'll ask."

Quimby reacted with fury. Didn't they realize he could hear? Didn't they know that Tandy was with him? Were they so goddamned arrogant they thought that, since he was black, it wasn't important how he thought or felt? South Africans would act that way. So would some Rhodesian whites who were still around. Superior bastards, contemptuous of the niggers around them. Goddamn their souls. But what was their accent? He couldn't hear it. They sounded like Rhodesian whites, troopies. *Who the hell were they?*

Tandy rested in the water at the end of the pool for several minutes, then moved to the stairs by the diving board and came out of the water. All three of the white men were sitting up now, muttering comments to each other. Her eyes on Quimby, she started to step by the three white men, and the older one caught her by the wrist, twisting her around to face him. "By God you are a beauty," he said. "How about we make pom-pom in my bedroom?"

The young men snickered loudly, and Tandy raked the face of the man holding her wrist with her fingernails. He swore and swung an open hand at her stomach that hit her in the thigh, and Tandy raked his face again, producing instant red marks along his cheek. The man said, "Why you fuckin' *swart teef!*" and he rolled to his feet like a cat, reaching for Tandy's free hand.

Then Quimby was there, going in crouched forward, arms up. He hit the man a hard blow on the side of the temple with the side of his fist, not wanting to break his hand on that hard-looking jaw. The white man let go of Tandy, reeled backward a few steps, then caught his footing, and focused murderously angry eyes on Quimby. His teeth pulled back in a mirthless grin; he bent to pick up a beer bottle and came at Quimby holding the bottle out at the side like a club. The other two were up and separated, advancing at Quimby's left flank.

Talk, damn you, Quimby was thinking. Call me names, let me hear you swear, let me know where you come from. He ducked the swinging bottle and brought his knuckles up under it into the man's throat. He stepped to the side, letting the heavy body pass him, and turned, realizing that the other had turned more quickly and was coming on again.

The younger men were at his right side now, coming in warily, and Quimby knew he was going to kick the nearest man's kneecap if he took another step. He would have to stop that one, then meet the man with the bottle head-on. On his left flank the elderly couple was getting up, hurrying away, and the teenagers were screeching. Tandy stepped to his right, interposing herself between him and the two younger men, and Quimby, amazed and grateful, concentrated on his opponent and that bottle.

From the door of the room behind the young men, a big-framed, blond man in a blue leisure jacket and khaki shorts, stepped outside. He spoke forcefully, his voice like the sound of a whip: "Jack! *Staan!*"

All three of the men facing Quimby froze.

The man in the leisure suit spoke into the quiet with the harsh authority of a man who knows he will be obeyed: "Get in here!"

The older man looked rebellious, but only for an instant. He walked past the other two and stepped inside the room, still carrying his beer bottle. The others followed.

The man in the leisure suit, remained in the doorway. Tall, rawboned, and angry-looking, he spoke stiffly in English to Tandy and Quimby: "I offer you my apology for the behavior of my friends. I hope that no damage was done to the young woman?" Watchful blue eyes stared at them from under a thatch of hair and a set of bushy eyebrows bleached almost white by the sun. He smiled, a forced turning-up of the ends of his thin mouth that did not change his stern expression, and he added: "Indeed, it seems my man got the worst of this. Forgive him, please. He is drunk."

He did not wait for a reply, but stepped back into the room and pulled the glass sliding door and its drapes shut.

Quimby turned with Tandy and they returned to their room, both of them grinning. *Swart teef* was Afrikaans for black bitch; *staan* meant stop. Those were South Africans, no doubt at all, and he was going to fight them.

THEY used the scuffle with the whites as an excuse to announce to the clerk that they would not spend the night in the hotel. "My wife has been insulted," Quimby told the clerk. "You're allowing white riffraff in your motel."

He refused to permit the clerk to call the police, or take any other action. They left the motel quickly, and at Tandy's

217

suggestion, Quimby drove into Marondera and found a grocery store. They bought bread and sharp chedder cheese, thinly sliced cold roast beef, cartons of milk, a packet of butter, paper napkins and a plastic knife for spreading butter, and they carried their food back to the car.

When they were out on the road, Quimby asked: "How does a woman get through life? Men see you and want you and grab at you. How the hell do you get through?"

"It's been goin' on for a long time," Tandy said, grinning morosely. "Of course, most of us want to be grabbed, but we like to have the option of deciding who and when. That's called 'freedom of choice,' Ole Chifamba. I think I marked that man's face up pretty good."

"A tiger couldn't have done better. I'm going to be more careful around you from now on."

"Don't you dare." She flounced her pale pink skirt across the seat and leaned back, arms over her head, breasts high, giving him a mock-passionate look. "You can grab me anytime, but gently. I didn't help much, getting involved that way."

"That wasn't your fault. I got us into a stupid situation, and we're lucky to be out of it. If that commander-in-chief type hadn't come out and stopped us, we could be in jail now, and I would have been responsible for ruining the whole show." He threw a look of dismay in her direction. "Well, for Christ's sake, Tandy, was I supposed to just sit there and let them manhandle you?"

Tandy put a hand on his knee, smiling her thanks. "So what now?"

"Well, they're South Africans, that's clear. I do the dry run with the men tonight, and tomorrow night we'll fight them."

Minutes later, Tandy asked a question she had asked before. "Back there, you were ready to fight all those men instantly," she said. "What makes you so involved . . . so aggressive?"

He answered defensively, "What about you? You covered my right flank in a hurry."

She did not reply at once. Instead, she looked away from him through the window at her side. From the corner of his eye he caught a glimpse of a taut cheek, the lower lip caught between her teeth, and he saw her lift a hand and hold it at her throat.

She turned to him and moved closer and put a hand on his shoulder. Speaking slowly, she said, "You have to understand; the white policemen killed my brothers for no good reason. They put me in prison, and . . . Taylor . . . you have a right to know: White policemen came and raped me, one after another, as if it were a joke, laughing about it as if I wasn't even there. I know the names of three of them. I have their addresses. I'm going to see them punished if I have to do it myself. It isn't just for myself, but for all the others. . . . In the meantime, no white man will ever touch me without suffering for it, and I live for the day when we govern South Africa."

She moved away from him and leaned forward over the paper sack on the floor between her feet, her face hidden, busying herself with getting out the food.

Quimby put his right hand on the back of her neck, wanting to console her, to let her know his sympathy for her; he gently massaged the muscles leading up from her shoulders into her neck, and tried to answer her earlier question: "You said a little while ago that a woman likes to have the option of deciding who and when. I suppose something like that explains why I'm involved: Even black people should have the right to choose their options in this crazy world."

He noted the time: seven-forty-five. Twenty-five miles to Harare. He wanted to work out the plans for the dry run tonight and get in touch with Chitepo, but he didn't want to go into Harare until it was dark.

As he drove the sun went lower. In the softening light, valleys turned to dark blue and misty-looking greens; the granite domes at the edges of the plateau began to turn black. Quimby finished the sandwich Tandy had made for him and looked over, and she had already put hers down and was building another for him, looking busy and contented, enjoying this peaceful, domestic work.

Later, she put the remaining food back into a paper bag, brushing crumbs off her skirt. She gathered up his napkins and brushed off his knees, and when her housework was done, she moved closer and looked up into his face, half-seriously, half-mockingly. "Mungu and I agree about you," she told him. "You really are a wild ngozi, one of those spirits whose people were cheated the last time you lived here. So now you roam the land, and you'll never be happy until what has been stolen has been returned. But I don't care what you are. I love being with you; I want to be with you forever."

WHEN they reached Tafara, Quimby drove to the shanty-type carport they had been using for the Toyota truck, and brought the Peugeot in under the canvas roof. He turned off the lights and opened his door, putting the ignition key in his pocket, seeing that Tandy was already out of the car and reaching back inside to gather up the sacks that had carried their supper. He opened the rear door to get the carryalls they had bought to hold their new clothing, heard Tandy gasp and call his name, and saw men on that side of the car grappling with her, one with his arm across her throat.

Tandy started to scream, and as she did he was pushed violently from behind so that he fell forward over the backseat; as he fell, half in and half out of the car, hands grabbed at his arm and legs.

220

Tandy went on screaming, a piercing, high-pitched shrill of terror.

Quimby twisted his body, attempting to get himself turned around, trying to face the men behind him and get his feet on the ground so he could fight back. To do that he let himself slide down between his attackers to the ground, slipping away from the hands that pulled at him.

He came up on his knees, aimed a good shot at a man's crotch, and heard the "ooff!" of pain. He clawed his way to his feet, shoving a man away, kicking another's knee, having trouble getting his hands free because the men he faced were not hitting at him but were holding on, trying to restrain him. He understood at once that they were not here to kill but to capture.

He made use of that knowledge by butting his head into a face, bent and bit the fingers of a hand holding his wrist, put an elbow hard across a nose, and swung his head and shoulders vigorously, trying to fight free. The weight of at least three men was on him. One clutched his legs just below the knees, lifting his feet, and the others wrestled him to the ground and came down after him, hanging on.

He cursed and bit a man's ear and took a fist on the side of the head. He pulled one leg free and kicked out, and for that he got himself banged on the jaw. Tandy's scream went on and on, and it seemed to his suddenly confused mind that he heard other sounds, other voices taking up that scream, yelling in the street. A second punch landed on his jaw, and he had a bright clear instant when he knew he was going out; then black night swirled down over his mind while Tandy screamed and those others multiplied the sound.

SOMEONE was holding his upper body off the ground, rocking him, sitting on the ground behind him. Quimby regained consciousness thinking that he was still fighting those three men. He jerked himself forward, pulling his torso away from the man behind him, trying to twist around to face him. Then he realized that he was lying beside the Peugeot, that the man squatting at his back, hovering over him, was trying to help, and he became sickeningly aware of the pain in his jaw that made his whole head feel lopsided, oversized, sensitive as an infected tooth.

He held his jaw and asked, "What happened?"

The man at his back replied quietly, "I don't know. We heard a woman screaming, and a bunch of us came hollering along to find out what was wrong."

"There was a woman with me. Where did she go?"

"The people who hit you ran off down the street. A car started up over there and went off pretty fast."

Quimby thought about that, and asked, "Will you help me up?"

He leaned back against the Peugeot, fingers searching his jawline for the center of pain, realizing that the man who had helped him was not alone, seeing a little cluster of men and women and several children standing in the darkness, forming a neat semicircle behind the car, staring at him. He put his head back, wishing that his mind would clear, that the throbbing in his head would go away, and he knew that in spite of the way his head hurt, he understood well enough what had happened and what the consequences were going to be.

Someone, probably Muzingi's boyos, had come after him, but Tandy's screams and the people in the street had scared them off.

They had wanted him. They had taken Tandy.

He was not sure whether the cold block of fear in his chest was caused by his concern for Tandy's safety, or for what Muzingi's having her could do to his plan to stop the commandos. He felt a stab of guilt because he was thinking about Victoria Farm instead of Tandy, and he told himself that he should be thinking only about her. But the two were inseparable. He had to get her back.

Muzingi would abuse her, punish her, torture her. Tandy knew all about the plans for tomorrow night, and Muzingi would be damn glad to beat the information out of her. She would talk, of course; she wouldn't be able to oppose that brutal bastard, and he would learn how many men and weapons were going to meet the commandos, where they would be placed, and the crucial fact that no ANC meeting was actually taking place. That meant the plan was ruined. Quimby heard himself groan aloud: He had failed Nkala. He had failed Tandy. He had failed himself.

He pushed himself away from the car and stood upright, waiting for the ground to stop moving, and he thought: *No, by God. Not until I'm dead.*

With a grin of fraudulent embarrassment, he spoke to the little crowd of people watching him: "It is a personal matter. My wife does not want me to be with this younger woman, and the woman's brothers feel the same way. They have taken her away from me, but I should be able to straighten things out in the morning."

He thanked the man who had helped him, and the others for coming to help, and he stepped into the Peugeot and started the motor. He waited a minute until the street was clear; then he backed the car out and drove through Tafara toward Mutare Road, but before he reached the highway, he stopped the car off the road and turned the lights out. He sat breathing deeply, praying for the pain in his head to lessen, and thinking out what he had to do.

"GET dressed," he told Florence Mubaka. "Put on something warm and do it in a hurry. We're going out."

He had come up the drain pipe and the brick wall to her little fake balcony and had broken through the French doors. He had found her in peach-colored panties with a thin red dressing gown over her shoulders, and when she scowled viciously and headed toward her lingerie drawer, he beat her to the drawer and put her pistol in his pocket. He showed her his knife then, and explained how they would leave the apartment together quietly and successfully, without disturbing the guard he had seen outside her building.

Her lips drew back to show her teeth and she squinted hard at him. She pulled her dressing gown tightly around her nakedness and made her counterthreat. "I'm going to scream," she told him. "We'll have the police here. I'll tell them you came to rape me—"

"And will you also tell them that you and John Kado are managing an assassination squad that's killing the ANC's leaders? Will you tell them you're responsible for the massacre that's going to take place at Victoria Farm tomorrow night?"

Some of the anger and arrogance went out of her face. Her busy eyes widened, searching his face as if she had lost something very valuable there; the horizontal lines on her forehead multiplied until they went all the way up into the hairline, and he saw that her fingers were suddenly flat and still along her thighs. Her voice rose stridently: "What are you saying?"

"That the details of your conspiracy are known. The ANC and the Zimbabwean Republic Police know what's going to happen tomorrow night, and they will stop it and capture your commandos. Your role, and Kado's, are known. You are going to be arrested tonight, and if Mugabe's court feels mean about refugees who kill secretly for the SACP and the Soviet Union—and you know it will—you're dead."

Her wide-set, beautiful eyes studied him as she might have studied a black mamba coiled to strike, calculating its reach and deadliness. She stood straight, feet a little apart, chin up, the nipples of her small breasts standing up hard against the flimsy material of her dressing gown. Her fingers became very busy—brushing at her brow, touching her hair, pinching the wide bridge of her nose, rubbing at one of her eyebrows, reaching to smooth her gown over her wide hips, then grasping one another tightly.

"I don't understand why you are here."

"I came to help you get out of the country. Save your life. Maybe get you to the United States."

"Why would you do that? Are you CIA?"

"I want information. A little while ago my woman, Tandy, the woman with the iron skillet, was kidnapped by Muzingi's men. Tell me where I can find him, and I'll get you out of here."

He thought she suddenly looked relieved, as if she had been offered a reprieve after she had concluded there was no hope. She continued to stand quite still, lips pursed, her calculating eyes flickering over his face, the red-nailed fingers of one hand rubbing steadily at the back of the other.

"I don't believe you."

"The police know about Jameson and the gun club, and the commandos you and Kado have working for you. They've arrested Seifert, and they've put troops around the Soviet Ambassador's house."

She licked her lips, studying his face. Her glance leaped past him into the corners of the room at his back, making him think of a rat getting ready to make a quick dash for safety.

He was fervently impatient, wanting to shout at her to move, but he stood quietly. She was not looking at him, and he sensed that she was considering his words, the proposition he had made, trying to reach a decision, getting ready to leap one way or the other. At the same time, he thought, she must be thinking what it would mean to desert the cause and turn informer, betraying her comrades to save her hide. Would a woman like her worry about those things? Probably. He didn't know. More likely, she was wondering what kind of deal she could negotiate with him, how she could trick him into a noose.

He said, "If we're not out of here inside the next ten minutes, you're done for. I don't intend to wait until the police get here."

She grimaced tragically and replied in a language he did not know, but he caught its overtones of bitter resignation and knew that he had won.

Ignoring him, she dressed swiftly in a dark woolen suit and put on a light, cotton coat. She hurried through the room, throwing papers and jewels and clothing into a traveling bag; she took a packet of money and her passport from a drawer, grabbed up her purse to stuff them inside it, and stood for a moment looking sorrowfully about the beautiful room. Then with an imperious toss of her head, she led Quimby into the basement of the apartment house and out a side door, helping him escape the man who was posted at the front.

He brought her to the Peugeot and started it up.

"What are you going to do with me?" Florence asked. "You said you would get me out of the country."

"Tell me where I can find Muzingi. Where does he live? Where does he work?"

Florence moved to face him in the car, and she sounded disturbed, as if she were afraid that her failure to give him useful information might cause him to abandon her. "I don't know. I only met him last week when John sent him to protect me. Honestly, I don't know."

"Would Kado know?"

"I'm sure he does."

"Give me your key to Kado's house."

She peered at him through the darkness, hesitating, then rummaged in her purse and handed him the key.

He drove her to Chitepo's house in Chitungwiza, moving the car well inside the carport Chitepo had built. He explained to Peter what had happened and what he wanted, and Peter left the house to find two ANC men who lived down the street and who could act as Florence's guards.

"We'll keep you hidden here," Quimby told Florence. "Too many things are happening tonight. I'll come back late tomorrow night and start you out of the country."

She stood with her back against the front door, her face tight and her eyes filled with hard suspicion. "You lied to me," she accused. "You kidnapped me, and you don't intend to help me at all."

"I do," he insisted. "But I told you I want information. Look, I think I understand about John Kado. He's power-hungry; he's dreaming of becoming the ruler of South Africa. But who's back of your operation? Who's running your commandos? You've got mercenaries coming into the country, the assault platoon of Umkhonto We Sizwe, the gun club. . . . How many people are going to hit Victoria Farm tomorrow night?"

Her eyes hated him. "I don't have any idea how John does what he does. I do know that he's clever; he gets what he wants."

"Is Colonel Seifert calling the shots? Is he doing the Soviet Union's secret work out here?"

"I have no idea," she repeated stubbornly, her face smooth and expressionless. "I've been loyal to my brother, but I've never wanted to go along with the violent things he's done. He's too ambitious, too ruthless. I'm glad to be out of this. . . ."

"And of course you're the innocent victim," Quimby said, giving her no sympathy. "But what were you doing all that time you spent at the party school in Moscow? And did you enjoy your KGB training? I'm beginning to think you're the kingpin of this whole operation."

"Think what you like. You're a fool."

"I'm going to offer Kado a trade—his queen for mine," he told her. "Will he play, d'you think?"

She did not reply, but it seemed to him that he saw a gleam of interest or hope in her eyes.

Chitepo came bustling in and Quimby spoke to the men he had brought back, emphasizing how important it was to keep Florence out of sight and be prepared for searchers who would use violence to get her back. Then he headed for Kado's house.

HE let himself into Kado's half of the duplex with Florence's key and found John Kado, round-shouldered in his shirtsleeves, sitting over a table strewn with papers.

Kado looked around, curiosity, then anger and resentment, showing on his sallow face. He jumped up belligerently, and demanded, "What do you mean breaking into my house? What do you want? Who are you?"

"I'm Quimby."

Kado reacted swiftly, lunging toward a chest of drawers against the wall. Quimby hit him across the face with his open hand so hard that Kado fell to the floor and lay there, looking as if he couldn't believe what had happened.

"Listen closely," Quimby said, talking down into the wide, frightened eyes. "I have your half-sister locked up where you can't find her. Victor Muzingi's men captured my woman tonight out at Tafara. I want her back. I want her back now, tonight, and I want her unhurt. Whatever Victor does to her, I'm going to do to your dear sister twice as bad. If Victor beats her I'll beat Florence; if he rapes her, I'll hire a bull to rape Florence. If he disfigures my girl, I'll give Florence a face she'll never take out in public again as long as she lives. You see where we are? You and I have to find Muzingi before he has a chance to hurt my girl, or your poor sister is going to suffer. . . ."

Kado, stiff-faced, staring as if he thought Quimby was crazy, got to his feet and lifted a trembling hand to his reddened cheek. He pulled his gray tunic from the back of a chair and put it on, wriggling his back to settle the padded, square shoulders.

Quimby kept talking. "And if you're thinking, 'What the hell, let dear little old half-sister go to the devil,' let's keep thinking. She knows all your secrets; she knows how you've been betraying and killing the ANC leaders to get yourself into the ruler's seat, and you can bet your bottom dollar she'll talk when I twist her arms and burn holes in her feet. I'll get her words taped and sworn to, and they'll burn you. But . . . help me get my woman back and I'll hand back your sister. I want a deal, and if you screw around trying to double-cross me the people who are holding Florence will kill her. D'you understand?"

Kado's eyelids blinked frantically over eyes that stared with shock; he nodded his head emphatically, and moved slowly toward a closet, watching Quimby closely, indicating with his hands that he wanted to put his shoes on.

"What's the matter?" Quimby asked. "Have you lost your voice?"

Kado shook his head, and Quimby saw that the man's whole body was shaking, with fear or fury. "No one has ever hit me, actually hit me, before," Kado said, his heavy voice trembling. "I've never been involved in anything physical before. If I could kill you I would, but I want my sister free."

IN the car, Kado seemed to gain control over his trembling body. He told Quimby where they would probably find Muzingi, and listened attentively while Quimby outlined how he wanted Tandy's release to take place.

"You go inside and send her out. I'll be outside somewhere. You tell her to come out and walk down the street, and keep walking. We'll see what the situation is when we get there. I'll take her off, and if you or Muzingi make any effort to stop me, you kiss your sister and your career good-bye."

"How do I know you'll—"

"Give your sister back? You don't. But if you doubt me, why don't you come out with my girl? I'll take you to Florence. You. Not anyone else."

Kado examined that proposition for a moment; then he said, "I don't think so." He paused, looking at Quimby's face, and continued, speaking more firmly. "Listen to me, Quimby. It is vitally important to me that Florence should be free. It is absolutely essential. No matter what you think, I'm prepared to do whatever I have to do to get her back. For the moment at least you and I are in agreement. I will help you, but *you must free Florence!*" He put a hand on Quimby's forearm. "Do you understand what I'm saying?"

To Quimby, the resonant baritone belonged to a professional liar, a big-time con man. He didn't believe Kado actually valued anything but his own self-interest, and that seemed to mean that if he was so damned anxious to get Florence back, she must be very important to him or to his work. At the same time, Kado's persuasive tone, the emotional throb in his voice, the intensity of the anxiety he expressed, made his words appear to come from the heart. Was he calculating or was he feeling?

"What's wrong?" Quimby asked. "Are you afraid Colonel Seifert will flatten your head if you don't get Florence back in a hurry?"

Kado retorted instantly, his voice thundering inside the car.

"Goddamn Seifert! He doesn't tell me what my duty is. I want my sister freed. I don't care what else happens, I want her back, safe. Tell me what I have to do and I'll do it, but if you fail to keep your promise, I'll hound you and see you die."

"You'll get her back," Quimby promised, puzzled by Kado's heat, but still not convinced that brother-sister love had anything to do with Kado's anxiety.

They drove to a cluster of workers' hostels just south of the railroad, and Kado pointed out a run-down building with broken windows where he said a contingent of Umkhonto We Sizwe was quartered.

They put together quick arrangements about which way Tandy would turn when she came out; then Kado went inside the building.

Quimby pulled the car away, found a parking place for it, ran back to the hostel, climbed on top of a garage across the street, and settled down to watch the doorway.

While he waited, he began to think more coolly than he had during this last hour and a half, realizing that what he was attempting was foolhardy. At the same time the passionate interest Kado had expressed about getting his sister free appeared to be a plus. Quimby wondered if brothers and sisters were ever that close. Did half-brothers fall in love with their half-sisters? Or was that guess he had thrown at Florence earlier, that she was the kingpin in this operation, close to the bull's-eye?"

Much more likely, he thought, Kado had some trick in mind, and that brought his own mind back to the question of foolhardiness.

If Muzingi was inside that hostel with Tandy, he had probably already learned about the plans for tomorrow night. Right now, he was probably persuading Kado to let him take his men out the back door over there, scatter them around these streets, and then let Tandy come down the steps. And when I pick her up, Muzingi's people will close in and try to grab us both, Quimby thought. Or he'll refuse to do what Kado says. . . . Maybe he can't; maybe she's dead.

He thought about that somberly and decided that he would have to go in and find out.

He saw Tandy in his imagination, dressed in her bright yellow swimming suit, raking that Afrikaner's cheek with her nails; he saw her contentedly making sandwiches in the car and talking about why she was in this fight, and later, screaming while those bastards tried to silence her. Those images mixed together with Tandy in her dancing costume, Tandy standing over him with that skillet in her hand looking like the wrath of God, Tandy on the mattress in her nun's quarters, making love, and he knew that he had to try very hard to think rationally, to keep his attitude cool and professional, because the way he was thinking about her could cause him to make some idiot play to get her free that would ruin everything.

Keep cool. Be patient.

Muzingi could be pounding on her, cutting her, burning her. Shut up!

He was back on the ground figuring out which window he would enter, when Kado came out.

Kado stood a moment, looking uncertain, peering up and down the street; then he moved down the steps of the building and turned and walked in the direction Tandy was supposed to have walked.

Quimby waited until Kado was past him, then crossed the street. He ran behind the hostel, watching every shadow, and went on beyond it, following Kado from the backs of other multistoried buildings, slinking along the walls, trying to avoid the refuse piled everywhere, expecting an attack at any moment. When none came, he went forward more rapidly and got himself ahead of Kado. He moved closer to the street at the forward edge of a house, and when Kado approached, he whispered, "Kado."

Kado stood quite still, not turning to look at him, and spoke quietly, none of his great rhetoric sounding. "Muzingi isn't here. Someone came for him, and he left this place half an hour ago. The girl isn't here either. We have to go where Muzingi went."

Quimby considered Kado's information, peering back toward the hostel, looking for the trick, still half-expecting an attack. There was no reason at all to believe Kado's words, but he had nothing else to go on. He said, "You know what will happen to Florence if you're giving me the runaround."

He got no reply, but had the impression that Kado was anxious to get moving.

"Turn left at the next corner," Quimby said. "Keep walking. I'll pick you up in a couple of minutes."

THEY coasted to a halt above the huge house in Alexandra Park, and sat looking at it for several minutes. Then Quimby drove past it, studying the heavy hedges, the jacaranda and beech and fir trees surrounding every house, and long, curving streets cut by others as straight as rulers. This was a plush area with very large houses and yards, swimming pools, and extensive servants' quarters in the back. The grounds were heavily landscaped with bushes and trees and flower gardens, and with long hedges that locked each estate into its own privacy.

Quimby drove back around to the spot above the house, tight with the pressure of his fear that Tandy was inside with Muzingi, that Muzingi could be doing anything he wanted to with her. He was desperately afraid that he had wasted too much time kidnapping Florence, too much time with Kado at that hostel, that right now he was taking too much time trying to work out an escape route that could get her away.

"All right," he said to Kado. "In you go. Tell Tandy to turn left as she comes out of the house and walk toward the corner down there; at the corner she's to turn right. Remember, if Muzingi wants to play games with me it's your sister's life he's playing with."

He drove past Kado as Kado approached the house, and he returned along the route he had taken before. Then he brought the car back almost to the same starting place, but parked it out of sight of the house.

He got out and ran to the house and moved along its hedges, looking for a vantage point that would let him see anyone who tried to sneak out of its various doors. One side was blind except for basement windows. He made the assumption that Muzingi would probably not try to slip people through the front door, and he found a spot inside the hedge that permitted him to see the doors and windows at the back and sides of the house.

He had no idea what to expect, no clear plan about how long he would wait. Kado had said this place belonged to a "supporter," and had thought Tandy could be here because Muzingi had rushed here when he received the message at the hostel. Theoretically, Kado was in there negotiating for Tandy's release, Quimby thought, but he was a twisty, cunning, deceptive, arrogant bastard; he and Muzingi were bound to be trying to work out some filthy trick.

He moved his position, beginning to study the windows, thinking what he could accomplish if he went inside, how he would go in, and how he would try to get back out with Tandy. Kado had said, "a supporter's house." How many people were in there? Muzingi and Kado, probably three or four of Muzingi's people. The owner and his family?

Every goddamned minute was one more minute Muzingi could be pounding on Tandy.

He moved again, wanting to see the front door, trying to guess where the people inside would be collected, thinking about breaking in. But Kado was in there and he had made it clear that he was frantic to get Florence back. Give him a few more minutes.

The lights at the front of the house went out as the door opened. Quimby saw Tandy in the doorway before the darkness closed down, wearing that pink dress they had bought in Marondera. He felt his heart leap, and knew that no matter what Muzingi did now, he was going to follow his own plan and get her away from here.

He saw her pale form move to the street and turn left, and he ran along the hedges and raced back toward the car. Kado had seen him drive the car on past the house; if Muzingi intended to make a play for him, he might be expecting to see the car approaching from that direction.

When he reached the Peugeot, Quimby jumped inside, and rolled the window down on the passenger's side. Instead of using the starter, he released the emergency brake and let the car roll forward, using its impetus to start the motor, and he rolled on with his lights out.

As he passed the house, everything seemed quiet. He saw Tandy ahead, still seventy yards away, and he turned on his lights and raced up to her, braked and yelled to her: "Tandy! Tandy! Get in! Get in!" He held the door open for her, pulled her in, got her seated and the door closed, and pulled the car away as fast as the 504 could move. And Tandy was laughing and crying and yelling over and over: "Oh thank God! Thank God! Thank God!" She was grabbing his arm and pounding on his left thigh, and screaming words that meant only that she was out of her mind to get away from there. The Peugeot was roaring down the road too fast, and he discovered that he was yelling too, hooting and laughing like a fool, so damned happy to have her back that there were tears in his eyes.

THEY sat for almost an hour parked between other cars at the back of the parking lot at the Newlands shopping center, while Tandy alternately shook and cried from her experience and laughed and exulted that Quimby had got her out of that house. They spent a little time explaining what had been happening to them, he having to admit that he hadn't been conscious when she was taken. He told her about his abduction of Florence Mubaka, the way he had broken into Kado's place, how worried he had been that Muzingi would hurt her to find out what she knew, and he repeated at least ten times how damned glad he'd been when he'd seen her come out of that dark doorway.

Fortunately, she told Quimby, Muzingi had been somewhere else when they brought her to the house in Alexandra Park. One of the men had gone after him, and that had taken time, so that Muzingi had not arrived until some twenty minutes before Kado got there. "He didn't hurt me," Tandy said. "I mean not really. He slapped me everywhere, and told me all the things he was going to do to me, and I was so scared that I just blubbered and thought about what he would do when he got really started. I'll never understand how a man can be so brutal—"

She sat very close to Quimby, letting him hold her, trying to get over her fears, explaining what had happened. "I figured that a hysterical-woman approach was about as good as anything I could do; so I was hysterical, and I cried and yelled and screamed and drove them kind of crazy. It got tougher when Muzingi came in, but when he started slapping me I shrieked as if I thought he was trying to kill me the way he said he would. He asked his questions, and I kept crying and saying I didn't know, and I slowed him down, but I didn't know why I was doing that. I guess I thought he would kill me when he knew the truth. I didn't have any idea at all that my black knight was about to ride in and save me. O Jesus, Quimby! I would have told him sooner or later, whatever he wanted to know. He's terrifying. He's evil. . . . He hates you; he hates us both. . . ."

They had asked her who Quimby was working for, and she had said she thought he worked for the CIA. And what did she do? She was his girl. She worked at the hotel and in the market and at The Chief's Den. She was his girl, that's all she was. And Muzingi had asked point-blank, why she had helped Quimby kill people, and she had hooted and shrilled and ululated and shrieked, and said she didn't know anything at all about anything like that, knowing all the time that when he began to bear down she would tell him everything she knew.

"Well, you see," Quimby said, joking with her, but still troubled with the way he had thought about her and the ruin of his plan simultaneously. "That's why I had to come get you. I wasn't worried about you, but I *was* afraid you'd give my plans for tomorrow night away. I couldn't let that happen."

"Ah, you wonderful bastard!" She hugged him and patted him and lay back, sighing and chuckling. "Didn't you come down that street, though! What now, Sir Galahad?"

"Well . . ." He was reluctant to say it. "I'm supposed to get back and meet Mungu and the others. We're doing a dry run tonight."

"Oh God! Don't you ever quit?"

"This is important. My people have to know exactly what

they're doing. Listen, we can't go back to the squatters' camp. Muzingi's people will be out there again. I'll put the car out on Goromonzi Road under some trees. You can sleep there until I'm through."

She leaned forward, silently bowing her head almost to her knees. He understood that she was fighting the fear of being alone, and decided that it was impossible to leave her after what she had been through.

"Why don't you get in the backseat and put on those field clothes we bought for you today," he said. "Jeans, boots, sweater, something dark around your head. Come up on the hill with me."

She sat quietly for a moment. Then he saw her shake her head. "No," she said. "I've had enough for today. I'll sleep in the car."

10

AT TEN o'clock on the evening of November eleven, Quimby and Tandy watched twelve men load into two safari minibuses outside the Selous Hotel at Selous Avenue and Sixth Street. Six men in each bus.

Quimby carefully followed the buses to the western edge of the city, to the Hunyani Motel, where four more men got into one of the buses; then they followed again, hanging well back, as the pseudocamouflaged yellow-and-brown minibuses crossed the city and entered the suburb of Borrowdale. On Huntington Road, they turned into a tree-lined driveway that led beyond smooth-cut grass to a large ranch house.

Quimby waited several minutes on a side street, then drove by the ranch house, and turned in at a driveway well beyond it. He drove back slowly, wishing that he could see the front of the house more clearly. He wanted to learn if one of the cars in the garage at the side of the house was the rental car with Mozambique plates he had spotted yesterday outside the Wedza Motel. That would mean at least four more commandos had arrived. But the night was dark, the trees and shrubs were dense, and he gave that up and drove out to Salisbury Drive to take the fastest route to Goromonzi Road.

"That place is probably their armory," he said to Tandy. "They'll pick up their weapons, put on their work clothes and boots, go over their plans again, and head for Victoria Farm."

Tandy was sitting with her legs under her, her face tense with anticipation. She nodded and gave him a weak little grin but did not reply. He thought he knew how she felt: guts knotted up, fear making her mind consider all the bad things about to happen. The fight was inevitable.

AT ten forty-five, the old brown-painted minibus that had served as the storage place for Quimby's weapons puffed up the rough lane leading to Victoria Farm, and six thick-looking black men dressed in formal business suits got down and filed into the farmhouse. Quimby had insisted upon this step because he believed it was highly possible the commandos would have an observer in the area who would report whether the meeting of ANC leaders was actually in progress.

If that observer was watching the heavyset men move into the farmhouse, seeing the light in one of the front rooms coming on behind drawn shades, he could now report that the meeting was definitely on.

He would not be reporting that once they were inside the

house, the six men quickly stripped off their jackets and began to unstrap the Uzis and Kalashnikovs that had been tied under their arms or across their chests; he would not be reporting that two of them were carrying hundred-round drums of ammunition for the RPD belted around their waists, nor that they all carried magazines for the Uzis and Kalashnikovs in every pocket they had as well as on their belts. Nor would he be reporting that the six men left the house immediately, by the side windows and the long veranda at the rear of the house, crawling on their bellies through the flower gardens and bushes, and going very cautiously on all fours when they came to the open grass. He could not report about these things because Quimby's people skillfully made certain that no one saw them.

Mutota led his two wiry recruits, all three of them armed with Uzis, along the east side of the house toward its front, then down the slope of the hill until they reached the ditch that paralleled the approach road, which was really little more than a narrow, blacktopped lane. They did not move into the ditch but placed themselves about ten yards apart along its eastern edge. If the commandos knew about the ditch and made their assault up that narrow defile, Mutota and his men were positioned to fire into its whole length from the east side and bag themselves some hostiles.

Panebondo took his men to the north side of the house, then beyond it into the buffalo grass on the slope of the hill west of the entrance lane. His men faced almost due west and intended to fire in that direction if the commandos chose to come up through the high grass, but they were also prepared to fire to the southeast, catching the SAs on the flank if they came up the road or if they were driven away from the ditch by Mutota's fire. Panebondo and his men carried AK 47s because they expected to be firing at

241

targets some distance down the slope, and their bodies were misshapen by the bulges of the several curving magazines each of them carried.

At about the time Panebondo got his men in place, Mungu, puffing hard, reached the crest of the hill behind the farmhouse. He and his men had come in on foot from the Mutare Road, following a native trail through rocks and uncultivated fields. Mungu carried the RPD, the light machine gun, with three ammunition drums belted around his waist. A Kalashnikov was strapped across his back. One of his men carried the RPG, the rocket launcher, or as he called it, the "bazooka," and he and his buddy each carried three high-explosive rounds for the RPG on their backs. Their chests and middles too were fat with magazines for the Kalashnikovs.

Mungu paused behind the half-completed fieldstone wall to catch his breath and wipe the sweat out of his eyes. The night was quiet and clear, too clear. He would have preferred a good storm or a cloudy night. He could make out the dark outline of the house because of a light that glowed very dimly behind heavy shades at a window on the east side.

He placed his two men at positions behind the wall they had selected beforehand, and he gave them each an encouraging pat on the back. Then he left the cover of the wall at its eastern end, reluctantly crawling on all fours through the high grass that fringed the close-cut lawn nearer the house, wondering if Muparadzi was right to believe the SAs had an observer here. With the two guns and the weight of his ammunition, crawling was hot, hard work, but he kept at it until he was about twenty yards away from the southeast corner of the house.

Although he could not see it, he knew that he was about twenty yards from the upper end of the ditch. He also knew that the machine gun, which he set up on its bipod, could fire straight down the ditch from this position, that from this spot he could just as easily cover the road, the ground on the other side of the road, and if worst came to worst—if the attack should come from the rear—the smooth lawn on the south side of the house.

The men he had left at the wall were there to signal an attack from the rear and give him time to get his RPD turned in that direction, or, if the big noisy-birds came, they were to kill them with fire from the RPG. Muparadzi, he knew, thought of those two as his reserve, because they could be moved to support Panebondo or Mutota or serve as a base for a strong point if the others had to move back to that wall, but Mungu was not much impressed by the idea of a reserve of only two men.

QUIMBY'S watch hands showed eleven-two when he stopped the Peugeot on the Goromonzi Road about a mile in from the Mutare Road. He grabbed Tandy's hand and squeezed it, and said, "Remember, the highest point—where you were before. Turn your radio on now, and when they go by, press the send button and click your tongue three times. I'll hear it. Don't make another sound or you may give us away. As soon as they've passed, get over to Chitepo and help him keep his visitors happy. Leave the radio on, and I'll call to tell you when we're coming in."

She was getting the straps of the radio over her shoulder, and she was almost invisible in her dark trousers and sweater. He felt a sudden pang of loss, hating to see her go, and he leaned closer to her, putting a hand on her warm hip, pressing, wanting to promise her that he would be back.

Tandy turned quickly and brushed his cheek with her lips. "You be careful up there, Ole Chifamba," she whispered. "God bless you." She stepped out of the car, padded across the road, and disappeared in the darkness.

He drove the Peugot on toward Goromonzi, past the tobacco

farms, past the turnoff to Victoria Farm, further toward Goromonzi to a grove of eucalyptus trees and a dip in the road that he had decided earlier would prevent anyone near the farm from knowing that he had stopped. He parked the car off the road and hooked his radio strap over his shoulder, turning the radio on with the volume low; then he went back along the dark road until he reached a tobacco field he had reconnoitered the day before.

He walked toward the east down plowed furrows for nearly two hundred yards, climbed over a fence, went on for another hundred yards, and came to a fence that cut across his path; he climbed over a locked gate and walked along a fence-line that turned south, and he followed it until it stopped at an uncultivated field; then, bending low, he went across a section where the grass had burned away. Beyond this section, he entered the land of the Victoria Farm.

He mounted a smooth slope for seventy yards, came to the entrance lane, crossed that, and moved along the hill with all the stealth he could summon until he was certain that he was behind Mutota and his men. Then he went straight up the hill toward the farmhouse.

When he was high enough, a dim light from the side of the house helped him get his directions, and he went down on all fours and crawled through the buffalo grass, pausing twice to make a faint clicking sound with his tongue against his teeth, warning Mungu that he was on his way in. When he heard the sound returned he veered slightly and came up to Mungu's body stretched prone behind the machine gun.

Mungu took hold of his hand and laid it on the Kalashnikov and four extra magazines, and Quimby stuffed the magazines into his pockets, pushing the awkward box of the radio over to his left side so that it would not be in the gun's way. He let his fingers roam over the functioning parts of the gun, making sure that it would shoot when he wanted it to, wishing again that he had been able to give his men extensive target practice, regretting that none of them knew whether their weapons would actually fire.

It was too late to worry about the training, but his mind went on thinking about all the other ways he could have worked to help prepare the men more effectively. In a small action like this, in the dark, the individual soldier's initiative was everything. Once the shooting started, control became damned near impossible. Every man on his teams knew what he was supposed to do; each man had vast experience in bush fighting; and they all knew why they were fighting, but when guns were banging away up close, aiming at them, trying to kill them, it would be hard to get them to pay any attention to signals. Coordinating this action was going to be difficult. . . .

He knelt on one knee for several minutes, studying what he could see through the darkness. Mutota and his men were down here at his left, only a few yards behind where Mungu's machine gun pointed.

Panebondo . . . over there . . . In his mind Quimby crossed the ditch, the lane, went past the house thirty yards away from it, and into the high grass: *there*. Panebondo would be able to see the action over here; he would know what was happening on this side of the road as well as on his own front and flanks.

In his imagination, Quimby walked at the edge of the grass behind the house. Mungu's two were behind the wall, which he could not see from here but which he knew lay behind that smooth flat lawn where helicopters could have come in but weren't going to now because the commandos were arriving in safari wagons. Those two had the RPG and its ammunition. He had insisted on having the RPG brought up, but it would probably not be useful now, unless the commandos tried to drive their wagons right up to the front door.

He heard Tandy's tongue clicking against her teeth—three times, too loud—and he turned the radio off. He flattened himself on the grass, listening intently for the motors of the minibuses, and he gave Mungu a warning tap on the shoulder. He watched Mungo pull back the cocking handle of his gun and push it forward. He took his Kalashnikov off safety, and they both lay still, waiting.

THE commandos must have coasted down to the entrance lane with their motors off.

One moment, there was nothing; the next, Quimby saw men running hard up the hill on the road, turning away from it, and disappearing into the ditch, which he knew was there but could not see. The tension in his gut went up another notch, and he waited, giving those men who had gone into the ditch time to get themselves up on their feet, time to begin to come up toward the house. He wanted them in a neat line.

He was acutely aware that other commandos were charging straight up the hill across the road, heading into Panebondo's right flank. Somewhere, he remembered, he had read a poetic line about how American Indians "flitted like shadows through the dark forest." The commandos weren't shadows but solid dark figures, and they weren't flitting worth a damn. He could hear their heavy feet pounding the ground, the grunt of effort and the hard breathing of men running all-out, climbing the slope as fast as they could move, determined to hit the house in nothing flat. He could not tell how many men were coming up on that far side, and that worried him; they could be throwing in their major effort over there. Panebondo would need help, and Panebondo was holding his fire, waiting for the signal from here. He could be overrun.

Quimby tapped Mungu on the bottom, careful not to jiggle his shoulder where he held the butt of the RPD tight against his cheek. He whispered, "Fire!" and felt Mungu's body tense.

Mungu pulled the trigger for a long burst down the length of the ditch, pulling the muzzle up a little as he tracked along it, and the ditch exploded. There were cries of pain and anger; someone commanded hoarsely: "Get the fuck out of here!" Then Mutota's group began to fire into the ditch from the side, each man raking the sections he covered best. The yelling went on, and the commandos' guns burst into a jagged line of flame with a hammerlike roar that made Quimby wonder if every weapon they carried was automatic.

Quimby had expected that the first fire he opened against the ditch would drive whatever men lived through it westward toward the road, out into the open where they would be sitting ducks. Instead, they appeared to be coming out of the ditch to the east, straight into Mutota's fire. Mungu fired three more bursts, then pulled up, hesitating to fire to the east of the ditch because Mutota and his men were there.

Quimby saw by the flashes of the Uzis that Mutota and his men were pulling back, firing as they went, falling away toward the east. He told Mungu that and Mungu began to fire into the grass along the ditch, and Quimby came to his feet and threw his own fire at the flashes there.

It was clear that the commandos' aggressiveness could end in their overrunning Mutota and this position up here, and Quimby poured fire down steadily, pausing only to try to see how far back Mutota was withdrawing.

The commandos returned his fire, allowing Mutota to get himself set in a new position, wherever the hell he had got to. Quimby got to his knees, and said, "Come on!" to Mungu. He scrambled to a new position and changed magazines and fired again and paused to look again and decided that the commandos were being pushed by a demon who insisted that they advance at any cost. They had to be taking casualties, but they were moving their line rapidly eastward, flanking him, flanking Mutota; they were almost so far east now that they were behind Mutota.

From the position of the flashes he could see on the other side of the entrance lane, the commandos were doing the same kind of thing over there, flanking, moving further to the west and north. They appeared to be far enough around already to be beyond Panebondo's little line. Unless Panebondo moved his men he would be flanked from the north, forced to turn his back on the action over here. Quimby understood that each piece of his miniature army was being isolated.

As he listened to the sound of the Kalashnikovs' dry, clacking reports and saw the flashes, he realized that Panebondo was already firing due north, and he saw the danger of what was happening. The commandos were running a double pincer movement, circling outside; they were apparently intent on destroying each separate position or crowding his people back into the cleared area around the house where there was no cover at all, where they could be shot down like the white rabbits on a chain at a carnival. They were making a swift war of attrition out of this, wanting everything—wanting his men and the ANC leaders who were supposed to be inside all dead.

He thought: Screw this! He wasn't prepared for a long fight; his people didn't have enough ammunition. Besides, if this thing went on too long, every unit of Mugabe's army would be out here shooting at anything that moved. He had to stop this blitzkrieg right now. He pulled at Mungu's shoulder, his mouth at Mungu's ear, yelling: "We move! Mutota needs help!"

He and Mungu ran to the east, radio and magazines and ammunition drums bouncing, and as they moved a little higher on the hill, they looked for the rifle flashes that would tell them where the enemy was, where Mutota was.

As well as Quimby could tell, Mutota had come up the slope. He and one other gun were firing from the forward slope of the hill only twenty yards away, and at least six guns were coming up at them. Holding onto Mungu's upper arm, Quimby pulled him further east, trying to get to a firing position where he could rake that commando line from its flank.

They fell together into a small declivity on the ground, and stayed there, Mungu working in the dark to remove an empty drum and attach a new one, pulling the belt through as they had practiced so many times, cocking the gun and settling down behind it to fire. Kneeling above Mungu, Quimby saw the tracer path of the gun's first burst, corrected Mungu's aim, and then shouted that he was on target. Then he began to rake that area with his Kalashnikov. He had flanked the flankers; they would have to run off to the south or the west now. At least he had broken up this end of the pincer.

He stopped firing for a moment and yelled, "Mutota! Up here!" And he kept firing while Mutota and one of his men came up through the grass and knelt at his side, breathing hard, swearing, wondering where they had lost Dikita, the other wiry little man in Mutota's team.

With his arm over Mutota's shoulder, he told him, "Drive those bastards back now. We've hurt them enough that they can't keep coming. Try to connect up with Panebondo across the road. And remember, *I want prisoners!*"

He pulled at Mungu again, and together they bumped their way back toward the west, along the slope in front of the farmhouse but above the ditch. They crossed the entrance lane and came up to the smooth grass in front of the house, hearing bullets crackling above their heads, unable to see Panebondo's line. They went forward on all fours then, still harassed by bullets snapping above their heads, and they saw that five or six guns off to their left were firing toward a clump of rocks higher up the hill.

Panebondo's Kalashnikovs were firing from the rocks, and Quimby pulled Mungu forward, feeling the shock when Mungu took a bullet from somewhere, feeling Mungu jolt and fall sideways, grunting with pain. He fell with Mungu, anxious about him, worried about the machine gun, and apprehensive about Panebondo and the fire that was pinning him down in those rocks just below.

"Where?" he whispered in Mungu's ear, and he let Mungu take his hand and pull it down to his right thigh. He felt the hole in Mungu's trousers, ripped at it, and pulled the rip wider. He felt the wound high in the thigh, dreading the discovery of shattered bone and blood pumping uncontrollably from a ruptured artery, but he found only a small neat hole high on the outside of the thigh, another at the back, and he was infinitely grateful. Even if the bullet had grazed the bone, Mungu would live, Mungu could function. With a feeling of intense relief and gratitude, Quimby realized how much he depended on this quiet, strong man whose loyalty was so absolute, who had fought under him so usefully. They had been together for a long time. . . .

He explained to Mungu what he wanted to do, and he took the machine gun and the last two of the ammunition drums from him. He handed Mungu his Kalashnikov and two magazines, and moved forward to the edge of the grass, set up the RPD, and began to fire at the flashes in the buffalo grass.

At their backs, high above their heads, a single blue flare exploded in the sky, throwing a blinding garish light over grass and farmhouse and fields as unreal as the artificial glare of an immensely powerful fluorescent bulb. Quimby ceased firing for a moment to look up and back at the flair swinging slowly downward on a little white parachute. Around him, other guns went silent while the men on the ground pondered the significance of that light.

He heard the throaty, unmistakable phut-phut of powerful engines and fast-turning rotors. Helicopters. And he knew instantly that he had been outthought and was about to be outgunned. The sons of bitches were bringing in reserves. Gunships or more troops. Maybe both.

It seemed to him that he should have known from the way the fight had been going that he was being manipulated; he should have understood that his people were being drawn out to the sides of the farmhouse, clearing the landing place in back so that a reserve could come in and cut his people down from behind. The choppers could hang in the air, put on their searchlights, track him and his people wherever they ran; they could throw down rounds from their 30- and 50-caliber machine guns, or blast away with heavy rockets.

He considered calling his men off, running with them into the buffalo grass before the choppers arrived, but that would be stupid and suicidal. Besides, he had to win; he couldn't give up; he had to have prisoners, evidence that would prove who these commandos were to the whole world. There had to be some way to beat these people. Agonized by the thought, he wondered how many of his men were still alive, how many would be alive when the choppers finished their work.

At his back, a commando's grenade launcher tossed a red flare on the grass behind the farmhouse, lighting the landing pad. The roar of the helicopters was louder now, and he guessed that they must have taken off from somewhere in Mozambique at a specified time so that they could arrive at this spot at just this moment. Someone in the grass must be talking to them right now, telling them where the "terrorists" were, telling them how to land. There would be more fighters coming off those damn things. . . .

Quimby pulled the bipod out of the ground and lifted the RPD. He wriggled backward a few feet and stopped at Mungu's side and asked the big man if he thought he could make a run to the house with him.

Mungo grunted a painful, "Let's go," and heaved himself up on his knees, waiting for the signal.

The two of them ran in the shadow of the farmhouse, across the front lawn, to the east side, where the van that had brought the pseudoleaders of the ANC was parked twenty yards from the house.

They crawled under the bus and moved forward so that they could see the span of grass at the back of the house lighted by the red flare that gave the whole area the unreal look of another planet or the lips of a volcano.

Quimby explained what he was thinking: "There'll be more men coming off those things. We'll cut them down from here; otherwise, the rest of our men are going to get it in the back."

"How many noisy-birds, Muparadzi?"

"Two I think. Maybe three."

"Different sound. Bigger sound than years ago."

"Yes."

"We won't get out of this, Muparadzi. Did we do well?"

"We've hurt a bunch of them. We *will* get out. We can't let them win."

It looked like a HueyCobra gunship. He hadn't been watching the changes in gunships these last three years; he wasn't sure what it was. Rocket pods clustered under short, vestigial wings, four on a side. It came in very low, no more than a hundred and fifty feet, and sat in the sky about two hundred yards away.

He watched the missiles flame and leap out—two, four, six, eight—all of them going into the farmhouse, exploding inside, blowing the windows outward, glass sprinkling against the van and on the ground, the sound of the explosions deafening because he and Mungu were so damned close. Heavy artillery, blasting the building apart. If anyone at all had been inside the house, they would have been killed by the first or second rocket. This was overkill.

He thought he was beginning to understand the commandos' plan. They had pulled those flanking moves to get out of the way of the rockets, but they were close enough to the top of the hill, out on the flanks, to come in when the helicopters had put their rockets into the house; they probably intended to come in and mop up his men and the men who were supposed to be inside the farmhouse. He and his men were caught inside the circle. He had to get them back down the slopes, but not while the helicopters were staring down at them.

The gunship fell away, going off to the east, and Quimby waited for the next one to come in, knowing that he and Mungu were lying right next to the target and that the van above them was itself an attractive target.

The noise of the helicopter coming in seemed twice as loud as the first one, and it came much closer, hovering above the house, blowing dust and grass around the yard, as if a small tornado-in-reverse was blowing downward against the earth. Its searchlights turned on suddenly, making the whole area almost as bright as day, giving every upright thing a strangely foreshortened shadow.

Quimby saw the greenness of the grass, the crazy-sharp lines of the shanties down beyond the grass, the edges of the dry buffalo grass where it drew its sharp lines around the yard, the coarse, wooden planking of a barn with its cracks and knotholes and sagging wide doorway, the half-constructed yellow stone wall off to his right, even the granite pebbles and red dirt around his fingers.

He inched forward, wanting to get a look at the chopper, hating the need to look up at what was going to kill him, knowing that the men up there could see the tiniest movement down here, knowing that they could spray more bullets in a few seconds than all his men had.

He had to stare a moment, trying to see up past the bright lights. A helluva big thing. Square, bulky-looking, a line of square windows. But not a gunship, only two parallel mounted machine guns on this side. It resembled the big ambulance choppers that had been used in Vietnam. He recognized the make. . . . It was a Bell Helicopter, the UH or HH-something, rigged as a troop carrier. A troop carrier, by God. Had a capacity of fifteen, maybe twenty men, how many exactly he wasn't sure.

Some three hundred yards away from the lighted troop carrier, another one hung back in the dark, its motor roaring, waiting for word to come in. Another fifteen or twenty men; too goddamned many . . .

The machine guns above him began to fire at the same time that the helicopter began its descent. The pilot left the lights on and came down carefully but quickly, like the pilots in Vietnam—brave but not exactly happy to be floating in the air with the whole world shooting up at them. The landing runners touched the grass and settled, but the rotor kept turning, slamming air and dust in every direction. The searchlights went out.

Quimbly settled behind his gun, sighting on the door that would slide back, and took a good breath, ready to pull the trigger when men started to pour out.

Someone slid the door open and Quimby saw the inside of the helicopter, lighted by the red flair. He caught his breath and let it out slowly, shocked. The chopper was empty. His mind raced in search of an explanation, looking for theories that would explain *that*, and he knew at once that he had misread this part of the commandos' operation. The choppers were here to take the commandos out of the country after their job was done.

He cursed himself for being stupid, for being chicken, for deciding that he was dead before he was hit, for running away after the first mortar round hit. He despised cowards, weakbellies, people who jumped at conclusions because they were scared, and he held himself guilty of all the charges. Like an hysterical old mammy. Like a dumb kid in a Detroit alley running from a cop with a short-range shotgun. All right, he knew what the score was now; he was fighting men from South Africa's Defense Force; that was clear from the insignia on the helicopters. This was what he'd wanted. And he was not going to let these bastards get away; they would go back to Pretoria and Johannesburg and get medals and spend the rest of their motherfucking lives bragging about how they went into Zimbabwe and killed a lot of *kaffirs* and flew merrily out. Piss on that! He was here to disgrace them and their whole fucking country and he was going to finish the job.

He shifted the RDP back to Mungu and unstrapped the ammunition drums he carried. He yelled into Mungu's ear, "I'm going across and put an RPG round into that helicopter. Do what you can to keep these people busy."

Mungu seemed to see the sense of that and grinned, white teeth and eyes in the darkness, and Quimby slid himself backward under the van until he was behind it. He stood up, crouching, and edged his way to the front end, then sprinted toward the stone wall, the radio box banging against his hip. He heard firing behind him. Mungu's. Other firing down the hill where Panebondo was. He heard the snap of bullets past his ear, and as he ran, he saw the pilot and navigator in the bubble of the helicopter looking out at him, felt the hard, hot wind from the rotor pushing down at him, and resisted the strong desire to bend low because of the helicopter blades, although they were at least six feet above his head.

Then he was over the wall, hearing bullets smash into the stones, looking down at Mungu's two men, one of them lying on his back, the other on his knees, doing something to the prostrate man's head.

Quimby grabbed up the RPG and felt in the darkness to make sure it was cocked. He touched the round the men had already placed in the launcher, making certain that it was up and in place. He felt the front end of the projectile: The nose cap had been removed, but the safety pin was still in the fuse. He went up on one knee so that his head and half his chest were above the wall; he removed the safety pin from the fuse, aimed at the huge body of the helicopter, and pulled the trigger. He remained there kneeling, hearing the bullets snap around him and feeling foolish and helpless and desperately frustrated because the projectile sat dead at the front of the launcher. Misfire.

He fell backward, that being the quickest way to get down behind the wall again, swearing when his elbow struck against a rock. He rolled to his hands and knees, reaching out to the man at his side, demanding: "Give me another round. Take this one out. Careful." He screwed the cylinder containing the propelling charge into the rear end of the new round, convinced that it was taking him far too long to get it done. He removed the cap from the head of the projectile and pulled the safety pin and took up his position again. And when he was in position, he cocked the launcher, thinking irrelevantly that here he was kneeling as if he were in church in front of a bunch of bastards who were trying to kill him.

As he aimed, meaning to put the round into the middle of the helicopter, its searchlights came on again, momentarily blinding him. The helicopter's motor roared and the huge body lurched awkwardly into the air.

Quimby thought exultantly: By God, I've scared him; he thinks I've got one of those heat-seeking missiles that can blow him to bits. He pulled the trigger, aiming now at the middle of the bottom of the helicopter. The round started with a good explosion and it hit the helicopter, blowing off with a sharp orange-white blast that he could not hear because of the noise of the motor.

He'd hit the damn thing; he knew he'd hit it, but the chopper, instead of blowing up in a great whoosh of red flame and black smoke the way they all seemed to do on television, simply continued to rise and turn, and begin its trick of falling forward above him, going away fast. He hadn't hurt it, only scared it.

Then he heard the high shriek of tearing metal, and a great sheet across the bottom of the chopper tore away but did not fall off, and the chopper moved off, sailing east but losing altitude. Its lights were still on. Quimby lay on his back behind the wall and watched the injured bird moving away but appearing to go lower and lower. At the end it seemed to be going down more rapidly, its searchlights probing the ground beneath it until it landed about two miles down the valley.

The pilot of the helicopter that had been standing back out of range had seen enough; he turned his ship and went after the first, flying high. He landed when he came to the place where the other chopper was down, and in less than a minute, Quimby heard the distant roar of its motor, and it was in the air again. On its way back to Mozambique and points south.

Quimby let the rocket launcher fall and cupped his hands around his mouth, and in the quiet left by the helicopters, he roared, "Commandos, it's over! If you're still alive, get up and walk in toward the house with your hands over your head. We're taking prisoners, but if you don't come in we'll kill you."

He paused, getting another breath, his mind feverishly beginning to think about all the things that had to be done now. He didn't expect many men to walk in voluntarily with their hands up; if they could crawl, they would be moving away like lizards, determined to make it back to South Africa. He cupped his hands around his mouth again, and yelled, "Panebondo! Mutota! *I want prisoners!* Bring them up to the van!"

THERE were five prisoners, three of them exhausted and angry but unharmed, filthy in their dark green fatigues, black boots, and tams, their faces white under streaked black greasepaint, rings of red around blue and hazel-colored eyes. Two were wounded, one very seriously with part of his chest shot away, the other holding his lower leg, where a burst of bullets had stitched three neat holes through the muscles of his calf. Mungu, sweating and limping, herded them into the van and got in to guard them, and Quimby checked with his other team leaders to learn what casualties they had suffered.

Three of his men were gone; he had to presume they were dead, two were scraped from falls they had taken rushing around in the dark. Mutota had been grazed along one shoulder blade by bullets and had been hit in the arm just above the elbow. Mungu had the leg wound, and one of Mungu's men had been hit in the face by fragments of that stone wall when bullets had sent a shower of splinters flying.

A high casualty rate, but Quimby believed that the commandos had suffered much worse. He tried to tell himself that it was worth lives to make the point that South Africa had to stop its murderous invasions, but the letdown from too much adrenalin and fear and excitement, too much all-out running, and the fact that the battle was over, was beginning to hit him. It wasn't possible to balance lives with the worth of a mission; the equation never worked; the missing men were friends, men he'd lived with and fought with; nothing was worth their lives, but there wasn't time now to mourn for them.

He handed the Peugeot's keys to Panebondo, who intended to drive it into the outskirts of Goromonzi, taking along all of Quimby's men except Mungu and Mutota, planning to hide them in a half-burned garage until late the next day when some of the excitement about this shoot-out might begin to die down. Only then would each man make his way to his home.

Quimby turned on his radio and said, "Chifamba calling Tandy. Over."

She was back instantly. "This is Tandy. Are you all right? Chifamba, are you all right? Over."

"We're as well as can be expected," he told her. "We're coming down now. Five prisoners, two of them wounded, one very seriously. Mungu's hurt and so is Mutota. You'd better call that doctor over in Ruwa. Over and out."

IN one of the rooms of an abandoned farmhouse three miles north of Goromonzi, Peter Chitepo had rigged a kind of courtroom. A battered table stood at one side, with two chairs behind it and a kerosene lantern at one end, lighting that side of the room. Across from the table, and facing it six feet away, sat a folding chair Chitepo had brought along, and behind that a smaller table and another lantern. Wallpaper hung in tatters from the walls. Vandals or squatters looking for construction material or firewood had stripped the walls to get the laths; a part of the wooden floor was ripped away, and the glass was out of the windows, screened now with layers of dark plastic.

Five men sat on two benches made of boxes and planks, facing the courtroom scene. Two of them held square Hasselblad cameras in their hands and carried 35-millimeter cameras hanging from their necks. Photographers' gadget bags lay on the floor.

The other three men were international correspondents of important newspapers in three non-African countries.

Chitepo had worked for a day and a half to get the correspondents into the house, and he had told Quimby earlier in the day that he'd had to move heaven and earth to get them to come. They had been suspicious but curious, afraid of being used for some kind of propaganda stunt, and chary about putting their lives in jeopardy. He had not told them what the meeting they were to attend was all about; he couldn't do that, but he had persuaded each man individually that the story he would get might be one of the most important he would ever write for this part of the world. Then, hours ago, he and Tandy had met with all three of the correspondents, refreshing their memories about the ANC's aims and organization and its uneasy relations with the threatened countries who were its hosts, and reviewing the facts about South Africa's persistent effort to drive the ANC out of the Front Line States.

The round-bodied, pug-nosed, cocky-looking man in jeans and a red, cowled sweatshirt was Robert Collins of the *New York Times*.

The safari-suited blond man with the tanned face and thoughtful blue eyes was Hans Schrecker of the *Frankfurter Allgemeine Zeitung,* and the cynical-looking baldhead wearing tan gabardine trousers, boots, a worn leather jacket, and making an aromatic stench with his curved-stem pipe, was George Arnwell of the *Manchester Guardian.*

Important men, representatives of newspapers that enjoyed immense respect around the world, powerful men who publicly judged and condemned governments and their great leaders every day.

Quimby had also wanted someone from the Chinese Communist news service, *Hsinhua*, and someone from India, but their correspondents were in Mozambique and had refused to come up to Harare without a clearer description of Chitepo's story than he had been able to give them. The three Westerners would have to do.

Peter Chitepo, his long face looking tired and excited, met Quimby as he came through the door. He listened to Quimby's quick account of the fight and the clear evidence of the helicopter's insignia that proved the commandos were members of South Africa's Defense Force, and he brought Quimby to the front of the room.

Facing the correspondents, Chitepo made a brief little speech, explaining the situation both to Quimby and the correspondents.

To Quimby, he said, loudly enough for the correspondents to hear, "I've explained to these gentlemen what has been happening up on the hill. They heard the shooting and the helicopters. They may or may not believe what I told them about it."

To the correspondents, he said, "This is the leader of the little private band of South African and Zimbabwean patriots who have prevented South African commandos from slaughtering the leaders of the African National Congress. His men have taken prisoners, and he is going to interrogate them here. I will ask you to remain silent while the interrogations are going on, although the photographers are free to take pictures. We do not know what these prisoners will say, but you must understand that they have come straight from the battlefield. Two of them are wounded and are receiving medical attention in another room. We will bring them in if that is possible. When the interrogations are over, you will be free to ask the prisoners any questions you wish for as long as you wish." He looked around at the faces in front of him. "Is this an acceptable procedure?"

The German, Schrecker, lifted a hand and leaned forward, peering hard at Quimby. "What happens to the prisoners after your interrogation?"

Quimby had been standing with his Kalashnikov held in both hands. He placed it on the table and turned back, lifting his shoulders. "Do you mean, are we going to shoot them? No. If you like, we'll hand them over to you. You will probably want to turn them over to Mugabe's police."

There were no other questions. The correspondents sat looking at him with skeptical "show-me" stares.

Quimby sat behind the table on the left side of the room. Chitepo went to the door and opened it, and Mutota, his arm bandaged, looking as wild and filthy and murderous as Quimby had ever seen him, pushed a man into the room by poking his Uzi into the man's back.

The tall, blond commando had black greasepaint streaked on his face and in his hair; powdery-pink dirt covered the front of his dark green fatigues. Mutota told him to sit, and he sat, making an obvious effort to be calm, his red-rimmed eyes looking fearfully around the tattered room, then flickering back and forth between Quimby and the correspondents. His whole body was shivering violently, whether from cold or shock or terror it was impossible to tell. His hands trembled in his lap, and he looked down at them curiously for a moment, as if they might belong to someone else; then he carefully placed both of them between his knees to hold them quiet.

Quimby had a good idea what Mungu and Mutota might have told the prisoners about these proceedings. In the old days the practice had been to let a man think that if his captors did not believe he told the truth, he would be shot at the end of the interrogation. He had always questioned prisoners immediately after the battle while they were still on a frenzied high, half out of their minds from seeing their comrades killed, terrified by being in the hands of the enemy, certain they were going to be killed. During that brief period they were usually ready to tell their captors anything they knew in order to keep themselves alive.

He plunged into his interrogation without explanation, harsh-voiced and demanding: "Give me your name, your rank, and the name and number of the unit you belong to."

The commando threw him a startled, black-faced stare, sat up straighter, and rattled off the information: "George van Devanter, corporal, two-oh-five commando regiment, three battalion, H company, Third Platoon."

"Where is your home base?"

"Phalabarwa."

"In what country?"

"Republic of South Africa. Phalabarwa is east of Pietersburg, close to Kruger National Park."

The correspondents began to write in their notebooks. One of the photographers left the bench and sat on the floor facing the prisoner, taking close-ups of that frightened, grease-stained face. The other moved behind Quimby, his flash working overtime.

Quimby asked: "How many men came into Zimbabwe with you from Phalabarwa?"

"I don't know exactly. Twenty, I think. There may have been others on the helicopters."

"How did you get into Zimbabwe?"

"That was all legal. We came across the borders as tourists."

"And your weapons were ready here in Harare?"

"Yessir. In a house. A South African lives there."

"What was the purpose of this invasion?"

The corporal pulled his right hand away from where it had been captive between his knees and rubbed it along his thigh. He took the hand away from his thigh, and scratched at his cheek and the back of his neck with trembling fingers, making new pink lines in the greasepaint. He moved his head from side to side, as if he were answering some argument he was making with himself, denying something almost desperately. Whatever that argument was, he settled it and stared at Quimby without speaking.

"Answer my question!" Quimby ordered, and saw the man's face stiffen with hopelessness, as if he were afraid of the consequences of what he was about to say.

"We came here to kill the men who run the ANC," the corporal said. "They're the terrorists who cause all the trouble in our country. They're trying to bring down our government, carrying on a regular war against us. We came here to defend our country."

Quimby nodded and smiled at him, and signaled Mutota to take the corporal away.

The second prisoner Mutota brought in was the slab-sided man Quimby and Tandy had scuffled with at the Wedza Motel. He came in, square jaw thrust forward, looking aggressive and defiant, one sleeve torn away, showing the hard muscles of his arm. The broad, flat planes of his black-painted face were marred by the parallel scratches Tandy had put on his left cheek, and though the night was cool, heavy beads of perspiration lay along his brow and his face. He sat stolidly, glaring at Quimby and the others in the room, an animate mass of explosive force looking for a place to detonate.

Quimby started the routine: "Give me your name, rank, and serial number."

"Jack Grobler. Sergeant. 4861070."

"What is your unit?"

"Fuck you. That's all you get. I don't have to answer your questions."

"Then I'll answer some for you," Quimby said. "We know quite a bit about you, Sergeant. You're from the two-oh-five commando regiment, third battalion, H company, Third Platoon, based at Phalabarwa. You crossed the border into this country from Vila de Manica and drove to Mutare two nights ago. You're carrying a Mozambican passport, but you're a South African. You spent yesterday and last night at the Wedza Motel outside Marondara, and I gave you a knock on the head yesterday when you made a pass at my woman. I know why you're here; I helped whip your commandos tonight, and I whipped another bunch that came to Harare on the twenty-seventh of October. I know all about you. Answer my question: Why did you and twenty other men come into Zimbabwe?"

Grobler's black-streaked face distorted with rage. He leaned forward, arms up, fists clenched, grinding out words of hatred: "You black son of a bitch! You've killed some of the finest soldiers I've ever had! All right, shit! Don't expect me to crawl on my belly for you. We came in to kill the leaders of the ANC who were meeting on that farm tonight."

"And were you successful?"

"Ah, fuck you!"

"Who gave you the orders to mount this operation?"

"Shit, you know the answer to that. The colonel."

"What colonel?"

"Johann Swart. The guy outside with the holes in his leg. Ask *him* your fucking questions. I don't get paid for answering questions."

"I'm asking *you,* Sergeant. What is your unit attached to? What unit does it report to?"

265

Grobler's eyes watched the photographer who came and squatted just in front of him. He sat up a little straighter, puffing out his chest, scowling defiantly into the lens, and he said pridefully, "Everyone in this part of Africa knows how we work. We're on detached service under Hendryk van den Graff. General van den Graff, Chief of Intelligence and Security Operations."

"And do you know who he is subordinate to?"

"Everybody knows that too. We've got a chart in the messroom that shows it. Our unit is right up there at the top. The general reports directly to the President and Prime Minister who's also the Minister of Defense."

"And how do you get your information about when and where the ANC leaders are meeting?"

Grobler leered at him, grinning malevolently at a thought he had, and said, "Spies probably. We've probably got a lot of fucking kaffir spies in your ANC."

Angered, wanting to hurt the man, Quimby taunted him. "Was that you commanding that stupid team I hit in Lusaka last week?"

Grobler's face dissolved into rage again. "Ah, you filthy black bastard! You fucking murderer!" He lumbered up from his chair and made for the table, but Mutota leaped forward to prod his throat with the Uzi and herded him out through the door.

Quimby leaned over to whisper with Chitepo. The pattern he had thought he was beginning to see through these last two days was clearer now, and he discussed with Chitepo how it should be presented. "I don't care whether we've got it exactly or not," he told Peter. "Present it the way we decided to this morning. Now we've got a name. Lay it on this van den Graff for all you're worth. Play him as a Communist traitor or a fool; he's the head murderer way up high in the SA government."

Peter stood up and began another little lecture to the correspondents.

This time he talked about the relationship he and Quimby had discovered between van den Graff, a crypto-Communist member of the ANC he did not name, and the Secretary-General of the SACP, John Kado. He put special emphasis on what he called "the incongruous cooperation between General van den Graff and the South African Communist Party," and he posed a series of questions about this relationship that, he said, had to be answered.

"We know all about this General van den Graff," he told the correspondents. "Chief of South Africa's Defense Forces Intelligence Service, and in charge of what the South Africans like to call 'police actions' in the Front Line States. But look very closely at what he's been doing. Why would this great general cooperate with the Communists to get rid of the ANC leaders? Is it possible that he's actually trying to strengthen the SACP? And if he's doing that, why? Is it because he is himself a Communist? Here you have this Afrikaner right up at the top of the heap, responsible for carrying out the government's covert operations, responsible for the intelligence that is the basis for such operations, and he's a Communist? In South Africa? That boggles the mind, but of course this kind of thing has happened before—in countries like Great Britain and West Germany and France. Or try another theory: Could it be that the so-called intellectual types he has so carefully gathered inside his agency are all Communists and that they and van den Graff are deliberately subverting the government's policies? Are they and he actually working for the Soviet Union?"

Quimby listened and approved. Peter was making the points the right way, twisting the truth a little, putting the main emphasis on South Africa's involvement and van den Graff's duplicity. He and Chitepo had hashed out earlier in the day how they would handle this thing if the commandos turned out to be South African troops rather than mercenaries or members of the Umkhonto We Sizwe assault platoon or Seifert's people. And they had discussed how their arguments could best be presented in each case so that they would win the sympathy and support of the correspondents for the ANC. He watched Chitepo smile winningly at the correspondents as he spoke, and he saw their sympathetic and understanding grins. They were beginning to appreciate the puzzle Peter was handing them.

"Or, still another interesting theory," Peter continued. "Do you suppose that van den Graff is as ignorant of our politics as so many other Afrikaners are? Could it be that he's not even aware that by killing the ANC leaders he's actually strengthening the SACP, giving it virtually absolute control over the ANC? Can a man at the head of South Africa's intelligence and security services be that naive, that incredibly stupid? Is it possible to believe that he is so politically illiterate that he honestly can't see the difference between the democratic ANC and the totalitarian SACP? Is he just an honest Afrikaner, so blinded by prejudice he can't think at all? You see the problem? The general is either an ardent Communist working to strengthen the SACP's control over the millions of black people loyal to the ANC, or he's an absolute political nitwit. We don't know which answer is correct, but we hope you will ask the prisoners questions that may help us get to the truth."

Quimby's hands were beginning to shake almost as badly as those of the first prisoner he had interrogated. Letdown, weariness, the suppressed fear of death raising its head after the danger was gone, and the memory of the men he had lost. He was so goddamned tired he was ready to die. He interrupted Chitepo, suggesting that they interrogate the colonel.

The colonel's leg had been attended to. He hobbled in with a hand on Mutota's shoulder, and sat stiffly upright, ice-blue eyes glaring at Quimby and the correspondents. His long-nosed, long-jawed face was set and haggard, the well-clipped beard was blackened with greasepaint and had picked up patches of white-looking dust and pieces of dried grass. The whites of his eyes were bloodshot, and the flat, raw-boned body seemed somehow brittle, ready to break up. After he sat down, he held on to his knee with both hands clutched above a heavy, white bandage, lips drawn back in pain that bared his teeth, obviously determined to show no sign of weakness to the enemies sitting around him.

Quimby recognized him. This was the man in the blue leisure suit who had ordered Jack Grobler into the motel at Wedza with such powerful authority.

Quimby spoke with sympathy and respect: "Colonel Swart, I know you're in pain. We'll get you to a hospital in a few minutes, but first I have a question I want you to answer. We know your unit, your mission in coming into Zimbabwe, how your men and helicopters got into the country, and we know that your unit is detached for special service to General van den Graff. What we don't understand is how the general could possibly bring himself to enter into an alliance with the South African Communist Party in order to get information that would help him kill the leaders of the African National Congress. How do you explain that?"

The cold blue eyes looked at him intently, but the colonel made no effort to reply.

"Colonel?"

The colonel's voice was low. "I don't understand what you're saying."

"I'm saying that van den Graff has been conspiring with the SACP, the Communists, to kill the ANC leaders on the National Executive Council, and he has carefully avoided killing the SACP members on that Council. The conclusion you have to draw is that he's a Communist himself, working to strengthen the SACP by killing the ANC leaders. He's been using, *misusing*, South African commandos—*you and your men, Colonel*—to strengthen the SACP, to give it total control over the ANC. Now my question was: How do you explain that?"

The colonel's lower lip thrust out and his jaw came forward, making him look grim and stubborn. "I don't believe any of this," he said. "I don't believe you're telling the truth."

"Consider the facts, Colonel," Quimby began to speak very slowly, wanting the colonel and the correspondents to absorb every word. "With the exception of one set of vengeance killings, every person your commandos have killed during the last six weeks were ANC leaders who were members of the National Council, but they were *not* members of the SACP, although eleven members of the thirty-man National Council are members of the SACP. In several attempts in early and middle October, you managed to kill three ANC leaders, all non-Communists. The unsuccessful attack you made here late in October was also made against ANC leaders who were *not* members of the SACP. The same was true in Lusaka. The man you assassinated in Maputo, Herbert Nkala, was one of the great ANC leaders, known by everyone to be an ardent anti-Communist, and the meeting you attacked tonight was a meeting of non-Communist ANC leaders. All this is fact, and so is our evidence that van den Graff's secret contact in the National Council, the man who gave him information about these meetings, is the Secretary-General of the SACP. Now I ask you again: How do you explain this?"

Swart stared at Quimby for a long time, the lines at the corners of his eyes so deep that they stretched back up into his dirtied red-gold hair. He turned to look at the correspondents busily writing down their impressions or gazing at him with a mixture of compassion and horror, as if he were a mortally wounded wild animal. He fixed his eyes on the lantern at the end of the table where Quimby sat for almost a minute, appearing to go into a kind of trance.

Quimby prodded at him. "Colonel?"

Swart turned back to Quimby. His face seemed to break up into a mass of wrinkles, and he shook his head vigorously, denying what he did not want to believe. He opened his mouth wide as if he wanted to shout, but made no sound. Abruptly, he put his hands up over his face and bent forward until the backs of his hands were against his knees, head down, face hidden. The men in the room saw the top of his head; they saw the way his back and chest heaved as if he were sobbing, but they heard no sound.

11

On the way from the abandoned farmhouse to Chitepo's house in Chitungwiza, Quimby let his exhaustion take over and dozed with his head on Tandy's shoulder. One phase of the struggle was over; he had clobbered the commandos and tied South Africa into a tangle of scandal that was going to hurt it. But he had to get back to Florence Mubaka. He wanted to understand how Kado had been able to command South Africa to kill for him; he wanted to bare that connection and cut it out forever so that the slaughter of ANC leaders could not happen again. Kado had to be exposed, and if the SACP was behind him, that had to come out too. Kado should be tried for murder.

And after that, Quimby thought wearily, I'll have to settle up.

The police and the government will be wanting answers. They'll put me in Chikurubi Prison for a thousand years, and I don't give a damn. . . .

He had almost completed what had to be done. As far as he could see, even with its dangerous relationship with the SACP, the ANC was still the best bet. The ANC people knew what the dangers were; hell, they knew the Communists' aims and the tactics they were prepared to use, but they were sure that they and the South African people were tough enough and dedicated enough to fight off those babies forever and create a genuine democracy. Nkala had believed that; he'd had faith in their stubborn good sense. . . .

If he had to go to jail, Quimby thought, so be it. What could he do?

Thinking about those things, he fell sound asleep.

CHITEPO brought the old van to a halt ten yards away from his house. He turned the rumbling motor off quickly and sat staring into the darkness for several minutes; then he reached over Tandy to press Quimby's shoulder.

Quimby came awake, straightening up in the seat slowly, yawning, and Chitepo said, "Muparadzi, something's wrong. We left two men to guard Florence Mubaka. One of them should be out here now, coming down here to give me an all-clear signal. There ought to be a light inside the house. I told them—"

"Wait." Quimby came wide awake, sensing danger. He sat for a moment studying the house and its yard beyond the low fence.

He leaned across Tandy, feeling her breast against his shoulder, aware of the beating of her heart, and he began to whisper, thinking out loud: "Kado promised he'd kill me if I didn't return Mubaka. He's probably sent Muzingi and his men looking. If Muzingi found her, and if she's told Kado what we know, then what? He can run, or leave the country, or hide for the rest of his life, but he won't do any of those things because he knows he's history's baby; he figures the great god of dialectical and historical materialism has picked him to be a winner. He would see that the only way he can suppress what we know about his assassination scheme is by killing us. I told Florence that the Republic Police and Mugabe's government knew the truth, but Kado wouldn't believe that because if it were true he'd be in jail. So . . . he can be thinking we're the only people who know what he's done, and if we're dead he's in the clear. . . . Let's look around a little, Peter. Carefully."

Chitepo whispered. "I wish to God we hadn't left all those weapons at the farm."

"You want to get picked up carrying a Kalashnikov in Chitungwiza?"

"Better than getting my ass shot off in my own front yard."

"Quitely now." Quimby had eased his door open and was stepping to the ground.

Chitepo came around to the front of the van and Quimby motioned him to move further to the left so that they could approach the house separated by several feet. They moved silently, both of them used to fighting in the bush, but this was open ground, light showed from houses some distance away; here in the street there was no cover.

Chitepo moved ahead on the graveled walk, and Quimby saw a figure hurtle out of the darkness and tackle him, bring him to the ground and climb on top of him, wielding a club or a knife.

Quimby rushed in that direction and brought the edge of his hand down on that man's neck. He heard Chitepo start to say something or cry out, but the sound ended in a sharp choking sigh as if his throat had been cut or he had been knocked unconscious.

Someone hit Quimby from behind, shoulders driving into the backs of his thighs, arms grabbing at his knees, trying to throw him forward on his face.

Quimby had been in a half-crouch, and his attacker's arms could not reach all the way around his legs. As he fell forward he rolled and grabbed a wrist and tore the hand from one thigh, bending the man's arm up behind him and yanking it up and forward, lying back as he did so, forcing his assailant to go sailing over his head.

The man had been trained for this kind of fighting. He did not go down flat on his face as he should have, but ducked his head and rolled and was on his feet before Quimby had completed his own roll. He came back at Quimby, slamming his club against Quimby's shoulder, rocking him back, and rushed in to hit him again.

As Quimby went down with the man on top of him, he was aware that a third person brushed past them, carrying Tandy in his arms, rushing into Chitepo's house through the open door. He rolled and came to his feet, and his assailant caught him in a bear hug, his embrace creating an excruciating, remembered pain where Muzingi had bruised those ribs only a few days before. This man was strong, but he was about Quimby's size, and he did not have Quimby's left arm inside the bear hug.

Quimby stabbed his fingers into the man's eyes and heard a grunt of pain; he stabbed again, and when the arms around him loosened, he reached out and grasped a chin with one hand, the back of the man's head with the other; he twisted hard and fast, giving it everything he had, hearing the vertebrae crack, guessing that he had seriously injured or killed the man even before he felt the body against him go lax. He dropped the man and moved swiftly to the scrawny hedge only a few feet away, wanting to be out of the gunsights of whoever was inside the house, and he crouched there, catching his breath, trying to put the situation together in his mind.

On the other side of the pathway, Chitepo lay on his stomach, completely silent. Here, closer, lay the man whose neck had just been broken.

Quimby had a memory of running feet and supposed that the man who had attacked Chitepo had run away. The other memory was less clear; he'd had that quick impression that a man had carried Tandy past him into the house.

He only knew one man big enough to do that and run so lightly, only one big man who would want to. *Muzingi*. He turned toward the door, knowing that he would have to go in after Tandy, and he wondered suddenly why Muzingi hadn't shot him. Surely he could see him standing here in clear sight against this thin hedge? Then he remembered that this wasn't Victoria Farm; it was the center of Chitungwiza, a few hundred feet from a police station. Muzingi didn't dare shoot.

Quimby drew his knife from the scabbard at his back and held the blade against his thigh. He stepped quietly along the hedge, planning to slip from there to the front of the house to approach the door.

As Quimby advanced, Muzingi began to speak from inside the house through the open door. The voice was strong, arrogant, taunting, and Quimby instantly recalled that louder taunt years ago when Muzingi had challenged him from a hilltop. "Hey, Muparadzi," Muzingi said this time. "I've got your good-looking woman. Do you want to guess what I'm going to do to her?"

Quimby fearfully made too many guesses too fast, knowing that whatever happened he would not let Muzingi abuse Tandy. She had already had more than her share of that. He made no effort to reply, although he was glad that Muzingi chose to talk, for the big man's words were helping to cover the sounds his boots were making on the gravel.

Muzingi's high tenor shrilled on: "You know what I ought to do with her, Muparadzi? What she did to me with that big iron skillet. Break her head. But first I have a better idea. Listen carefully. I want you to hear this. . . . Be very quiet and listen. . . . Quiet . . . very quiet. . . . There! Did you hear that? I'm breaking her fingers, Muparadzi. . . . Listen . . . Listen to them crack."

Quimby could not hear the sounds of finger-bones breaking; he *did* hear Tandy's scream, muffled to a moan, probably by one of Muzingi's big hands.

"And when I finish with this," Muzingi said, "I'm going to do to her what you did to me. I will tear off her ears. How will you like that, Muparadzi? How will you like your woman with broken fingers and no ears? Why don't you come and—"

Quimby lunged through the doorway, looking to his right, because from outside that had seemed to be where Muzingi's voice was coming from. His eyes caught a dark flurry of movement where Tandy was trying to pull herself away from Muzingi's grasp; then he was there, with the knife held low, intent on halting this big bastard's sadistic torture.

Muzingi hurled Tandy forward and came after her, bringing a short club straight down on Quimby's right hand, sending the knife flying. He struck again, at Quimby's head, but in the darkness the club slipped down the length of Quimby's arm, and Quimby reached with his left hand for the hand holding that club and took a big knee hard in the thigh.

Quimby pulled back, aware that Tandy was on the floor, silent. He retreated across the room, reaching for anything—a chair, a shelf off the wall, the box-table he remembered. He found a chair and lifted it in the dark and charged with it into Muzingi's middle. Muzingi dropped his club, tore the chair from Quimby's hands, and slammed it back at him, and a corner caught Quimby on the forehead and fell away to the floor at his back.

Muzingi came in with his hands forward, reaching; he raised a knee into Quimby's crotch, finding the vulnerable target, and Quimby fell away gasping, knowing that he had to find a weapon of some sort, searching the room in his mind—the little kitchen alcove over there, the wood-burning stove—perhaps a skillet like Tandy's, or a grate, or a piece of wood big enough to use as a club. . . .

He knew he could never outpower this Muzingi. He faded toward the stove, and Muzingi kept after him, beating him, pounding on him with heavy, crushing blows, managing to give the impression even in the dark that he was enjoying himself. Quimby had the thought: Old Victor wants to kill me bare-handed. I've chased him through the hills and torn off his ear and screwed up his chances to be a big muckety-muck in South Africa. He must think I'm the ngozi sent to ruin his life. Maybe I am. . . .

His eyes were growing accustomed to the darkness and he saw that Muzingi had a strip of white gauze around his head, reaching down on one side where his ear was supposed to be. Quimby opened his hand wide and slapped that white patch as hard as he could, and felt encouraged when Muzingi squealed a curse and lost a beat in the pounding he was administering. Quimby hit the ear again and stepped back hurriedly, reaching to the floor by the stove where Chitepo kept his woodbin.

His hand closed around a small bit of something wooden. Too small. It would splinter against Muzingi's muscles. He wondered if it would make sense to let it go ahead and splinter; maybe he would get something sharp he could stab the bastard with. Too many separate steps: He couldn't tell what kind of splinter he would get, probably a toothpick. He felt further, taking a brutal pounding on his back and the back of his neck, and he found a larger, stronger stick, two inches in diameter, nearly two feet long.

He scrambled backward across the room, moving the way an outclassed fighter backs away from the man with the better punch, hoping to last until a chance to score offers itself. Muzingi turned with him, whining with rage, and came in reaching as before. Grasping the stick in both hands, Quimby rammed it into Muzingi's middle, driving the air out of him, and Muzingi hesitated long enough to grunt. Quimby raised the stick and tried to bring it down on Muzingi's head, but missed and hit a shoulder, and Muzingi yelled and reached out and twisted the club away from him.

Muzingi stepped back and swung the stick at Quimby's head and Quimby raised his arm to protect himself, felt the club slam into his arm, and felt and heard simultaneously the bones of his left arm break above the elbow.

He knew from the pain and the sudden, stinging paralysis of his left hand that his arm was broken, and he wondered frantically what he was going to do with only one arm.

The club was coming at him again, and he ducked and found himself off to Muzingi's right, halfway behind him. For want of a better idea he went up on Muzingi's back, wrapping his legs around the hard middle, his broken arm dangling at his side while he flailed at the bandaged side of Muzingi's head with his right fist.

Muzingi raised himself straight and thrust himself back against the wall, banging Quimby's back and neck, trying to shake him off. That didn't work, and he took a few steps forward and reared back again, slamming Quimby against the set of shelves where

Chitepo kept his sculptored works, trying to scrape Quimby off his back.

Remembering desperately, Quimby reached back along one of those shelves. Not this one. Lower. This one. His hand closed over Chitepo's little red-granite rhinoceros, a solid handful, heavy, graspable, with its legs and body making a good handle. He hit the top of Muzingi's head with the rhinoceros' nose. He hit him again, bringing the solid granite piece down desperately. . . . He beat Muzingi to his knees and went on beating until the giant was flat on his face, and he kept on until he knew Muzingi was dead.

Even after he was sure at last that the man was dead, he continued to sit astride the broad hips for several minutes, breathing with an agonizing wheeze, trying to remember what the other things were that had to be done. He had lost Mubaka; he could not find out now how Kado had managed his conspiracy. . . .

His left arm was sending signals of agony to his mind and body, and the pain in his ribs made getting enough air into his lungs impossible. He felt confused, punchdrunk from the blows he had taken. There was something he had to remember. Tandy. He had to remember Tandy. Oh, God, Tandy!

He dragged himself away from Muzingi, crawled to her on his knees, and knelt by her side. She was unconscious, but breathing. He touched her face and head, thinking that she might have fainted from the pain in her fingers, or that Muzingi must have hit her. He wanted to touch her fingers, but he was afraid he might hurt them somehow, and he was sickened with the thought of what that bastard had done to her. He had to get her to a hospital.

He climbed to his feet, hearing the labored sound of his breathing as he moved, and stumbled outside. Chitepo was still down on his face, not dead, but moaning. Hurt bad, had to be helped . . .

Quimby went into the street, getting his bearings. He looked at the van and remembered that Chitepo had been driving. He went to the van and felt at the ignition switch for the key. It wasn't there, and he shuffled back to Chitepo, knelt to get his hand into Chitepo's right trousers pocket, and found it.

He went back to the van and got behind the wheel, groaning when his broken arm bumped against the door. He started the van and drove down the long row of almost identical houses until he came to the corner; he turned left and went on another block until he saw the light of the police station. Then he stopped the van out in the middle of the street, got down, groaning again, mounted the two steps to the entrance, holding his left wrist to keep the broken bones from grating against screaming nerves, and pushed open the glass-paned door with his right shoulder.

Inside a bare room, with a single light and a long table, a policeman with a sad, loose face like a bloodhound's sat eating something out of a greasy paper bag. He jumped up when he saw Quimby's face, exclaiming, "Man, you hurt! You hurt bad! You had an accident?"

Quimby sat in the policeman's chair and leaned his chest forward until it touched the table, trying to take a breath that would not pull that hurting rib right through his lung. "We need an ambulance," he said. "Two people at least are hurt worse than I am. And some are dead. You'd better get the ambulance first; then the city police; then the Republic Police because this is a political thing. I'll take you to the house when you're ready."

12

THEY set his bones and put a cast over them and rolled him into a room of Presbyterian Hospital, which he realized after the male nurses helped him into bed, was to be his room. Part of his confusion arose from the fact that the place was full: officers from the State Security Services and the Republic State Police, intelligence men from Zimbabwe's Central Intelligence Organization.

He was pretty well bombed out on a sedative the doctors had given him, but the police went to work and kept after him through most of the rest of the night, trying to get his complicated story straight. It was near dawn when a doctor came in, raised hell with them, and gave him a shot of something that eased the pain in his arm. He went out like a crushed light bulb.

When he woke about ten o'clock in the morning, other police were there; different faces but the same rough impatience. A nurse brought him toast and milk and two boiled eggs, which he ate ravenously before he went back to answering questions.

He kept Nkala out of his story, and Mungu and his other fighters, but he filled his questioners to the ears with details, explained his motives, and told them what he had guessed about John Kado and Florence Mubaka and Heinz Seifert and the South Africans.

By midafternoon he began to believe that every high-ranking policeman in Zimbabwe had been through his room at least once. He was beginning to fade again, but he asked if they had collected Kado and Mubaka and Seifert through the night. They told him nothing, looking at him with a special look he decided they had practiced for use on incorrigible criminals and psychos.

He asked a Republic Police captain about the connection between the sports club and South Africa, and got an answer.

"You'll be reading about it in *The Herald*," the captain told him. "Those Rhodesian fellas were planning a rebellion, you know, back to white rule. They were acting as helpers for the SAs, sizing up ANC meeting places, providing transportation and safe houses, hiding weapons, and for that they were expecting South Africa would give them help when they started their rebellion. We nabbed most of 'em. Fella named Jameson got himself shot in the butt crossing into Botswana last night."

IN the evening, Tandy visited him from the women's ward, trailed by her own guards. They sat together on a screened veranda apart from the policemen.

Her right hand was in a sling, with three of her fingers locked in a cast. Muzingi had broken those three. Quimby apologized over and over for not having got himself inside Chitepo's house more quickly. Tandy of course insisted that the broken fingers were nothing. She sat looking at him with worship in her eyes and laughed at the T-shaped cut in his forehead where Muzingi had hit him with the chair. That, she insisted, was her permanent brand.

They talked gloomily about what would happen to them now, both assuming that Mugabe's government would send them to court on ten or twenty charges ranging from possession of firearms to murder. They speculated about what their punishment would be, dreading the idea that they could be executed, and discussed what kind of life they could put together some time in the future if they were given long prison sentences.

"I don't care," Tandy repeated several times. "It had to be done. We stopped the SAs and made fools out of them, and we taught the SACP a lesson."

Quimby didn't find much he could add to that, and they walked to another ward to find out how Chitepo was. He lay gaunt and hollow-eyed, barely conscious, suffering from a severe concussion.

LATE on the second day in the hospital, Quimby's secretary managed to get to him, bringing him business decisions to make and the international editions of several foreign newspapers. The November twelfth edition of the *New York Times* carried Robert Collins' four-column story about the events in Zimbabwe on the second page, and Quimby was delighted with it. The first paragraphs closely followed Chitepo's lead:

> South Africa's latest effort to break up the ANC, the African National Congress, known to be the largest and most popular opposition party now leading blacks against South Africa's white apartheid rule, has ended in fiasco.

Last night's attack on a meeting of the ANC's National Executive Council at a farmhouse just east of Harare in Zimbabwe was driven off by a small group of Zimbabwean freedom fighters. The cost to the South African commandos was at least thirteen men killed, several wounded, loss of a giant Bell helicopter, and potentially disastrous consequences for the agency inside South Africa responsible for carrying out these raids.

This writer was present during the interrogation of South African prisoners immediately after last night's fighting.

Information was uncovered that leads observers to believe a major national scandal may be brewing among high government circles in Pretoria.

General Hendryk van den Graff, Chief of Intelligence and Security Operations, has allegedly masterminded previous cross-border operations against the ANC in Mozambique, Botswana, Zambia, and Zimbabwe, the most important heretofore being the three-pronged attack last May against Zambia, Botswana, and Zimbabwe. According to the prisoners' testimony, he also ordered last night's attack against the ANC, as well as five others during the last six weeks.

Observers believe that van den Graff's ANC targets were carefully selective. The significant fact last night's testimony brought out was that Communists have not been present at any of the meetings attacked during recent weeks. In fact, all the members of the National Executive Council who have been killed have been non-Communist members of the ANC.

Experts consider this to be damning evidence that van den Graff himself has been working to strengthen the hand of the SACP within the ANC. An international ANC conference is scheduled to meet in Lusaka on November 15, and it is evident that had the latest commando attack been successful, the SACP would have been in position to establish a two-thirds majority in the National Executive Council and thus exercise virtually absolute control over the ANC.

>Some intelligence analysts are asking if this once stalwart Afrikaner and close friend of the President and Prime Minister is himself a Communist, working to strengthen the Communists' hand in this most important opposition group, with the aim of supplanting the apartheid rule. Others have suggested that it is possible that van den Graff was simply not aware of what was happening.
>
>Most commentors this reporter interviewed believe that van den Graff might prefer being branded a Communist to being known as their dupe.

Collins proceeded to make much of his presence on the scene, describing the "distraught faces" of the prisoners, providing verbatim accounts of some parts of their testimony, and detailing their replies to his questions after the formal interrogation. He went on to report the furious protests against South Africa's behavior that were being expressed by Robert Mugabe, Kenneth Kaunda of Zambia and Chinchano of Mozambique, the Organization of African States, and other Third World members of the UN.

In the *Frankfurter Allgemeine Zeitung*, Hans Schrecker had a two-page philosophical survey of the history of apartheid and the seventy-four-year history of the ANC. Discussing the case against van den Graff, he concluded that it was indeed possible that a man of van den Graff's background and family might be a Communist mole working to undermine a government he despised. His conclusion was that if the general was not a Communist it would be very difficult to find a rational explanation for why he had operated as he had.

In the *Manchester Guardian,* George Arnwell's analysis of the brutal bombings, shootings, and assassinations carried out by South African commandos in more or less helpless countries was as dry as something out of *Jane's Fighting Ships* and as ferocious as an antipersonnel bomb. His treatment of van den Graff, "the crypto-Communist and/or boob/or dupe," painted the general as a ludicrous but bloody-handed man with the morality of an eel and the ambition for power of an imbecilic weightlifter.

Quimby read Arnwell's concluding paragraph several times, enjoying every word.

> Officials in Whitehall who do not wish to be identified point out that since Robert Mugabe's government had no part in this fighting, and indeed, was unaware of the events until after the fact, South Africa can have no justification for retaliatory action against Zimbabwe. It is thought, on the contrary, that the Boers would do well to count themselves fortunate if they succeed in retrieving their prisoners and wounded. As for the fate of General van den Graff, the South African government has established a high commission to unravel the threads of his conspiracy while he bleats pitifully that he is the victim of a Communist conspiracy. Whether the government has been irremediably damaged by van den Graff's defection remains to be seen.

He had hurt them, Quimby decided. He had whipped their commandos, made their intelligence chief look ridiculous, and publicly embarrassed the government, and now other people in the world were up in arms at South Africa's brutal interference in the affairs of the ANC. How long that would last was anybody's guess, but for now at least the SAs had to back off.

The police continued to press him, coming back again and again to check information he had given them or to prod at his mind for more. In turn he tried to learn what they intended to do with Tandy and Chitepo and himself. He got nowhere.

He tried all afternoon to find out what had happened to John Kado and Florence Mubaka and Heinz Seifert, but no one would discuss that subject. Even men he had known very well in the past treated him like a condemned criminal.

He had told the Republic Police about those people during the first minutes after they had come out to Chitungwiza, but nothing had appeared in the papers about their arrest. He was beginning to believe they had escaped scot-free, or that the government of Zimbabwe, embarrassed by the charges he had made, was deliberately refusing to take any action, preparing to whitewash the role of the SACP in order to avoid difficulty with the Soviet Union.

In the evening, he sought out Tandy, and they went to visit Chitepo. Peter was sitting up in bed, looking pitifully weak, but his doctor had encouraged him to walk, and they marched slowly through the bleak halls, three sorry-looking ambulatory patients, trailing their little escort of policemen. . . .

ON the afternoon of November fifteenth, the International Conference of the African National Council met in Lusaka, and Quimby and Tandy and Chitepo listened to the proceedings on the radio. The Chairman of the SACP, present at his own request, took the podium and denounced the absent John Kado for fathering his own personality cult, and described how Kado had tried to take control of the ANC and the SACP to satisfy his overweening personal ambitions. He announced Kado's expulsion from the SACP, and also the dissolution of a special platoon of Umkhonto We Sizwe, which, the Chairman said, had been created to serve as Kado's personal guard.

Amid great consternation and applause from the assembled delegates, the Chairman eloquently repledged the SACP's solemn support for the ANC Freedom Charter, going to great lengths to emphasize that the SACP had always kept the faith, and that a single person, John Kado, working with a few henchmen, had betrayed both the ANC and his own party.

Quimby guessed that there had to be members of the ANC leadership who believed that at least some of the guilt laid upon Kado should have been shared by other leaders of the SACP, but these thoughts were not mentioned. Noisy demonstrations went on in the hall for nearly twenty minutes; then a series of speakers representing many different groups spoke from the floor, making impassioned pleas for united action to achieve a truly democratic government in South Africa.

Just before the delegates recessed for the evening, eight non-Communist ANC candidates were elected by acclaim to an expanded National Executive Council, giving the ANC's non-Communists more than a two-thirds majority in the membership of that body. Thereafter, each Communist member of the newly constituted Council formally swore to abide by the Freedom Charter and the will of the people of South Africa as that will was expressed to ANC representatives. For the near future at least, a cowed SACP was to be compelled to play by ANC rules.

ON the morning of the sixteenth, Enos Karwi, Zimbabwe's Minister of State Security, came into Quimby's room, greeted him formally, as "Mister Taylor Quimby," as if he had never seen him before in his life, and placed his sizable bottom on the straight chair next to Quimby's bed.

Karwi, Quimby knew, had been educated in England in something like philosophy or politics, and he had completed his work for the law in Zambia immediately after the war. He was tough and smart and immensely hard-working; he had risen rapidly in Mugabe's government, and in Quimby's judgment he deserved every bit of his success because he was incorruptible and courageous. With his fine, square face and black mustache, his dark eyes partially hidden behind glistening gold-rimmed glasses, he looked the personification of Mugabe's best senior civil servants.

Because Karwi had addressed him as if he were a stranger Quimby sat up, prepared for the worst, and he returned Karwi's greeting with equal formality: "Mr. Minister. This is a pleasure."

Karwi smiled stiffly, flashing even white teeth, wagging his head with a look of compassionate understanding. He said, "Muparadzi, you had to destroy one more time, didn't you?"

They gazed at one another a moment, Quimby waiting with considerable dread for the boom to drop. He had no experience with prisons, wanted none, saw no way out of his predicament, but knew he would not beg for favors or leniency.

During these last five days he had argued strenuously to persuade the officials who questioned him that, given the situation, it would have been impossible for either the ANC or the government of Zimbabwe to fight off the commandos. He had refused to name the men who had fought for him, warning Tandy and Chitepo to do the same, but he had given the investigators almost everything he knew or guessed about the conspiracy to kill the ANC leaders. He had not tried to defend his own actions because he knew perfectly well that he was guilty of organizing a group of fighters, arming them, and killing with them. There was no way to get around those facts. Looking at Karwi's sober face, he felt doomed, and he waited silently for whatever judgment Karwi had come to deliver.

But no one had told him what had been done about Kado and Mubaka and Seifert, and he burned to know. Moved partly by the desire to put off the sentencing, he put his question directly: "Enos, I suppose you've come to tell me and the others how we are to be punished, but first, please, tell me what happened to Kado and his sister, and to Heinz Seifert."

Karwi nodded calmly. "They've told me that you keep asking. Kado is under arrest and will be tried for conspiracy to murder and a lot of other things. I have no doubt he will be condemned. Heinz Seifert has been expelled from the country. Florence Mubaka has evaded us; we believe she has left the country."

"I think she was the leader of the whole conspiracy."

"We think so too. Kado has talked a great deal. He says that she and Seifert were KGB; little sister, apparently, was a lot meaner and brighter than Kado. He says she called the tune for a plot worked out in Moscow designed to put both the SACP and the ANC under Kado's control for an early revolutionary effort in South Africa. He was just the front man, the voice. He told us that he was frantic to get Florence away from you because without her he knew he would be unable to function. Apparently the Soviet leaders are impatient with the elected leaders of the SACP; they want a Communist South Africa as soon as possible, and Florence Mubaka had promised to get it."

"I guess I'll never know how she persuaded the South Africans to do her killing for her."

"Kado says she finagled them into recruiting her to spy for them. He says the Afrikaners are so blinded by fear that for them every black person who wants change is lumped into the same red Communist pot; they're hysterical about Communists and dissident blacks, and the hysterias get all mixed together until they can't separate the one from the other. He says Florence pointed this van den Graff at the non-Communist ANC leaders and that he didn't seem to know the difference; as far as he was concerned everyone in the ANC was Communist. Florence simply hoodwinked him by pretending to work for him."

"And she's out of it," Quimby said, regretfully. "And now we know how anxious the Soviet Union is to carry the fight into South Africa."

"In this part of Africa we've known for a long time that we have to work out our own destiny while the powers around us try to force us to do what they want. Times haven't changed."

"No." Quimby shifted his body to face Karwi more squarely. "Well . . . And the verdict for me and my people?"

Karwi leaned forward and placed a plane ticket folder on the bed by Quimby's right hand. He said: "You have forty-eight hours to settle your affairs, starting at noon today; then you are to be out of the country. Robert Mugabe asks me to send you his thanks for your service during our War of Independence and for this little war you have just completed. You did us a big favor by taking this fight out of our hands and telling the world about it. You will understand, of course, that we cannot publicly condone your illegal acts by permitting you to remain in Zimbabwe. Some of our dissidents might see this as an invitation to dig up their weapons and start their own wars again, and our neighbor to the south would accuse us of harboring terrorists and think it had a new reason for crossing our borders."

A great weight lifted from Quimby's mind. He knew that he was suddenly grinning like a fool. He took a huge breath of relief, ignoring the pain in his ribs, wanting to shout with pleasure, but his mind filled immediately with questions and thoughts about all the things he had to do.

"And the others?" he asked. "Chitepo and the girl?"

"They go with you." Karwi smiled suddenly, looking embarrassed. "Incidentally, although we have arranged passage for all of you and secured these tickets, we expect you to pay for them. After all, Zimbabwe is poor—"

Quimby picked up the tickets and read his destination: London—one of the great centers of the ANC's operations. He and Chitepo and Tandy would find work to do there. But right now he had to go and tell them what the verdict was; he had to get up and out of here, arrange to sell his house and his car, transfer his business to someone, pack and ship, clear up a thousand details in a hurry.

To Karwi he said, speaking formally again to hide his excitement: "Enos, thank you. I hope you will give my deep thanks to Robert Mugabe for the opportunity he gave me to serve our cause, and for this most recent favor. I have been privileged to fight for Zimbabwe. And tell him . . . please . . . tell him I want to return one day. We still have a long fight ahead."